HAPPY FOR YOU

HAPPY FOR YOU

Claire Stanford

VIKING

VIKING

An imprint of Penguin Random House LLC

penguinrandomhouse.com

LIBRARY OF CONGRESS CATALOGING-IN-PUBLICATION DATA

Names: Stanford, Claire, author.

Title: Happy for you / Claire Stanford.

Identifiers: LCCN 2021039455 (print) | LCCN 2021039456 (ebook) |
ISBN 9780593298268 (hardcover) | ISBN 9780593298275 (ebook)

Subjects: LCGFT: Novels.

Classification: LCC PS3619.T36488 H37 2022 (print) |
LCC PS3619.T36488 (ebook) | DDC 813/.6—dc23

LC record available at https://lccn.loc.gov/2021039455

LC ebook record available at https://lccn.loc.gov/2021039456

Printed in the United States of America

1st Printing

BOOK DESIGN BY LUCIA BERNARD

For my parents, Don and Michi

I

ONE

When I went to my interview at the third-most-popular internet company, I tried to make myself look like a real person. I bought a suit and put it on my body. My interviewer was a woman around my age who appeared to also be half Asian. I couldn't determine what kind of half Asian she was, nor did I mention the fact that we were both half Asian. Neither did she, though for her to mention it during a job interview would probably have been illegal.

The project, she said, was happiness.

Happiness? I said.

Happiness, she said. They wanted to understand it. To measure it. To help their users grow it, like a muscle that could be toned. They were looking to add out-of-the-box thinkers. She asked me what I thought I could contribute.

I told her about my wide-ranging philosophical grounding, my study of the mind-body problem, of the theory of emotions. These were the phrases I used, phrases I had practiced in the mirror the day before. She nodded, making a note.

"I see you haven't finished your PhD?" she said.

"Not quite," I said. She nodded and made another note.

"Why do you want to work here? Why leave academia?" This was the question I had practiced the most.

"I want the work I do to matter. I want to do something tangible, to be part of something that affects people's daily lives, that improves them."

She asked me more questions, I gave her more answers. I came back for more interviews, met more people, sat in more conference rooms, talked more about my research.

A few days later, I got the call that I was hired.

TWO

The third-most-popular internet company was not the company that most people I knew used when they used the internet, but it must have been used by enough people in the world every day that it could somehow stay in business, and also maintain the hope that it would one day overtake or at least equal the company that I and billions of other people saw when we called up our home screens. I wondered why the company even existed. Apart from the obvious evils of monopolies, and particularly information monopolies, what need was there for a number two internet company, let alone a number three?

This was not something I could ask at my interviews.

Up until this point in my life, I had done everything possible to avoid a desk job. I was thirty-one years old, and I had spent the past eight years in a PhD program in philosophy, the last four years of which had been spent struggling with my dissertation on the mind-body problem. It was a centuries-old question, the subject of countless dissertations—did the mind exist separate from the body?—but my specific angle was asking how it had been complicated by recent technologies. Social media, virtual reality, artificial intelligence. How important was our physical body to our mental processes: thoughts, feelings, consciousness?

My argument, in short, was that the body was not very important.

My dissertation argued that our online selves were an extension of our consciousness, that they were so deeply enmeshed with our cognitive processes, they had become part of our minds. I wasn't sure I entirely believed my own argument, but when I had suggested it, my advisor had been excited. It was hard to get my advisor excited about anything; she had already turned down several of my earlier ideas. I didn't mind that I didn't totally believe my own argument. Did Berkeley really believe that material substances didn't exist? That tables and chairs were only ideas in the mind of the beholder, that they did not exist if they were not perceived? I highly doubted it.

A month before my interview at the third-most-popular internet company, I got an email about a job recruitment fair. These recruitments usually were aimed at engineering students, sociology students, students who were studying something that had any practical application. Not philosophy students. Normally I would have swiped the email right into the trash, but lately, I had been considering a change.

I had begun to rethink things that spring, after I presented at philosophy's biggest conference. I had been submitting abstracts for years without receiving an invitation. Finally, I thought, I had made it. I spent endless hours on my paper, on my slides, on my delivery. I flew on a red-eye to Florida and took a crowded shuttle to the conference hotel. I dutifully went to panel after panel, taking notes, trying to network, drinking seemingly infinite cups of complimentary coffee from an urn in the lobby. The night before my presentation, I couldn't sleep, my body buzzing with caffeine and adrenaline. In the morning, I drank more coffee and practiced my talk one more time. There were six people in the audience. Was this, I wondered, what I really wanted? It had been four years, and I still hadn't managed to finish my dissertation. Maybe there was something else out there for me.

At the recruitment fair, the vast room was warm with the heat of ambitious bodies, with nerves and handshakes and undergraduates in suits and ties, in tasteful heels, each holding a sheaf of carefully formatted résumés. I had graduated from college during the recession, but I had been sheltered from its worst effects by the amniotic safety of graduate school. These students were different. They were hungry. They knew what they wanted to do in life and they were ready to do it. The booths were mobbed—labs, consulting firms, start-ups. I saw a booth for the first-most-popular internet company, and the second-most-popular, both surrounded. But the third-most-popular had a momentary lull.

I told the recruiter about my research.

"We've been looking for people like you," she said.

※

In September, instead of going back to school, I took an indefinite leave of absence. Normally, the hiring manager for the third-most-popular internet company had said, they wouldn't give a job to someone who hadn't completed their PhD, but my work was so relevant to the project, they were sure I would make a good addition to the team. Still, they hired me on a six-month trial contract—I would have to prove myself worthy of a permanent position.

The contract did not stipulate how, exactly, I would do this.

Even during this trial period, the amount of money they would be paying me multiplied my graduate student stipend by several factors. I had lived on the stipend for so long that the number they said was almost incomprehensible to me. My boyfriend, Jamie, was excited for me. My best friend, Sharky, sent me a firecracker emoji when I texted him the news. My advisor was the only person who didn't approve. She said she couldn't stop me, but that she was disappointed. My work, she said, was poised to make a significant contribution to the field.

On my first day, I woke up hours early. I sat in the living room with a cup of coffee and thought about whether this was what I really wanted to do. It wasn't too late to take it all back, but also, really, it was. I had told everyone I knew that I was leaving academia, that I was starting this job. I was proud that the third-most-popular internet company wanted me; I was excited to feel useful.

When Jamie woke up an hour later, he found me still sitting, already fully dressed, on the sofa. He came and sat next to me, his body warm and loose, the left side of his face still creased from the pillow.

"Nervous?" he said.

I nodded.

"It's going to be fine," he said. "You'll be great."

I nodded again and felt something inside my chest relax. Jamie always thought everything was going to work out, and he had a way of making me feel like that, too.

"You're so smart and so thoughtful and you're going to bring something to them that they've never seen before," he said. "You're taking a risk, trying something new, and that isn't easy. I'm proud of you."

"I'm proud of you, too," I said.

"You're proud of me? For what?"

"For being you, I guess."

"You guess?"

"Not I guess," I said. "I know."

"That's better," he said, and then he grabbed me in a bear hug and pulled me into his body.

THREE

The third-most-popular internet company occupied a building downtown that was all metal and glass. In the lobby, an enormous sculpture hung from the ceiling; it was brightly colored and abstract, meant, I thought, to confer liveliness and excitement onto its otherwise sterile environment.

I pressed the employee ID I had gotten at orientation to the scanner at the security turnstile and waited the requisite split second for the light to flash green. At the orientation, I had filled out paperwork for my health insurance, which, though I was a contractor, was still surprisingly excellent. I had taken a tour of the building, gotten my photo taken and my security badge printed, picked up my company-issued laptop, and met a few members of the team I would be working with, none of whose names I remembered except for the head of the project, Alethea Luce, who would be my boss. She was in her mid-forties and enormously tall—easily over six feet—with curly red hair that went down to her shoulder blades. She wore a pair of thick-rimmed glasses that made her look extremely fashion-forward, though it was not clear to me whether they were a conscious style choice. She had a PhD in neurochemistry, and I was basically in awe of her; she had sat in on several rounds of my interviews, asking questions that were difficult and provocative, nodding intently as I gave my answers. I had read up on her research when I was interviewing for the job; her dissertation argued that emotions were physical processes triggered by external stimuli. Her work advanced the claim that each emotion was housed in a specific location in the brain, and that once that location was found, the emotion could be targeted much more effectively—by medication, by electrotherapy, by an array of other interventions. This was a controversial stance; studies had shown that a group of people would say they were all experiencing the same emotion—anger, for example—but MRIs of their brains would show entirely different regions lighting up. The truth was that emotions were still an utter unknown, in philosophy, in psychology, in neurochemistry.

I took the elevator to the seventh floor and stepped out into the open office space. I looked at the rows of clean white tables, the ergonomic mesh chairs, the sleek computers, many already whirring with the day's work. Our desks were not assigned, and looking out at the open seats felt not unlike trying to choose a spot in the cafeteria as the new girl at school. Somehow, they hadn't covered this detail in the orientation.

Just then, a woman came up to me, a broad smile on her face.

"Evelyn, right?"

I nodded.

"I'm Sabine," she said, sticking out her hand. I clasped it with my own. The woman looked like she was a couple of years younger than me; her face was dewy and bright, and a small diamond stud sparkled on the left side of her nose. She was very petite, inches shorter than me, but I could tell already that she had a big presence. She appeared to be South Asian.

"I knew a new person was coming today, and you looked just lost enough," she said. "We're in the same research group. Come on, I'll show you where we sit."

I followed her to a far corner of the office, where a white man a few years older than me was sitting. He had curly black hair and wore glasses with clear frames. He looked slightly disheveled, but in a way that I suspected might be more crafted than accidental.

"This is Josh," Sabine said. "He's also part of the emotions research team. It's the three of us now."

"Welcome, welcome," Josh said. He turned from his screen to shake my hand and then immediately went back to the document he was working on.

"He's in the middle of something," Sabine said. "Anyway, it's open office, but we basically sit here. You can take this desk, it's next to mine." She motioned to an empty workspace across from Josh. I put my bag on the desk she had pointed to, and we sat down in neighboring chairs.

"Philosophy, right?" she said. I must have looked at her quizzically. "You're a philosophy PhD, right?"

"How did you know that?" I asked.

"Oh, we know everything about you. Right, Josh?"

From the other side of the computers, Josh made an assenting sound.

"I heard you haven't finished," she said. "That's pretty rare. They must have really wanted you."

"I guess so," I said. "I don't know."

I asked her about her background.

"Sociology," she said. "I mostly do quantitative user experience research, but some qualitative. Basically it means how people are using the product, what they want from the product, what they need from the product." She went on, telling me about software stacks and development servers, standardized markdowns and open-source programs. I didn't understand much of it, but I figured I would soon. Josh, she said, had a PhD in psychology. He mostly worked on meta-analysis of users' emotional fluctuations.

"We've never had a philosopher before," she said. "What's your specialty?"

I told her I worked on the mind-body problem. Before I could explain it, she nodded knowingly. "Ah," she said. "I thought you were going to be an ethics person. That's what we both thought, right, Josh?"

The same assenting sound came from behind the monitor.

"An ethics person is what they really need around here," she went on. "But those decisions are above my pay grade." She must have sensed my discomfort, because she hurried to add that she was sure I'd have a lot to contribute to the team.

"Oh, I almost forgot," she said, opening a drawer at her workstation. "HR dropped these off for you." She handed me a long rectangular cardboard box that was surprisingly heavy. Inside was a sheaf of business cards. Everything else at the third-most-popular internet company was digital, of course. But the cards were a throwback, printed with raised letters on heavy cardstock.

I ran my hand along their top ridges, watching them flip forward and backward. I pulled a single card out of the box and traced the letters of my name with my finger.

It read:

EVELYN KOMINSKY KUMAMOTO, RESEARCHER

A company—and not just any company, but the third-most-popular internet company, a company that was globally recognized, even if it was not globally dominant—had decided to invest in me, to present me with these thick cards with these raised letters, to give me this desk space and a shiny new computer with a screen so large it dwarfed my body.

I looked at the card in my hand. It didn't feel real.

※

That afternoon was our first team meeting. I went with Sabine and Josh to a large, glass-walled conference room, where the other employees who had been summoned were assembling: designers, programmers, engineers, copywriters. The meeting room was large and airy, its outer wall composed of floor-to-ceiling glass windows that looked out over the bay, and as we waited for the meeting to start, I watched the sailboats skimming across the water, bending low to the waves, their decks cutting almost perpendicular to its surface.

The room was filled with a whispered excitement. It was the official launch of the happiness project, the project I had been hired to work on, but no one knew much beyond that.

The glass door swooshed open and the whispering immediately quieted. Dr. Luce entered. Even though everyone else at the third-most-popular internet company went by their first names, apparently Dr. Luce insisted on being called Dr. Luce.

Standing at the front of the room, Dr. Luce picked up a remote and clicked a button. The screen behind her lit up. After a moment, the words HOW TO MEASURE HAPPINESS? appeared.

"I'm very pleased to introduce our newest product focus," she said. She paused for a beat, looking around at us, her audience. I tried to look engaged, attentive, ready to contribute.

"The premise is simple," she continued. "None of us, not a single one of us, truly knows how happy we are. Some of us fool ourselves into thinking we are happy, when a few small changes might bring us real happiness. Others of us have convinced ourselves that happiness is out of reach, when in fact we may be in the top tenth percentile of happiness and not even know it. If a simple algorithm could tell you how happy you were—objectively how happy—wouldn't you want to know? And why shouldn't we? We have algorithms that tell us which books we will like, which TV shows we should watch, which groceries to buy. We have algorithms that tell us traffic patterns and weather forecasts, when to buy plane tickets and when to sell stocks, even who will win the World Series. These algorithms make our lives better. More seamless. This research is a natural progression. Who wouldn't want to know if they were truly happy?"

Around me, my fellow employees were scribbling notes. My note-pad was blank. I could not imagine how an algorithm could capture something as complicated and ephemeral as happiness. How could a concept philosophers had struggled, over centuries, to even define be compressed into numbers and functions? I supposed that was what I was at the third-most-popular internet company to learn.

I should write something, I thought.

I wrote: *Happiness = World Series?*

I thought for a minute and then added, on the next line:

Happiness = Seamless life?

"This project is very important to me," Dr. Luce continued. "I believe it's no less than the future of the company. And if we don't do it, someone else is going to. You can bet on that. There are other research labs working on this right now. There's money in emotions, you know. A lot of money. If we know what emotion the user is experiencing while they are using our platform, we can predict their behavior to the nth degree: what they'll click on, what they'll buy. Everyone wants to be happier, so that's where we're starting: happiness. But happiness is just the beginning."

She clicked another button, and the screen changed to a list of numbers and measurements: body temperature, skin temperature, cortisol levels, dopamine levels, facial musculature, pupil dilation. These biometrics, she said, were one way we would build a measure for happiness.

"The other way is where our researchers come in," she said, looking at me and Sabine and Josh. She wanted us to come up with a prototype for a self-assessment. We couldn't just ask the user if they were happy, or if they thought they were happy. We had to make it more detailed. What questions should we ask? How should we word the questions? And what scale should we use to measure their responses? That was up to the three of us.

"They are our experts," she said. "They'll have full intellectual freedom in crafting the self-assessment."

I wrote: *Being happy vs. thinking you are happy—are these the same?*

"Our mission is to locate and improve happiness," Dr. Luce said, concluding. "Any questions?"

I wrote: *Where is happiness located?*

Where did happiness live? Head, heart, lung, liver? Small intestine? Wherever it was, it was somewhere interior, somewhere pink and squishy, somewhere pulsing with blood and cells and spleen, somewhere uncontrollably repulsive, somewhere immeasurably delicate.

It would not last long if brought to the surface.

FOUR

On my way home from work, I stopped and bought a soft white cheese that came nestled in its own straw box, and I felt instantly very sophisticated and, possibly, Parisian. I put a bunch of flowers that were labeled RANUNCULUS—a flower I had never heard of—into the shopping cart as well, because even though I would never be home to look at them during the day, I liked the image of myself as the kind of person who had fresh-cut flowers on the dining-room table. A woman with fresh-cut flowers on the dining-room table was a real woman, a real person. And for eighteen dollars, I could be that person—a person who it had never before occurred to me to be.

Jamie worked as an environmental surveyor for the state. We used to subsist primarily on his government income, my stipend covering only a meager portion of our rent. Now, suddenly, I was making considerably more money than he was. Now, suddenly, I could afford to buy all the groceries I wanted at the organic market down the street, where the vegetables were arranged to look like a farm stand, where an entire refrigerator case was filled with fermented beverages that promised numerous intangible benefits to your body, beverages whose labels said things like REJOICE! THIS IS A LIVE FOOD.

We had met at a grad student mixer when Jamie was in the last year of his geology PhD. He had a very all-American look to him—tall and white, with a broad, easy smile. He was the kind of person who did not typically approach a person like me, and when he came up to me at the bar and asked me which department I was in, at first I thought he was just killing time with me until he found a more appropriate match, possibly blond but more likely brunette, a person with the same automatic confidence that came from never having to feel on the outside. But one drink turned into three, which turned into tacos the next week, which turned into a hike that weekend, which turned into a movie and more tacos—it turned out he loved tacos—which turned into us moving in together when he finished his PhD and moved to the city for a government job.

When I got home, the lights were on and the apartment had been tidied: the magazines neatly stacked, the throw pillows on the couch fluffed. Jamie had said he didn't understand the need for the throw pillows, but I had insisted on buying them. I'd read that they completed a living room. Did our living room look complete? A jazz record I didn't recognize was playing on the stereo. Jamie came out of the kitchen wearing a blue and white-striped apron.

"Dinner's almost ready," he said, coming over and giving me a kiss on the cheek. "Roast chicken and vegetables, salad. To celebrate your first day. How was it?"

"I'm not sure," I said. He had been about to pivot back to the kitchen, but stopped and looked at me with concern.

"I'm not sure good or I'm not sure bad?"

"I'm just not sure," I said as I took off my jacket. Usually I threw it onto the couch, but now everything was so nicely fluffed, so neatly stacked, that I walked over to the closet and hung it up properly, on a hanger. "Everyone else is so excited about this project—measuring happiness—and it's not like I want to be the downer, but I don't really see how it's possible."

"Maybe that's why they hired you," Jamie said.

"To be the downer?" I said.

"To ask questions," he said. "To push them to think harder."

I heard a timer go off.

"To be continued," Jamie said, squeezing my arm. I followed him to the kitchen and stood in the doorway. I watched him open the oven and pull the tray out, a whole bird resting upon a nest of diced potatoes and carrots, resplendent and golden.

While the chicken rested, I unpacked the small cheese and put the ranunculus in water. We sat at the table and ate the roast chicken and the vegetables and the salad, and drank a red wine that Jamie said was a little bit of a splurge. He would not tell me exactly how much it cost, but apparently he wanted to make sure I knew it was a splurge—how else would I know it was good? I had to admit, it did taste better than the five- or ten-dollar wine we usually drank, though it was unclear if it would have tasted better had he not forewarned me that it should.

Over dinner, he asked if I wanted to talk more about the third-most-popular internet company. I shook my head, no. He was right, I thought. I was there to ask questions, to push myself and the team. I was there to help them build something tangible, something real.

When we finished, Jamie stood up and put on an Al Green record, which I thought was a little cheesy, but I didn't say anything. Jamie was a person who, if the mood struck, would play Al Green unironically. Sometimes I wondered if Jamie would be better off with someone who would also play Al Green unironically, someone spontaneous and light. Sometimes, when I was with Jamie, I felt like maybe that person could be me.

The record started out crackly at first—we had found it while trolling garage sales one weekend, and it had some light scratches on its surface—but soon, the words began to come through, lines about loving you forever, whether times were good or bad, happy or sad. Jamie came strutting back to the table and stuck out his hand, beckoning me.

I laughed, but he shook his head, insistent. I stood and took his hand, a little tipsy from the wine. I let myself be guided through a series of twirls and dips, Jamie's warm body leading mine. He smelled like schmaltz.

We had been together for four years, and we had talked about marriage somewhere around the midway point of year two. That is, we had talked about it in an extremely abstract sense. I had said I didn't want to get married until I finished my dissertation. Now, of course, I might never finish it. I wasn't sure if Jamie even remembered what I'd said. But recently, when the topic of marriage came up—in a TV show we were watching, or a movie—I could feel some kind of static coming off him, vibrating between us in the air. I did not ask him about the static. I didn't know why I didn't ask him about the static. I didn't want to be with anyone else, nor did I foresee wanting to be with anyone else.

My long-term boyfriend, whom I loved, was possibly getting ready to ask me to marry him. He had made this nice dinner, he had bought the wine that was a bit of a splurge, we had danced to Al Green. I knew I was supposed to be happy about this. I had been told, over and over again, that I should be happy about this. And yet when I thought about marriage, I felt only a hollow pit deep in my solar plexus, a vacancy that seemed to be mine alone. Everyone else I knew seemed so sure of what they were doing: the people they were marrying, the houses they were buying, the children they were birthing. When would I be sure?

The song ended. We stood in the middle of the living room for a beat. Was this the moment the static was going to end?

"Well," Jamie said, "I'm going to do the dishes."

I felt awash with relief.

While Jamie started on the dishes, I stayed at the table, drinking the wine and eating the cheese, surveying our living room. In the corner was a tower of books that no longer fit on our shelves, a tour of the stages of my intellectual failure: Aristotle and Plato and Hume and

Descartes and Kierkegaard and Leibniz, all those men whose thoughts on thought I knew inside and out.

How was it possible that I knew so much about how to think, but so little about what to do? On some level, I knew I was overthinking things, but from where I stood, it seemed as if everyone else was underthinking things and I was thinking about them the right amount. Still, there were no answers in sight.

Perhaps I would need to rethink my approach.

※

After we cleaned up dinner, Jamie went to the bedroom and I sat in front of the TV. I wanted to watch something, but I didn't know what. I clicked through the channels for a few minutes, a small, time-wasting pleasure I would never have indulged back in my dissertation-writing days. Eventually, I came across a nature documentary and quickly became absorbed in it. I hadn't watched nature shows since I was a child, when I wanted to be a nature photographer for *National Geographic*— a profession that was exciting and physical and outdoors, entirely the opposite of where I had ended up. The show was called *Misfits!*, and each episode featured a creature that was often overlooked: animals that were not celebrated for their speed or strength or beauty. No sharks or lions or peacocks here; these were animals who marched to the beat of a different drummer, said the voice-over.

The first animal profiled was the big-headed mole rat.

Out of thirty-seven species of mole rat, said the voice-over, thirty-six live entirely underground. The big-headed mole rat was the one species who ventured aboveground to feed. They did not have a good sense of sight, nor did they have a good sense of hearing. I watched as, on-screen, a big-headed mole rat poked its blind head out of the earth. Nearby, a wolf, its muscles taut, began to approach the mole rat's burrow.

But eating the fresh grasses and shrubs must be worth the danger from predators, said the voice-over.

The mole rat snuffled about in the grasses, the wolf slinking closer and closer. I felt the muscles in my body tightening.

Suddenly, a bird chirped, and the mole rat, alarmed, dropped its enormous head back into its hole, safe.

"The big-headed mole rat has a secret weapon," the voice-over said. "A sentry in the form of a bird called the moorland chat." The bird lived off the grubs and worms that were exposed in the mole rat's excavations, and in return, it chirped an alarm when wolves got too near.

I had happened upon a marathon, and I watched several more episodes, about the Japanese mudskipper, whose evolution had gotten stalled somewhere between fish and lizard; the Arctic woolly bear caterpillar, who took up to seven years to store enough resources to turn into a moth and whose whole body went into deep freeze each winter, its blood turning to ice. I watched the mating progress of the minute leaf chameleon, no bigger than a fingernail. Because it is so small, the voice-over said, it is immensely difficult for the minute leaf chameleon to find a mate—they simply do not encounter other chameleons very often in the wild. If a male chameleon does manage to find a female, he climbs onto her back and won't let go until mating is complete.

"Finding a mate is tough," the voice-over said, "in this giant world."

When I finally got into bed several hours later, Jamie was making the soft snuffling sounds of deep slumber. I had been sleeping next to this person for years, but suddenly I felt shy about lying next to him, about exposing my half-clad body to his. I thought about how strange it is that we trust ourselves in slumber to other people.

And then he shimmied his body over to mine, enveloping my form in his. I put my head in the crook of his armpit and let my body rise and fall with his breath.

FIVE

I went to visit my father once a month. We rarely communicated between visits, and if he ever called me, which he never did, I would have assumed it was a life-threatening emergency. Sometimes Jamie came with me, sometimes not. This time, he had to work, and so I drove down the 101 on my own. My father lived in a ranch-style house about an hour south of the city, in one of those gated complexes where all the houses look the same—not exactly the same, but different from each other in ways that are only barely distinguishable. It was my childhood home, and yet every month, it felt less and less familiar. As I pulled up to the curb, I slowed down and stared at the house. I knew I was in the right place, but the house looked even more foreign to me than usual. The formerly grassy lawn had been pulled up, leaving a barren patch of dirt in its place, punctuated by a few rocks. It gave the whole yard a naked, bald look.

I parked the car on the street, even though the driveway was empty. I rang the doorbell, even though I had a key. No one answered. I rang again, tempted to press my finger to the bell repeatedly, like a child, making it ring out spasmodically through the house, demanding to be heard. I looked around me, at the quiet, wide street. Half the houses had grass lawns, half looked like my father's—stripped. For a moment, I stood on the front step looking out. A man in late middle age wearing acid-green running shorts jogged by, slowly. I put my key in the lock and turned it.

"Hello?" I called. The house was silent, but smelled strongly of food, food that had been cooked recently—fried onions and something meaty. My father never cooked. He lived an antiseptic existence of takeout salads and sushi, of microwave dinners and soup from cans, Special K with skim milk every morning for breakfast, the bowl and spoon carefully washed and set on the drying rack before he left for work.

I went into the kitchen. A new rice cooker sat on the counter, releasing a jet of steam as it bubbled away, the digital timer ticking down the seconds. A pan sat on the stove's back burner. When I lifted the lid, I saw that it was filled with flat strips of cooked meat. I picked one up with a fork. The taste was vaguely familiar, sweet and caramelized. Just then, I heard a car pull up. I watched through the window as my father exited the driver's seat and a woman I had never seen before exited the passenger side. My father waited for her and they walked to the front door together.

I didn't know where to go, what to do. Stay in the kitchen, go to the living room, wait by the front door. I wished I could crawl out a window and reapproach, ring the doorbell like I had before, my father opening the door seconds later, anticipating my visit, his only daughter. I heard the door open and close, the murmurings of quiet conversation in the hall, words I couldn't make out. I called hello right away and went out to the foyer.

Instead of his usual Sunday attire—T-shirt tucked into jeans, running shoes—my father was wearing pleated khakis and a pressed polo shirt with loafers. Next to him was the woman. She was Asian, but I couldn't tell what kind of Asian she was. I was a failure of an Asian in that way. She looked like she was in her early fifties but was dressed in a way that suggested someone much older, or perhaps not much older but somehow out of time: a floral skirt that fell to midcalf, a pair of white sandals with blocky heels, a fitted denim jacket. A silver cross studded with either real or fake diamonds hung prominently around her neck.

When she saw me, the woman smiled widely and spread her arms to embrace me, grabbing on to my body before my father and I could even do our usual pat-on-the-back stand-in for a hug.

"You must be Evelyn," she cried. Her voice had a trace of an Asian accent, also unidentifiable, at least to me. "I've heard so much about you." Even with her blocky heels, her head came only to my shoulder. Her body felt warm and smelled like lotion or shampoo. She stepped back, her hands still circling my wrists, and looked at me, as if waiting for me to say something. I looked to my father, who was standing by the front door as if he might be able to melt away, his hands in his pleated pockets.

"This is Kumiko," he said, keeping his eyes trained on her, the bashful smile on his face not unlike that of a sixteen-year-old boy. "My girlfriend."

※

While Kumiko heated up lunch, my father and I sat at the dining-room table and drank iced tea. He apologized for not being there when I arrived; they had been at church, he said, which explained the way he was dressed but only made him seem even more like a stand-in for my actual father. My actual father did not go to church, had never gone to church. I tried to imagine him sitting in the wooden pew, prayer book in hand, but the image wouldn't come. They had met online, he said when I asked. He had been online dating for a few months now, he continued, but nothing had taken before. I tried to imagine him going on dates, sitting stiff-backed with a glass of wine or a cup of coffee.

He had never mentioned dating to me before, not once. As far as I knew, my father had never been involved with another woman, not since my mother. I wondered how long he had been thinking about it; I wondered what had prompted him to finally sign up; I wondered which photos he had posted, which women he had messaged; I wondered what his profile said.

"Lunch is ready," Kumiko called from the kitchen. My father rose from the table to retrieve bowls of rice, chopsticks, plates, cloth napkins I had never seen before. Kumiko brought over the sizzling pan of meat and spooned it onto our plates, bustling about authoritatively as though she already knew this kitchen, this home, well.

I watched my father as he ate. Sitting next to this woman, shoveling meat and rice into his mouth with a set of long-unused chopsticks, he looked relaxed, easeful. I had not seen him look this way in a long time.

I asked her questions, about what she did for work (legal secretary), if she liked the work (it was fine), what she did in her free time (went to church, cooked), where she lived (just a few miles away, very convenient). She did not expand on any of her answers, and I ran out of questions quickly. The questions I really wanted to ask—how long she had been online dating, what drew her to my father, had she been married before, were things serious between them, how did she feel about him—didn't seem like the kind of questions I should ask the first time I met her.

My father asked me about my new job. I said it was good, and he nodded. We had not spoken about my decision to leave the PhD program; I had announced it unilaterally, and he had only asked me if the new job had dental insurance. I wondered if he would ask me anything else, but instead he stood up to get seconds, something he never did when I cooked. He had gained a little weight in the month since I had last seen him; his stomach stuck out slightly over his belt.

I complimented Kumiko on the food and asked what it was called. She frowned slightly.

"This?" she said, jabbing at the meat with her chopsticks. "You don't know this dish?" I shook my head. She yelled something toward the kitchen in a language I assumed was Japanese. I did not know that my father still knew how to speak Japanese. He walked back into the dining room with a full plate, put his hand on her shoulder, said something incomprehensible back to her.

"You don't speak Japanese?" she said. I shook my head, said no. I had studied French in high school, German in graduate school. "You don't know gyudon?" she said. I shook my head, no, again. I remembered eating it at a Japanese restaurant once or twice, but I didn't eat Japanese food very often.

She said something else in Japanese to my father, who shook his head.

"I'll show you how to make it," she said, turning her attention back to me. "The secret is the sauce. You have to get the right brand of mirin."

"That would be nice," I said, knowing full well that I would never take her up on the offer, never stand in the kitchen with this six-inches-shorter-than-me Japanese-talking Japanese-judging woman, watching her lay strips of beef in sizzling oil with the same hands she used to touch my father. "By the way"—I turned to him—"what happened to the lawn?"

He finished chewing an oversize bite.

"Decided to put in a drought-resistant yard," he said. "Grass is a waste of resources. Cut my water bill in half."

Kumiko nodded enthusiastically. Clearly it had been her idea.

"It looks a little sparse right now," he said, "but the succulents will be planted soon. Drought-resistant yard makes the property value go up. Everyone in the neighborhood is putting them in."

"What happens to the grass?" I asked.

"They truck it out somewhere, I guess," he said. I imagined a pyre of grass somewhere in the barren flats of central California, a monument to all the land once was, its famed fertility.

"You know what I read?" my father said, picking up a slice of beef with his chopsticks and holding it there, this meat of resource consumption, of CO_2 emissions, of *E. coli*–poisoned groundwater and rain forest depletion. "It takes a gallon of water to grow a single almond. Can you imagine? A single almond. What's so great about almonds, anyway?"

SIX

The city was going through its October heat spell, and the hills were covered not with the usual thick, cold fog but with a gloaming haze. The sidewalk tables were full of brunchers, twentysomethings sprawled out in Dolores Park in states of semi-undress, lines for strawberry-balsamic ice cream stretched around the block. The mid-fall heat wave was logging record temperatures, surpassing previous highs by a full five or even ten degrees on some days.

A month had passed since the happiness project kickoff. I had spent the time reading and rereading various philosophers' views on happiness, generating a list of possible areas for self-assessment: pleasure, purpose, community, belonging. Next to me, Sabine and Josh were doing the same for sociology and psychology. At the end of each day, we would confer briefly, considering points of comparison and overlap, growing our master list. I couldn't believe this was what I was being paid to do, and being paid so well at that. I drank complimentary seltzer after complimentary seltzer, marveling at the staggering array of brands offered in the communal refrigerator; I ate complimentary lunches of quinoa and salmon; each Friday, Sabine brought a bottle of craft beer to my desk at three o'clock—complimentary also, of course—and the three of us would toast to nothing in particular before continuing our research.

One day during my lunch break, I went for a walk down Geary to accompany Sharky on one of his trend forecasting surveys. He had been working as a trend forecaster for a year or so, after finally giving up on trying to make it as a filmmaker in Los Angeles. He said he liked trend forecasting. It was like film, in a way—you had to be good at noticing detail. And you could make it big as a trend forecaster, too. His boss had been the one to predict kale.

He walked slightly ahead, bobbing and weaving through the crowds of tourists, his arm extended, phone out, snapping photos continuously. I was struggling to keep up, when I heard a voice say my name. Female and faintly British, it seemed to be coming from close by. I stopped and looked behind me, but there was no one who appeared to be addressing me. Tourists streamed by, unnoticing, their arms weighed down by shopping bags—CHANEL, LOUIS VUITTON, BALENCIAGA—their heads bent toward their screens, where thousands of micro-algorithms were operating simultaneously to direct them to the next shop, the next restaurant, the next place to consume. The dollar was low; the tourists were hungry.

"Evelyn Kumamoto," the same voice said again, with the exact same inflection. Now it seemed to be coming from right next to me. But all that was next to me was a bus stop. On the side of the shelter, an illuminated screen displayed an interactive map of the bus system. I took a step toward it and watched as the image changed from the map to a photograph of a white-sand beach, green-fronded palm trees, cerulean waters. No one else noticed, no one else was stopping; they continued sidestepping me and moving on. Up ahead, Sharky was talking to a young Asian woman. All the trends, he said, came from Asia.

I looked back at the screen. Now there was an image of a buffet line, smiling, red-faced people piling their plates high. I could hear something about an all-inclusive resort.

I moved a few feet back, and the screen returned to the bus system map.

I moved back in, and the promotional images returned. This time, I watched the ad all the way through, the voice promising me the vacation of a lifetime. At the end, words scrolled by fast, in small print: SPONSORED BY THE HAWAII BOARD OF TOURISM.

An ad for an electric toothbrush was just beginning when Sharky doubled back to where I was standing. I could see him in my peripheral vision, but I didn't look away from the ad. My father was a dentist. Was it possible this ad somehow knew he was a dentist? Every time I saw him, he asked about my teeth. Maybe it was his way of asking about me—about my overall well-being—or maybe he really did just want to know about my teeth, my gums, the possibility of any cavities.

"This bus station map is talking to me," I told Sharky. I pointed to it. "Look." I was strangely mesmerized by the spiraling bristles. It did look like a good toothbrush. Nine and a half out of ten dentists recommended it.

"Whoa," he said, excited. Sharky was always excited, but now he seemed especially so. "ADAPT. Adaptive advertisement. I heard they were rolling out the beta test."

He pulled out his phone and began filming the ad. Around us, the crowd kept streaming by.

"Why is no one else stopping?" I asked. Sharky was poking some buttons on his phone.

"They already have ADAPT in Asia," he said, still working. "There." He showed me his phone, the video already uploaded to his social media. On the bus shelter, the toothbrush ad was playing again, the one on his screen echoing it in a slight delay. He had posted it thirty-two seconds ago, and it had already been viewed seventeen times.

He proceeded to explain, in his most reverent tone of voice, the way ADAPT worked, the way it looped into my internet searches and built a composite identity for me based on those searches. When I passed a certain kind of billboard, he said, it wirelessly connected to my phone and triggered the ads.

"A composite identity?"

"Yeah, like it's not quite you, but it's the you based on your searches, so it's also kind of more than you."

"I didn't agree to that," I said.

"You definitely did, or it wouldn't have happened."

"I definitely did not."

"You just don't remember agreeing to it, but you definitely did. You must have."

On the screen, the toothbrush ad ended and the Hawaii ad started again.

"But look," I said. "This is an ad for Hawaii, and I don't even like the beach."

"Still has some kinks to work out, I guess."

"Did you agree to it?"

"Of course! But I haven't been able to trigger one yet," he said. "Scoot over." I took a few steps back, and the screen returned to the bus system map. Sharky stood directly in front of the screen, but it remained static.

"Maybe they just haven't been able to pin down the elusive figure who is Sharukh Bhakerjee Teitelbaum," I said, but Sharky was already moving on. He continued down the street, stopping in front of the next screen just long enough to see if it knew who he was.

I had met Sharky on the first day of college, when we were randomly assigned to the same orientation group. We sat cross-legged on the leaf-strewn New England ground in what Sharky would later repeatedly refer to as a liberal arts feelings circle.

"Tell us something about yourself," said our group leader, a junior still suffering from wretched acne. "Only what you feel comfortable sharing."

A few people introduced themselves, giving their name, their place of origin, a fun fact. The introductions moved quickly around the circle, each of us giving only a few details, each of us still deciding who we were going to be in this new place. That is, until we got to a boy sitting across from me. His full name was Sharukh Bhakerjee Teitelbaum, he said, but everyone called him Sharky. Born and raised in Nashville—an origin that registered mild surprise on a few faces, given that he was distinctly South Asian in appearance, though maybe not entirely South Asian, possibly South Asian with something else mixed in, surprise that, given that this was a good liberal arts feeling circle, and, of course, all kinds of people could be from all kinds of places, everyone hastened to cover up—he played basketball, point guard. His high school team, he said, with a slight Southern accent, though his rapid-fire speech left little room for drawl, had been state champions four years in a row, and Southeast champions his junior and senior years.

Here was where everyone else had left off. But Sharky kept going. He loved fried pickles and country music, and he defied anyone to name a musician superior to Hiram King Williams, better known as Hank. He was the youngest of six children, all boys, all lawyers or in law school, but he wanted to be a filmmaker, documentaries, more Les Blank than Werner Herzog. Here he did what I would later realize was a Werner Herzog impression—severe, heavy, Germanic—but at the time, neither I nor any of my other seemingly worldly peers recognized it. He had made his first feature film when he was twelve and had made eight more since then. He was working on casting his next one, he said, looking around the circle meaningfully, taking in each person's face, if any of us were interested in auditioning. His top three favorite films other than documentaries were *The Big Sleep, Chinatown,* and *Double*

Indemnity: he was a lover of noir. Still, his parents said they wouldn't pay for him to go to college just to watch all the movies he'd already watched all over again, many of them for the tenth or twentieth time, and so he was majoring in economics, which he thought was basically the most boring subject possible—no offense to any other econ majors or potential econ majors out there—but he was thinking he would just make a boatload of money in the first few years after college and use it to finance his first feature film.

He paused for a second and looked like he was simply gathering his thoughts, but the pimpled group leader jumped in and thanked him for sharing, nodding encouragingly at the next face in the circle. The introductions continued on, moving from one quirky high achiever to the next, everyone besides Sharky saying only a sentence.

When this was done, the group leader left us to talk amongst ourselves until our next scheduled activity. Talking amongst ourselves was an area in which I did not excel, though I did excel at looking off into the middle distance and pretending I didn't notice no one was talking amongst ourselves with me. I was just beginning to lengthen my gaze and let it fuzz when a face appeared at short range: Sharky, the South-Asian-appearing, film noir–/Hank Williams–/fried pickle–loving point guard from Nashville.

"Jubu?" he said.

"Excuse me?" I said. His eyes were wide and eager.

"Ju . . . bu," he said again, enunciating each syllable. "You know. Jewish Buddhist. Like me, half Jewish, half Indian. Hebrew school, bar mitzvah, the whole deal, Torah portion was Noah and the flood."

I had never met another half-Jewish, half-Asian person.

"Evelyn Kominsky Kumamoto," I said. "Half Jewish, half Japanese. Torah portion was Moses parting the Red Sea." I stuck out my hand to shake, but he intercepted it with a fist bump. "How did you know?"

"I've got Jubu-dar," he said.

From then on, we were inseparable.

※

By the time I managed to tear myself away from the screen, Sharky was waiting for me, impatiently, at the next corner. I had made us miss the light. A few feet away, a man stood next to a giant poster board, ringing a bell like a Salvation Army Santa and yelling about the end of the world. Fornicators, sodomizers, time to repent. On the board, he had written a variety of words in capital letters of different sizes. FORNICATORS was the biggest, in the middle. Also: JESUS, HELL, HEAVEN, AVARICE, JUDG-MENT. There were other words, too, that I couldn't make out without getting closer. When I was twelve, thirteen, just beginning to explore the city with friends, I had frequented this area, and there had also been a man around then, with the same kind of poster, the same proclamations of impending doom. Was it possible this was the same man, all these years later? That he had withstood gentrification, had withstood the police, had withstood hunger and rain and the city's wet cold? That he had found a place to sleep every night, a place to wake, a place to ready himself, over and over again, for what he considered his sworn duty? That he had been standing here all this time, hoping for a day of apocalypse that would make all he had worked for come true?

The passersby gave the man a wide berth. Sharky was standing an arm's distance away, either utterly absorbed in his phone or pretending to be. I hurried to catch up, and as I approached, I accidentally caught the man's eye. He looked at me with what appeared to be complete lucidity. For a moment, he held the bell still, quieting its incessant ring.

"Young lady," he said, not with his usual fire and brimstone, but in a low voice tinged with pity. "Judgment is coming for you, too."

SEVEN

That weekend, Jamie and I went camping. He had been in the office all month—no fieldwork—and said he wanted to get outdoors. I wasn't sure that car camping counted, but it was the best we could do, so we drove to a campground, set up our tent on a pre-groomed square of dirt, built a fire in the premade fire pit, and grilled some steaks that we had purchased at the grocery store down the road—steaks that were decidedly not local or organic or grass-fed but came in a Styrofoam tray, bloody and absurdly cheap, the product of farm subsidies that we paid for with our tax dollars because farmland fit our vision of America as a place of plenty.

When we woke up the next morning, our tent filled with the slightly fetid humidity of two bodies breathing and sweating and doing all the other things bodies did, I heard a light tip-tapping on the tent.

"What is that?" I said, rolling over into Jamie's armpit.

"I think it's raining," he said. His eyes were still closed.

Rain had not been in the forecast.

I unzipped the tent and stuck my head out. The campsite was covered in a low gray mist. I slipped on my boots and grabbed my rain jacket—I had brought it just in case, of course. I looked at our pile of firewood. If I could get a fire going, I thought, it should be able to keep burning; it wasn't raining hard enough to put it out.

My mother had been the one to teach me how to build a fire. We had gone camping for a few days every summer, from as early as I could remember up until she got sick. We left my father at home; he was not interested in sleeping in a tent. It was a special couple of days for me, this time when I had my mother all to myself. This was before smartphones, before cell phones, even, and so, for those few days, she was utterly unreachable, no office calling her night and day. Instead, we spent our days hiking and swimming, making hot dogs and s'mores, and telling scary stories around the fire, stories that involved hooks in car door handles and vanishing hitchhikers. She made a fire every night, showing me how to arrange the kindling so that air could flow underneath, how to stack the bigger pieces of wood, how to blow on the flame so it would catch.

In the years since, I had noticed that building fires was not considered the purview of women. On camping trip after camping trip, the men I was with assumed they would make the fire and I would gather the kindling. I did not like being a kindling-gatherer. Jamie was the first man who had asked, on our first camping trip, if I wanted to make the fire. I said yes, I did.

I pulled my hood over my hair and crouched down next to the pile of wood, sorting through to pick out the least damp pieces, the ones that had been sheltered from the rain. I balled up some newspaper and arranged the smaller sticks in a tepee around the paper balls, as many sticks as I had the patience to place. Then I took the largest log and laid it horizontally as a base, just touching the edge of the tepee; I leaned two more logs against the large one so they rested over the kindling, but with enough space that they wouldn't suffocate it.

I struck a match and lit the base of the paper, watching as it flared up, the flame bright and alive against the gray mist that shrouded the campsite. I blew on it as gently as I could, willing it to spread. If the kindling was too wet, it wouldn't catch, but I watched as the flame moved to one small stick and then another, until the paper had burned out and the center was still alight. I began to blow harder, sticking my face closer to the flame, blowing into the growing fire and then turning my head to inhale fresh air before blowing again, making my body into a bellows. The fire continued to grow, the edges of the logs beginning to glow orange, the stray curls of wood lighting and then going out but not before they had concentrated a little more heat on the log, urging it to combust. And then, just a few breaths later, came the moment when I was sure the fire was going to catch. It had not caught yet, but somehow, I knew that it would.

I watched as the fire grew, moving from one log to another, until it was burning steadily enough to withstand the light drizzle.

✳

We spent the morning sitting under a tarp we strung up near the fire, drinking coffee and reading, watching our fellow car campers packing up and going home. Most of them were families, and the prospect of a rainy day spent in the confined space of a tent with children was too much for even the most devoted parent. When the rain stopped after lunch, Jamie announced that he wanted to go for a walk. It was too late in the day to go far, so we walked along the road to a lake that was meant to be one of the top features of the area. On a sunny day, I imagined it would have been filled with children playing, with beach balls and footballs and barbecues and multicolored beach umbrellas, but today, with the sky still overcast and threatening more rain, we had the beach entirely to ourselves.

I suggested we take a different trail back, one that cut through the trees. It started out as a well-groomed path, wide enough for us to walk side by side. Everything around us was still and glossy with raindrops, like the landscape had been cleaned. The air smelled verdant, of dirt and greenery. It was silent except for the occasional rustle in the grass, a chipmunk or a squirrel fleeing at the sound of our footfalls.

After a little while, the trail narrowed and we had to walk single file: me in the lead, Jamie behind. At the start of the trail, the grass had barely crested the top of my boots, but here it was hip high, arcing over the path from both sides, and as I pushed through it, I felt the cold droplets of water that had been resting on the blades transferring themselves to my body.

By the time we emerged on the other side—out on the road, not far from our tent—my pants were soaked from the knees down, my shoes squelching. Jamie looked similarly saturated.

"Let's get back to the tent," I said. We each had a change of clothes in the car; we could build another fire and warm our feet. Jamie nodded, but then he paused, staring at me—not at my face, but at my leg.

"What's that?" he said. We both bent over to look. It was a tick, clinging to my pants, trying to find a way through to my skin. He flicked it away. I turned to walk back to the campsite.

"Wait," Jamie said. And then I felt his hands on me, brushing me with increasingly frantic motions. "They're everywhere," he said, a note of panic in his voice. "They're on me, too."

He swiped one from the back of my knee; I flicked one from his thigh. There were more, on our pants, our shirts, our shoes. One tick I could handle, even two. But I had never seen this many ticks before; it was as though they had swarmed our bodies in a great horde. If we were finding this many on our clothes, some must have made it underneath. Ticks existed for no other reason than to find flesh; that was how they survived.

We ran to the bathroom, a concrete structure with pit toilets. We locked the door and stripped off our clothes, pulled off our shoes, for once not caring about putting our bare feet on the dirty floor of a campsite bathroom. We checked each other's backs and legs, looked in the creases behind our knees, between our toes, behind our ears. I combed through the hair in Jamie's armpits; he did his best to check over my scalp. We pulled off ticks, not yet latched, and crushed them with our thumbnails. We took extra care looking at places with moisture and warmth, places a body would want to go for shelter, places a body might seek protection. We pulled the folds of our genitalia this way and that; I had probably never been as intimate with my own body as I was in that inspection. After a moment's hesitation, we each bent over and separated our butt cheeks, allowing the other to peer into the crevice there, a different kind of intimacy than sexual intimacy, in which bodies are staged, prepared.

After we put our clothes back on, Jamie said we should get married.

"What?" I said. We were still in the concrete bathroom. This was not the way I had thought the static would culminate, but something about it felt appropriate. I wasn't someone who needed—or wanted—a fancy proposal, down-on-one-knee, a big diamond.

"We should get married," he said again. His face was serious. "There's no one I would rather face down a swarm of ticks with."

I was standing barefoot on the cold concrete in wet clothes, but suddenly, I felt very hot. Logically, I knew, the thing to say was yes.

"I don't know," I said.

Jamie laughed, his eyes crinkling at the corners in the way I loved.

"I know you need to think about it," he said. "You need to think about everything. It's okay that you need to think about this, too."

I felt a little less hot.

Who was this person who was capable of so much love and understanding? And why, out of all the people in the world, had he decided to love me?

Probably, I thought, that was a question with no logical answer.

EIGHT

The third-most-popular internet company's holiday party was held on a Saturday night in early December at the Natural History Museum. I guessed this was a purposeful decision, to host the party at a place that represented evolution, science, progress, the moment that a four-legged amphibious lizard came out of the sea and decided to try walking on two legs instead. Of course it was also incredibly grand.

"This should be something," I said to Jamie as we walked toward the Grecian-style building. I was wearing heels, and the balls of my feet were already beginning to throb. I had to lean on Jamie a little in order to get up the stairs. There was a photographer at the door, shooting pictures for the *Chronicle*. It seemed strange that society pages, which must have been a vestige of gold rush times, of new money that wanted to be old, still existed. We didn't stop for the photographer.

Simone de Beauvoir wrote that authentic love—ethical love—was one in which two lovers were able to walk side by side as equals, neither seeking subordination from the other. According to de Beauvoir, this kind of love was hard for women to achieve, conditioned as they had been from birth to believe that they must do everything they could to please a man, to make themselves worthy of his love. I thought of this as I hobbled beside Jamie in the heels I had felt compelled to wear because I was a woman and this was a fancy party.

More than a month had passed since the camping trip, and Jamie had not brought up marriage again. Mostly, I was relieved. I wanted things to stay the way they were. But I knew they couldn't stay the way they were forever; I might allow that, but Jamie would not. Jamie's life was a life with forward momentum. My life seemed to me to circle around in illegible squiggles.

We entered a vast rotunda. In the center was the skeleton of a blue whale, cordoned off with velvet ropes as though it were a celebrity. Even lacking flesh, it was massive, each rib the size of my entire person. I wondered what it would be like to be swallowed up whole, trapped in the belly of the whale. I knew this wasn't possible—the baleen, etc., a myth, etc.—but still, I pictured its giant mouth consuming me, sweeping me up with the plankton and the krill, ferrying me into an underwater netherworld of phosphorescence and silence.

When we entered the ballroom, it was already packed with people: men in suits and women in cocktail dresses and heels, bodies festooned with expensive watches and jewelry. In the center of the ballroom was a fountain where hundreds of Champagne coupes were tiered like a monolithic wedding cake, liquid flowing down their sides in what I hoped was a recirculating system. Along the fountain's periphery stood half a dozen waiters, also tuxedo-clad, each bearing a tray of full glasses, lest anyone make the mistake of trying to actually take one of the coupes, which would send the whole fountain crashing down.

"I'll go get us some drinks," Jamie said.

I told him I'd go with him.

"You don't have to do that," he said. "You work here. Find someone you know and make work talk."

I must have given him a look of panic.

"You can do it," he said, squeezing my hand and taking off for one of the several bars.

I had always found the small-talk portion of parties—the part before people are properly drunk, when everyone is still tense and inhibited—tiresome. I moved through the crowd, trying to look like I belonged. I did belong. And yet I still felt like an interloper.

"Evelyn!" It was Sabine, moving toward me through the crowd. I felt a jolt of relief. She came over, holding a glass of Champagne. "Bottoms up," she said, and then quickly downed her whole glass.

"Whoa," I said. "Someone's celebrating."

"Hardly," she said. Her eyes rapidly scanned the crowd. "Didn't you hear?" she asked in a low voice. "About the researcher they fired in AI?"

"What?" I said. I had not heard. "We sit next to each other all day, every day. How do you know this and I don't?"

"It just happened," she said distractedly, beckoning a waiter over. She gave him her empty coupe, plucked two glasses of Champagne from his tray, and handed one to me. "She wrote a paper for a conference that was an ethical critique of language models and racial bias, and they wanted her to retract it. She refused, and poof, no more job."

She took a sip of her Champagne, and so did I. I felt the bubbles hiss on my tongue. It tasted expensive.

"Something else must have happened," I said. "Are you sure you have the full story?"

Sabine looked at me for a long moment.

"I'm sure I have the full story, Evelyn," she said.

"Okay, sorry," I said. "But, still, that's a different department. That's not Dr. Luce."

Sabine raised her eyebrows. The party thrummed around us, the din of conversation echoing off the high stone ceilings.

"You're fooling yourself if you think Dr. Luce wouldn't do the same."

"She told us that we had full intellectual freedom," I said.

"Right," Sabine said. "Just like they told Theresa."

Theresa, I assumed, was the AI researcher. I tried to remember if I had ever met her, but I couldn't come up with anything. Despite being only the third most popular, the company was still vast. So far, I didn't recognize a single face at this party other than Sabine's.

"What do you think this means for us?" I said.

Sabine shrugged.

"I don't know," she said. "They want to pretend this whole thing never happened. I wish I could quit, but without this job, I wouldn't have a visa. I'd have to go back to Karachi."

She sighed, scanning the crowd and taking a sip of her Champagne.

"What about you?" she said, turning back to me.

"What about me?"

"You could quit," she said. "But most people don't. It's too much, to leave all this." She gestured at the scene around us, the tuxedoed waiters, the laughing faces, the air of plenty, of confidence, of surety that we were doing powerful and influential things.

After we talked for a few more minutes, Sabine told me she would see me on Monday and merged back in the crowd, no doubt to gather more information. I admired her tenacity. I finished my glass of Champagne and took another coupe from one of the waiters next to the Champagne fountain. I made my way along the periphery, looking for Jamie. I couldn't see him anywhere; only crowds of people, bodies talking and laughing and shaking hands with a powerful grip—everyone knew, by this point, to use a powerful grip—ready to celebrate the next innovation in technology, the next big thing. I was now one of those bodies, even if I tried to tell myself otherwise, tried to say I was a researcher, a philosopher, that I was different. I was not ready to give this all up.

I walked past a full prime rib, meat red, fat glistening, uniformed caterer at the ready should anyone desire a slice. When he saw me walk by, he straightened a bit, ready for action, and I felt I was letting him down when I didn't stop. At the far end of the ballroom was a raw bar, a long table with twelve kinds of oysters, their shells strikingly primordial in this epicenter of the digital and new. Around the oysters were piles of clams and mussels, curls of preshelled cocktail shrimp, fresh crabmeat, slices of tuna, yellowtail, whole scallops. Arrayed here and there around the table were sea urchins, their spiky shells broken to expose the custardy lobes of uni inside.

I put a few pieces of fish on my plate, a scallop, a shrimp. A delicate chopstick-full of crab. I put my drink down on the corner of a nearby table and ate, but within seconds, everything was gone and I was still hungry. I returned to the raw bar, stacking my plate with slabs of fish, as many as I could fit, the pieces threatening to fall off the edges. I stepped to one side and pressed them into my mouth, feeling their flesh give between my teeth. Still, I was not done. I moved to where a man in an apron was shucking oysters, his movements perfected and mechanical. As he put the shucked oysters on the table, I picked them up, sucking down one after another, awash in their salty brine. I didn't stop to sauce them, not with the cocktail sauce or the mignonette, but drank them down, pure and unvarnished. I went back for more: more of everything.

I picked up my glass again. A waiter took my plate. No evidence remained of the mass quantity of seafood I had just ingested. I had the power, I felt, of many tiny shrimp. Or maybe even one big tuna.

"There you are." I heard Jamie's voice behind me.

I turned and there he was, holding two coupes. I felt a want for him that I had not felt in months.

"Let's get out of here," I said.

"What? I haven't even eaten anything yet," Jamie said.

"Let's go home."

"What?" Jamie repeated. "Why?"

Clearly, I was not expressing myself well enough. I leaned over and whispered in his ear.

He put down the drinks and we left the party.

NINE

A few weeks later, after the holidays, I went to my father's house. Jamie and I had done Christmas just the two of us, our tradition since graduate school, when flights during the holidays had been too expensive for our stipends. Now that we were both working, we could afford the tickets to visit his parents in Michigan, but we stuck to our routine: a small Christmas tree in the apartment, a Christmas Day hike in the woods on the other side of the Golden Gate Bridge. It was one of those unusual years when Chanukah overlaps with Christmas, so when we got back to the apartment, we started grating potatoes for latkes. I still made them the way my mother had taught me, with only a tablespoon or so of matzo meal, just enough to bind the potatoes and onions together. For a few years after my mother passed away, my father and I had tried to keep celebrating Chanukah—frying latkes, lighting the menorah—but after I left for college, all eight nights usually fell during my final exams, so our attempt to keep the tradition going had ended.

I hadn't been back for my usual monthly visit since September. It might have been the longest we'd gone without seeing each other in several years, but my father accepted my excuses without question; it seemed like he might allow me to keep making excuses for the rest of my life. When he wrote back to my emails, he simply said it was fine, he would see me another time. He hoped work was going well. No one, it should be said, was forcing me to make these excuses. My father didn't ask anything of me, ever. It was me who felt I should be visiting on a certain schedule, who felt the tug of filial piety.

But then he emailed me, saying he wanted to turn my room into a home gym, and could I come sort through my things? I had a hard time picturing what things there were to sort. I was not one of those people who still had endless possessions stored at their parents' house, a teenage bedroom ready-made to step back into, should they need it. I rarely even went up to my room when I came to visit.

This time, I went down on a Saturday instead of a Sunday in an effort to avoid the subject of church. I entered the streets of almost-identical houses, their sidewalks curved according to carefully mapped coordinates. At my father's house, the bald patch of dirt was now pocked with green, where the succulents had been planted. I wondered if he had done it himself or if he had hired someone to do it. I couldn't quite picture it either way. He had always mowed the lawn when I was growing up, pulling the mower out of the garage every Sunday, and I assumed he had kept up this weekly routine right until the grass had been ripped out by the root. Before, the drought-resistant yard had been drought-resistant because there was no life there to die of drought. Now there were the beginnings of life. Something that needed sun and water, if only once a week.

The whole drive down, I had felt mildly annoyed that I had to spend my day sifting through my belongings—belongings that I didn't even remember leaving behind. But once I was there, on my father's cul-de-sac, I was relieved. Relieved that, for a few hours at least, I wouldn't have to think about marriage. I had been thinking about marriage a lot since the tick incident, but I had reached no conclusions. I still did not feel sure. But was anyone really sure?

As I walked up to the door, I could hear music playing. Music never played at our house. I didn't think my father even had a means with which to play music. I rang the doorbell, but it was drowned out by the sound. I pulled my key out of my purse and turned it in the lock. The music was much louder inside. I slipped my shoes off. The Rolling Stones. *I can't get no. Satisfaction.*

I walked through the living room, toward the kitchen. A record was spinning on a turntable. The record player looked vintage, but I had never seen it before. Next to the turntable was a pile of records: the Beatles, the Animals, Jimi Hendrix, Joni Mitchell, more Rolling Stones. As I thumbed through, there were more obscure albums, too, by artists whose names I didn't recognize: Fanny, the Chambers Brothers, Robin Trower, Louie and the Lovers.

From where I was standing, I could see through the doorway into the kitchen. My father and Kumiko were standing by the sink, doing dishes. Kumiko was wearing yellow rubber dish gloves and my father had rolled his shirtsleeves up to the elbows, apparently on drying duty. He seemed utterly absorbed, enthralled even, with their task. Kumiko was doing a standing-in-place dance, dish in hand, wiggling her shoulders and shaking her head from side to side, my father belting out the lyrics as he wiped a glass casserole dish with a dish towel. The sink was full of suds, far sudsier than seemed strictly necessary, and bubbles drifted lazily up through the air.

It did not seem to me that they were getting the dishes done with much efficiency.

The song ended, and Kumiko shook the water off her gloves, turning toward the living room to come out and flip the record.

When she saw me standing there, she gave out a little "Oh!" and jumped back, recoiling. My father turned then, too. He seemed, for a second, not to recognize me.

"I'm sorry," I said, stepping forward. "I didn't mean to startle you."

"It's okay, it's okay," Kumiko said, pulling off her gloves and bustling over to me. She gave me a tight hug. She released me and turned back to my father. "Stephen, you didn't tell me that Evelyn was coming today! I didn't cook." I hadn't heard my father referred to by his first name in many years.

The record was still spinning, unattended, on the turntable, making a gentle *whish whish*.

I had emailed my father the night before, but he said he hadn't checked. I told them I could clear out whatever needed clearing out from my bedroom. They looked at me blankly. "The exercise room?" I said.

"Ah, the home gym," my father said, giving a little nod.

"Home gym," Kumiko repeated. They both said "home gym" as if it were one word. *Home-gym.*

"Right," I said. "The home gym." I pronounced it decidedly as two words.

"Stephen will take you up there while I finish the dishes," Kumiko said, giving my father the kind of look that is more of a physical nudge. Together, they looked matched, like a set. A happy Japanese couple, who could have been together all their lives.

I wanted to say this was not necessary, I knew where it was, but something about the way Kumiko had looked at my father made me stop. I didn't know what it was about, but I could tell there was something. My father walked by me to the record player, lifting the needle and letting the record come, finally, to a stop. He placed the needle carefully back on its rest and put the cover on the turntable. There was still a stack of dishes next to the sink, but Kumiko didn't say anything about the music. She gave me a smile and returned to the basin of suds, and I followed my father's padding footsteps across the floor of the house I had grown up in, the house I once knew so well.

My childhood bedroom was painted light yellow. My parents had let me choose the color when I was eleven years old, and I remembered going to the hardware store with my mother to pick it out, to collect the rollers and the blue painter's tape we needed, the brushes and the primer. I remembered helping her as she meticulously covered the molding and the baseboard with strips of tape, as we painted over the off-white walls over the course of a weekend, windows open and music playing, paint spattering our clothes, our shoes, our hair, our skin.

My room was still the same light yellow my mother and I had painted it. But now there was an elliptical, a rowing machine, a stand holding dumbbells ranging in weight from five pounds to fifty. Who in this house was lifting a fifty-pound dumbbell? My father trailed me into the room, almost sheepishly.

"Those came as a set," he said when he saw me looking at the weights. "I'm not sure we'll get much use out of the big ones, but Kumiko said it was a better deal than buying them individually."

I nodded. We'll get much use out of. Kumiko.

"I didn't know you rowed," I said. I leaned down, pulled back the handle of the rowing machine and felt the flywheel spin. There was higher resistance than I expected.

"Kumiko does," he said. He was looking sheepish again, or maybe bashful. "She's going to teach me. She said it's good for me. Low impact."

"Like the elliptical," I said.

"Like the elliptical."

I was still holding the handle of the rowing machine, and we stood, silent, for a moment, as the wheel finished spinning and went still.

"Where'd that record player come from? Whose records are those?"

"Oh!" my father said, his face brightening. "Those are mine. You don't remember? We used to listen to them, when you were little. You used to dance around and pretend to sing along. You'd put on a little show for us."

For us. Him and my mother.

I didn't remember.

"Anyway," my father said, "I put them away, after. I had forgotten about them, but then Kumiko and I were talking about college the other day, and I was telling her how I spent all my time listening to records in my room, and then I remembered. I thought they might be damaged after all these years in the basement, but only a few got warped. The rest still sound good as new."

It was possible this was the most my father had said to me in one go in at least ten years. He had helped me, in those first few years of adulthood, to do my taxes; he had taught me to change my own oil; he had gone over the health insurance plan offered by the university, reading every sentence to make sure I would be covered in the case of any contingency. But he had never shared anything about what college was like, what he did there. I had never pictured him at college, but now an image flashed into my mind of eighteen-year-old him, standing alone on the Cal campus, lost and alone. Or was it the opposite: Was he exhilarated, liberated from home and his stern Japanese parents—my late grandparents—for the first time, free to spend his time however he wanted, browsing the record stores on Telegraph Avenue, building a collection, gathering with friends in his room to listen to LP after LP? These were things it had never before occurred to me to ask.

My father had been rustling around in the closet, and now he pulled out a cardboard box.

"Here," he said. "This is what Kumiko wanted me to show you." He put the box on the beige carpet in front of me, like an offering. It was labeled EVELYN. I instantly recognized the handwriting. My mother's.

I couldn't think what could possibly be in it. School papers? I kneeled down on the floor. The box had been packed with care, its flaps folded under each other so they would stay down. Was there a word for that kind of fold? I pulled on one of the flaps and all four opened out.

Inside was fabric—silk—in a herringbone pattern, from the '80s, maybe, but elegant. Below it was wool, linen, more silk. Clothes. My mother's.

"We found these," my father said, "way in the back of the closet. She got rid of a lot of her clothes, before. But I remember these. These were the things she thought were special. I remember her boxing them up. She thought you might want them."

I lifted the silk herringbone out of the box and unfurled it. A blouse, with an oversize collar and mother-of-pearl buttons. I had always thought she was so stylish, when I was twelve, thirteen, fourteen. And then she was gone, and all her beautiful clothes were, too. I hadn't known some of them were folded up in this box, waiting for me.

The shirt looked like it was my size. I knew that my mother and I had similar builds. Small shoulders, flat busts. I wanted the shirt to fit, I wanted to like it, but it was a lot of look for me. I held it up to my body.

"That was one of her favorites," my father said.

"I'll give you some time," my father said.

I heard his footsteps retreating down the hallway, down the stairs. I lifted the next item out of the box, a gray wool skirt suit. The fabric felt soft and luxe, a subtle pinstripe running top to bottom. But when I held up the matching jacket, I could tell that something about it was no longer right, the shoulders too big, the lapels too wide. This had probably been my mother's nicest suit, the one she wore to court when she argued a big case. I held the jacket and I pictured her standing in front of judge and jury. She had been so full of life, so full of joy. How was it possible that I still had this jacket, and yet I didn't have her?

I pulled the rest of the clothes out of the box. Each had been folded impeccably. I had the feeling that if I didn't pull them out now, I might never do it, might leave them preserved forever with their perfect creases, my mother's last communication with me. It was a small box, and yet it seemed to hold an extraordinary amount: sweaters and slacks, skirts and jackets, a trench coat lined in plaid. Occasionally, a bit of tissue would fall out, the soft paper crumbling, covered with the glittering remains of desiccated mothballs. Even in her final weeks, my mother had thought of everything.

I reached the bottom of the box. There, wrapped in plastic, was one last thing. Orange, the color of a ripe peach. I knew what it was from the photos: her wedding dress. I had wondered what had become of it. That was something I had always known about her—that she hadn't worn white at her wedding. She was not the kind to follow rules, my father had said, on one of the rare occasions when he spoke of her. A nice Jewish girl from the Midwest, she'd been on her way to law school at Stanford when she married the Japanese man she'd met in an anthropology lecture senior year. They dated for just six weeks before they got married, at the courthouse in San Francisco.

Her parents, my grandparents, surely would have preferred someone else. But as long as she would raise her children Jewish, they said, they would accept it. Really, they had no choice. By the time she told them, the marriage license had already been signed.

Clothes were splayed all around me on the beige carpeting, shirts and jackets and skirts and dresses that had once held my mother's body. I laid down on the rug next to the empty box. One by one, I picked up the clothes I could reach and placed them on my torso, on my hips, on my thighs, the fabric draping over my flesh, cradling me.

❄

Because Kumiko hadn't known I was coming, she hadn't had time to cook. She would have made me something nice, she said as we drove to the nearby sushi restaurant, something special. Did I like sukiyaki? She hadn't made that for me yet. I didn't know what it was? She would make it next time. It was good. One of her specialties. She would get fresh quail eggs from the market and we would crack them on top, the way they did in Japan. I just had to let her know a day ahead, so she could have the butcher slice the meat right: thin and against the grain.

I nodded along from the back seat. My father was driving. I had put the cardboard box marked EVELYN in the trunk of my car, which I had left at the house.

The restaurant was small and narrow, tucked into a strip mall with a tanning parlor and a smoke shop. I had not realized there were tanning parlors anywhere in Northern California.

Inside, the restaurant was full, but the host seemed to know Kumiko, and my father, too, but only as an annex of Kumiko. I couldn't be sure; they were speaking in Japanese. Every face at every table was an Asian face. The host led us to a table I couldn't see from the door, one hidden behind a screen of fake bamboo. In the window of the restaurant, I had noticed, were bowls of plastic ramen, boxes of plastic sushi. A pair of chopsticks dangled above the ramen bowl in the window display, holding up a string of plastic noodles. Truly, they were being held up by the noodles; the whole thing was one piece of plastic, with the unmanned chopsticks attached at the top.

We ordered sushi, teriyaki, gyoza. All foods whose names I knew, though many of the individual words for the sushi were foreign to me. My father and Kumiko each ordered a large Sapporo, and so did I. The beers came quickly, in enormous frosty mugs.

"Kanpai," Kumiko said, holding up her glass. My father raised his glass, too, but I was slow to react, and they waited for me, their glasses poised in the air. "Cheers," Kumiko said, when I brought my glass up to meet theirs.

"Kanpai," I said, and drank a large sip. I never drank Japanese beer. It tasted sweet and thin. My father asked me about Jamie. I said he was fine.

"Jamie is your boyfriend?" Kumiko said.

I said yes.

53

"You are not married?" she asked.

I told her no, we were not.

"But you live together?"

I told her yes.

"You have lived together for several years?"

I told her yes, again.

"I would like to invite you to come to church with me some Sunday," she said, her voice solemn. The look she gave me was full of import.

I thanked her for the invitation, and then told her I was Jewish, that I had been raised Jewish. It was odd that she didn't know. Hadn't my father told her that, I wondered?

"Of course I know you are Jewish," she said. "Bat mitzvah, right? But that does not matter. You can still come to church. Same Old Testament."

I told her I would think about it. I wasn't sure she would leave it at that, but the waiter came by with a plate of edamame. He deposited it on the table and asked if everything was all right, if we needed anything, and that interruption seemed to signal an end to Kumiko's talk of church.

They asked me about work. I said it was fine. I explained about the app we were trying to build, about how difficult it was to define happiness. As I spoke, I found myself slipping into the tone of surety that I heard every day at the third-most-popular internet company's offices; I wanted Kumiko and, mostly, my father to believe in the project. Kumiko nodded along, her face a mask of enthusiasm, though it was hard to tell if it was real enthusiasm or faked. I couldn't tell what my father thought. As I wrapped up my spiel, I found myself getting nervous, awaiting his judgment, desiring his approval.

"I don't understand it," he said finally. "Happiness is not one's goal in life. This obsession with happiness," he said, "it's an American obsession."

"I am American," I said. "You're American, too." His family had moved from Japan when he was seven; he had been an American citizen since he was ten.

"I suppose that's true," he said.

Just then, the food came, a waiter bearing a wide tray. As we served ourselves, I thought about what I might say to make my father understand. I took a dumpling, some strips of chicken, a piece of an elaborate sushi roll that was probably not strictly Japanese. I was only a few bites in when Kumiko carefully laid her chopsticks down, so that the tips rested on her plate, somehow signaling with this action that she wanted our attention, my attention. I put my chopsticks down as well.

"Speaking of happiness, we, in fact, have some happy news," she said. I couldn't help but think this was not the best segue, considering my father had just derided the very notion of happiness, but Kumiko seemed to have forgotten our earlier conversation entirely. She seemed flushed, her cheeks turning rosy, though it might have been from the beer. It made her look younger, and softer. Kumiko looked to my father before she spoke again. He had put his chopsticks down, too. He put his hand on hers and nodded. She turned back to me.

"Your father and I are getting married," she said. My father smiled that same bashful smile as when he first introduced her to me.

I didn't know what to say. I felt like one of the plastic replicas in the window out front, a plastic replica of a human being. Wouldn't a person who was not a plastic replica feel happy for her father?

I opened my mouth to say congratulations, but instead of saying congratulations, I just sat there, looking at my father with this woman who looked like she should be his wife but who was not, in fact, my mother.

TEN

When I woke up the next day, I felt intensely, inexplicably nauseated. I made my way to the bathroom, where I stood in front of the toilet and willed myself to throw up, but my body would not cooperate.

"Could you be pregnant?" Jamie said, after I had gone back to bed and he had brought me some tea. I felt a note of what sounded like hope in his voice.

"Not possible," I said. I had been on birth control since college. "Maybe I ate some bad sushi last night."

Jamie lay in bed with me most of the day, reading a crime thriller. It was a crime thriller that had been highly regarded, the author a woman who avoided the usual torture porn that male crime writers inevitably found themselves exploiting. I was reading a book that I had thought would be a thriller, too—a woman's soon-to-be ex-husband had disappeared in Greece, she had gone to track him down—and yet it was not so much a thriller as a meditation on marriage, an examination of how well we really ever know another person. I found it page-turning nonetheless—is there such a thing as a philosophical thriller?—but as I read, I looked over at Jamie's body next to mine, and I wondered how long my father and Kumiko had known each other. Less than a year. How had they known? How could they be so sure of themselves, so sure of each other?

In the afternoon, Jamie went out for groceries, and I turned on the TV. An episode of *Misfits!* was on. This one was looking at the kakapo, a large, flightless parrot native to New Zealand. The kakapo had evolved over many lifetimes to be a ground animal because it had no natural predators, but then settlers brought a scourge of invasive species: weasels, cats, rats. Its only method of defense, the documentary voice-over explained, is to freeze, hoping it won't be noticed if it stands very, very still. There were only 125 of them left in the wild.

I heard the front door open and then close, footsteps moving across the hardwood floor. I heard the refrigerator door open and then close, the cabinets opening and closing, Jamie putting away the sustenance he had secured for us. Finally, the door to the bedroom opened and Jamie entered.

If I lay very, very still, was it possible Jamie would forget about me? The problem was, I didn't want Jamie to move on to other prey.

I scooted over in the bed and pulled my body into the shape of a question mark, our signal for him to come spoon me. I couldn't see him, but I could feel the bed shift under his weight. And then I could feel the warmth of his arms around my waist, the heat of his breath on my neck. I could smell the particular scent of his body, the smell of truffles and head oil and other scents that were hard to describe but that I knew belonged only to him. I could not lose those scents.

Judith Butler wrote that to say "I love you" is to submit to a cliché; that we are willing to submit ourselves to that cliché only for certain people. But she also wrote that to say "I love you" is to try to put what is in the body into language; that to say "I love you" is to try to transmit a feeling in your body to another person through a speech act; that to say "I love you" is, in fact, to expose yourself bodily, to risk exposure in ways that might seem impossible to bear.

"I love you," I said. I had said it before, countless times, but, still, sometimes, the words felt strange and difficult in my mouth. Since my mother had passed away, since my father had disappeared into his grief, I had learned not to rely on other people. Other people could leave, even if they didn't want to; even if they wanted to stay, there was no guarantee.

"Did you say something?" Jamie said, his mouth pressed into my hair.

I turned to look at him, our faces inches away from each other. I could see his pores and the wrinkles at the corners of his eyes and the odd hairs that sprouted above his eyebrows.

I said it again, louder, and let him pull my body closer to his own.

※

By Monday morning, I felt much better. On the bus, all the seats were taken, and I stood clutching the metal pole. I took my tiny screen out, too, and scrolled through the news. A pigeon had been found near Lake Merritt with a blow dart lodged in its head. The article quoted an expert from a local bird sanctuary saying this was an adult pigeon, which was mated to another pigeon, trying to egg-sit and raise babies. The Animal Legal Defense Fund was offering a $5,000 reward for information.

A visibly pregnant woman boarded the train. No one so much as looked up from their devices, alight with their texts, their emails, their sports scores, their stock prices. She found a place standing next to me, one of her hands above mine on the pole, the other already scrolling through her own tiny screen. I had never heard the term "egg-sit" before. I looked it up on my tiny screen, expecting something scientific, an explanation of bird gestation and incubation, but all I found was a series of egg-shaped chairs that my phone thought I would like to buy, at prices ranging from two hundred to eight hundred dollars. Though the descriptions did not say so explicitly, it was somehow clear to me that they were meant to simulate being back in the womb. Still, the only chair that was explicitly called a Womb Chair didn't look womb-like at all, at least not to me.

When seats began to open up, I looked around for the pregnant woman, but she was already gone. I found a window seat, climbing over the legs of a teenager engrossed in the videos on their screen. In the row ahead of me, a man in late middle age pulled a point-and-shoot camera out of his backpack and aimed it out the scratched bus window. Possibly he was a tourist; it was impossible to tell. We were nowhere special—no candy-box Victorian houses lined up on a hill, no Chinatown fish vendors, no downtown skyscrapers—but he was taking photos all the same. From where I was sitting, I could see the camera's screen, and I watched as the man chose his shots, framing them carefully, waiting for just the right moment to press the button that would freeze the image. He was not indiscriminate, but I could not figure out what his logic was. He took photos of trash cans, of passersby, of nondescript apartment buildings, of traffic-stalled intersections. Because we were on a moving bus, the pictures all came out gray and blurred, but nevertheless, he looked at each photo after he took it and gave a small nod of satisfaction before lifting his gaze back to the wide plexiglass window and starting all over again.

After this had gone on for some time, the man paused to scroll through all the photographs, quiet but distinct beeps punctuating his progress through the camera's memory card. When he reached the final frame, he gave a last nod and made as if to put the camera away. But then something grabbed his attention, though I couldn't tell right away what it was.

He turned the camera toward the front of the bus. I could only see the back of his head, but even that looked more alert, the muscles in his neck stiff. When he lifted the camera, I finally saw what it was that had so piqued his interest. At the very front of the bus, mounted on the partition that separates the driver from the riders, was a large television screen on which our own images were being projected, seen slightly from above. I had never thought much about these screens; I had simply accepted them as part of my surroundings. But now I looked at the bus's screen, framed in the camera's screen. I picked out my grainy, black-and-white image, mirrored back to me and slightly distorted. I had always assumed that the screen was for our safety— and it was, in a way. Any crime would be recorded. But we didn't need the screen for that. Really, it was there to let us know we were being surveilled.

Every seat was taken, but no one else seemed to be paying any attention to the man. He zoomed in on the screen and took a picture. He zoomed back out and took another, and another. Then he put his camera back in its case and rang the bell to get off the bus. I felt a strange sense of violation—he had my image, grainy and irresolute, but nonetheless distinctly mine. It didn't feel right, somehow, that he should now be able to look at my face—at this image that included my face— whenever he so chose. But there was nothing to be done about it, and I wasn't sure why it mattered to me, anyway. A search on any internet browser would turn up dozens of images of my face, dozens of images of anyone's face. We had all been cataloged, long ago.

※

I spent the morning working on a new report that Dr. Luce had asked me to write on the ways different countries in the world thought of happiness. Did happiness mean the same thing in every country? My guess was that the report was looking ahead, to ensure that when the third-most-popular internet company's happiness project was ready to go global, it would resonate with an international audience. I read through years of the World Happiness Report, a project sponsored by the United Nations that ranked 156 countries by how happy their citizens perceived themselves to be. Asians, the report showed, tended to evaluate their own happiness negatively, with East Asian countries consistently ranking surprisingly low on the Global Happiness Index. But researchers still didn't know: Were East Asians actually less happy than the rest of the world? Or did their cultures dictate that they say they were not happy, skewing the results? I thought of my father, saying that happiness was an American obsession. Was happiness the United States' next great export, one that we would impose on the people of every nation in the world, along with the products they could purchase in order to attain it?

I skimmed through journal articles, databases, news stories, interviews. I ended up on a page that listed other languages' words for feelings, ones that we did not have in English. Everyone knows *schadenfreude*, of course, but there were so many more: *iktsuarpok*, from Inuit, the anticipation one feels while waiting for someone, when you keep going to check if they've arrived; *gigil*, from Tagalog, the irresistible urge to pinch or squeeze someone because they are loved or cherished; *litost*, from Czech, a state of torment caused by the sudden sight of one's own misery. If we didn't know the word for a feeling, could we still experience it?

I remembered a story I'd heard on a podcast a few years before about an anthropologist in the 1960s studying an isolated tribe in the Philippines who were known for beheading their enemies. When the anthropologist joined them, he and his wife—also an anthropologist—began to learn the tribe's language, but there was one word that baffled them: *liget*. One day, out in the jungle, he saw a young man bounding along the trail; that, the tribesmen told the anthropologist, was *liget*. The anthropologist thought he understood. *Liget*.

Vitality. But then, several weeks later, the anthropologist was in a hut with some members of the tribe when they asked to hear his recordings. They listened to many voices, but when the voice of one of the tribe's elders came on, the men changed utterly. The elder had died recently, and the men said that hearing his voice again made them feel *liget*: it made them feel like they wanted to take a head.

Thirteen years later, these same anthropologists were studying another tribe, also in the Philippines. They had brought their two young sons with them. They were supposed to go on a hike together, but one of the boys fell sick, and so the parents played rock, paper, scissors to see who would stay with the child and who would go. The wife won. She went.

Hours later, a woman came bursting into the anthropologist's hut. He had to come immediately, she said. He ran after her, along the trail, until they reached a sheer drop-off—a 65-foot cliff. At the bottom lay the body of the anthropologist's wife.

Some time later, the anthropologist was back in America. After the funeral, after the complicated work of packing up the body and shipping it back to the States, the customs forms and the airplane tickets that make an already terrible death into a bureaucratic black comedy, the anthropologist was driving along the freeway, not far from where I was when I listened to his story. And he felt inside him a feeling well up that he could only describe as *liget*. He pulled over to the side of the road and let out a primal scream.

We have no word in English for a feeling as powerful as *liget*. We have only grief, sorrow, sadness, anger, rage. But what of grief that is so strong, it makes you want to cut off another human being's head—that it not only makes you want to do it, but makes you actually do it? This was a level of grief I did not know, that I had perhaps never allowed myself to know, or perhaps simply couldn't, not being a headhunter myself.

And how, I wondered, did the anthropologist's wife feel in the moment her foot slipped, in the moment her body fell to the riverbank while her heart flew up to the sky? This we have no word for, either.

※

After lunch, I signed into the social media website that I always signed into after lunch. This was my small act of resistance: waiting until after lunch to give the social media website my traffic. I had only recently learned to log in and log out, to never leave the window open. Until I learned this, I had spent years letting it collect data on me, letting it monitor my every digital move. Sharky, of all people, had been the one to tell me to make sure to log off, Sharky, who never appeared to not be logged in.

In an ideal world, I wouldn't use this social media website at all. Every so often, I toyed with the notion of quitting entirely. But even though I posted infrequently, I liked things a lot. I commented sometimes. If I was no longer on the site, how would people know I existed? If I was no longer on the site, would I still exist?

Really, these were only half-joking questions.

My dissertation was based on the extended mind thesis, a philosophical argument from the '90s that aspects of human cognition could be externalized beyond the boundaries of the individual. An example from the original paper looked at a man with Alzheimer's who relied on a notepad to find the address of the museum he wanted to visit; the philosophers, Clark and Chalmers, argued that this act was not cognitively any different from someone else checking the same fact in their mental memory bank. The notebook was simply a piece of extended mind, just as our phones have become, our screens, the many technologies we rely on in daily life. Other philosophers had picked up on the extended mind argument and expanded it to a digitally extended self: the notion that even as our corporeal bodies become less and less important to cognition, we are reembodied virtually, through our avatars, our digital photos, our videos—all the ways we perform our identities online. My dissertation drew a distinction between extended mind and extended self; I argued that our increased reliance on digital tools did represent an extension of mind, but that the self was not such a porous thing—the self remained intact and whole, ultimately impervious. I believed in my argument, but sometimes, as I scrolled and clicked, taking in all the ways my acquaintances and I performed our identities online—built and shaped them for wide consumption and approval—I could feel my conviction waver.

Years ago, the site had introduced a feature where users could choose an emotion from a drop-down menu to accompany their news: *feeling elated, feeling hopeful, feeling happy.* I scrolled through my feed. Lots of photos of babies, lots of photos of houses. This was the stage of life I was in, the social media site was telling me. I had done nothing to get here except get older, possibly the most passive action one can take. The only action one cannot choose freely, the only force we had not—yet—found a way to defeat.

The far-right column showed an ad for Hawaii, the same one I had seen on the ADAPT screen months earlier. The same cerulean waters, the same white-sand beaches, the same swaying palm trees. SPONSORED BY THE HAWAII BOARD OF TOURISM. Why was I suddenly being targeted with these ads? Was Hawaii experiencing a tourist drought? It seemed unlikely. Nothing in my search history would suggest that I was a good candidate for this ad. I was not a beach person.

I chalked it up to a glitch in the algorithm and kept scrolling. In the middle of the page, Sharky was live-streaming something. The sandwich he was eating. A complicated construction involving multiple meats and cheeses. Twelve other people were watching, then ten, then sixteen. Then the deli added his live stream to its page and his numbers started to climb: thirty-two, forty-six, sixty. He was my best friend. Did that mean I had to watch him eat the entirety of this sandwich?

I liked it and scrolled on.

I scrolled past more babies, more houses. I scrolled past links to articles on how to refinish your porch, on the top nine traits of super-productive people. I scrolled past people who said they were feeling excited, people who said they were feeling blessed, feeling amazing, feeling blissful, feeling proud, feeling motivated, feeling hungry. There were options, too, for other emotions: feeling anxious, feeling hopeless, feeling frustrated, feeling incomplete. But no one I knew was feeling those feelings, or at least no one was saying they were feeling them.

Where would all these feelings be recorded? Where would they be stored? I had seen photos of the places where the social media site kept its servers, warehouses spread throughout the country, throughout the world, in the high desert of Oregon, the wide cornfields of Iowa, the icy expanses of Sweden, the lush green fens of Ireland, each with seemingly infinite rows of cold storage, little boxes glowing blue with data, climate controlled by giant fans that swept along the sides of the buildings, keeping our memories intact, keeping them safe and ready for retrieval. The storage was primarily for photos, those massive consumers of data, but I wondered if emotions would be filed away there, too, until someday we had vast warehouses of feelings, guarded like seed banks, protected from extinction.

Could a feeling go extinct? Could a feeling disappear, lost from disuse?

ELEVEN

A few days after New Year's, Dr. Luce sent me an email about an upcoming conference, one she said would give us a good handle on the emerging happiness market. She wanted me to go with her. She had been impressed, she wrote, by the most recent report I had written, the one on different cultures' understandings of emotions. She wanted me to represent the third-most-popular internet company on a panel called "What Is Happiness?"

A week later, on the flight to Los Angeles, Dr. Luce and I were sitting next to each other in business class.

"Are you ready for your panel?" she asked midway through the flight. She was sipping a Bloody Mary she had ordered before we even sat down.

I told her I was ready. I had spent the week prepping nonstop, attempting to anticipate every direction the discussion could take.

"Good," she said. "I'll be there, of course. I don't want to put too much pressure on you, but this could be the thing that helps me make the case for you to go permanent. What you say is up to you, of course— you're independent. Be true to your own theories, your own research. But you will be mentioning the way our technology is poised to increase happiness, I assume? Less friction, more happiness."

"Sure," I said. I had not been planning on mentioning that, but now I would.

"Of course, the panel is your first priority," she said, draining the rest of her Bloody Mary and shaking the ice in her glass. "But I'd like you to also go to as many of the events as you can. Meet people. Bring back new ideas. I'm going to be in meetings most of the weekend, so you'll be my eyes and ears on the ground. Bring me the latest in happiness. Whatever it is, no matter how out-there it seems, I want to know about it."

※

The Fifth Annual Global Happiness Summit was being held in an immense hotel conference center just south of LAX. It was the world's premiere conference on happiness, or at least that was how it billed itself, the Davos of joy. There were three days total, a packed schedule in booklet form that a smiling volunteer handed us when we arrived. There were dozens of overlapping panels on topics like how to change your world from the inside out, how to optimize your brain, how to change your story/change your reality, how to ignite your vital energy, how to go beyond superhuman, how to refire to rewire, how to wow yourself and your community. There were talks about minimalism and mindful consumption, mindful eating, mindful sex, mindful meditation, mindful performance; talks about the importance of doing nothing, the importance of play, the importance of laughter. There were workshops on laughter yoga and restorative yoga, on Reiki and healing touch, on crystal healing and crystal energy, on acupressure and acupuncture. There were one-on-one life-coaching sessions, one-on-one financial wellness consultations, one-on-one energy readings. There was a group Zumba class and a #ChooseHappiness cocktail party and a concert, and that was all just the first day.

Down in the lobby after stowing my bag in my room, I rifled through the scheduling booklet. The number of events at any given time was overwhelming. So many ways to practice happiness, to grow happiness, to restore happiness, to breathe and dance and even eat happiness, via supposedly mood-boosting foods like sardines and avocado and blueberries and dark chocolate. What would Dr. Luce be most interested in hearing about? I had no idea. I put the booklet in my bag and followed the sound of laughter down one of the hallways. Laughter was always a good thing, it seemed to me. I tracked it to one of the smaller conference rooms. Every room was named for a desert. This was the ATACAMA. The strange thing was that the laughter didn't seem to have changed much, if at all, in the time it had taken me to find its source. It was the same in tone and volume, a steady thrumming, like a beehive gone vaguely berserk. I registered this oddity just before opening the door, and without taking the time to think about it, I stepped inside. The room was about half full, which meant maybe twenty-five people, sitting scattered in the rows of chairs. A white man who looked to be in his mid-sixties stood at the front; he was very lean, with thin hair that fell in silvery wisps across his head. His hands were pressed to his stomach and he was emitting a rhythmic noise that resembled laughter but was not quite laughter, a staccato drumming that acted as a metronome for the assembled conferencegoers, who also held their hands pressed to their stomachs, mimicking his almost violent exhalations of the word "HA," their faces serious and unsmiling, dedicated to the correct execution of their task.

I was about to back out of the room, to find some other mode of happiness enhancement taking place in some other global desert, when the lean man at the front spotted me. His face did not break its mask of concentration, nor did he break his pace, but he lifted one hand from his abdomen and gestured for me to take a seat, pointing at one of several empty chairs along the aisle. Having missed my chance at a clean breakaway, I followed the direction of his pointing hand and sat.

I was still deciding where to put my hands when a voice next to me whispered:

"Why do you think there are always so many white people at these things?"

I looked to my right, surprised. A man, maybe a few years older than me. Good-looking, with light stubble across his chin. Asian. Unlike everyone else in the audience, whose faces were fixed with determination, sitting bolt upright in their chairs, he slouched loosely in his seat, a small smile playing at the corners of his mouth even as he held his hands to his stomach, even as he continued the stream of HAs. He leaned toward me and whispered, "This is my third happiness conference this year, and it's always the same. All white people."

The lean white man at the front looked at us, but it would have been impossible for him to hear anything over the chorus of HAs. Nonetheless, it was clear that he did not approve of any small talk. In one smooth gesture, he moved his hands from his abdomen to either side of his face, so his fingers rested on his cheeks and jaw. The room moved their hands in response, and so did the man sitting next to me. I put my hands on my face and joined in. There didn't seem to be any other choice. It looked like a room full of people imitating that painting with the figure on the bridge, *The Scream*.

As I looked around the room, I realized my indeterminately Asian neighbor was right: it was all white people. We were the only two people who were not white, and since I was just half, that made the ratio something like 24½ to 1½ white to not-white, with me splitting down the middle but nonetheless adding an important ½ contribution to the minority stakes. Was that half of me the half that felt such skepticism toward this exercise? But more than half of me felt skeptical, I thought, as I continued dutifully reciting my HAs. Maybe the Asian half of me was the half that, despite my skepticism, was unwilling to stand up and leave, unwilling to risk offense.

At the front, the lean white man looked exaggeratedly around the room, as if to signal something. Then he took a longer pause, and when he spoke again, he said "HO" instead of HA, his hands still clamped to the sides of his face in a Munchian pose. A few straggling HAs came out on the next round, but soon the room transitioned fully to HOs. Next to me, my neighbor was also holding his hands to his face. When he caught me looking at him, he wiggled his eyebrows at me, a gesture I would not have found particularly funny in most circumstances but that in this circumstance almost made me laugh genuinely, a sound I managed to suppress, since it surely would have broken the effect the lean white man was going for. I looked away, facing front.

"HO HO HO," I chanted, an obedient half-Asian lady Santa Claus.

※

The indeterminately Asian man's name was Henry. He introduced himself after the laughter workshop, as we stood in the carpeted hallway between ATACAMA and GOBI. He worked for an energy bar company based in Seattle, and when I expressed puzzlement about why someone who worked at an energy bar company would be at a happiness conference—let alone at three this year—he told me, without a trace of irony, that they were trying to break into the happiness market.

"Let's go down to the fair," he said, after we had exchanged niceties.

"The fair?" I said.

"It's the whole reason anyone comes to these things," he said, which didn't answer much of anything for me. I had been mildly interested in the talk on unsealing your inner fire—what would this entail, I wondered, and did everyone have an inner fire to unseal?—but I followed him to the escalators anyway, down to the basement level.

We entered a vast windowless space, seemingly a ballroom, though who would want to host a ball in this windowless space was a mystery. The room was filled with hundreds of booths, each with a table and a sign, a salesperson or two shilling product that was at least tangentially related to happiness. A guard at the door checked our badges; only conference attendees were allowed in.

I walked the aisles, trailing behind Henry. He seemed to know what he was looking for: he would walk quickly, scanning the stalls, then zero in on one and approach, chatting with the booth's proprietor for several minutes, holding up their product, whatever it was, tasting it or testing it or touching it to his skin. I lagged behind, surveying each booth in turn, trying not to make eye contact.

There were crystals and gels and elixirs, displays of tiny bottles with names like RELEASE FEAR and FOSTER SERENITY. Three drops on the tongue in the morning, three drops at night; or you could take it in your water or your tea, herbal recommended, preferably peppermint. There were cold therapies and heat therapies, there was something called vibrational therapy, which looked to me not unlike the vibrating band popular on infomercials when I was a child that promised astounding weight loss in just fifteen minutes a day. I didn't get close enough to see exactly how this variety of vibrational therapy worked, but it seemed very possible that it was just salvaged from those now largely defunct weight loss therapies, an overstock of bands that had found new purpose. There were cranial massagers and back massagers and foot massagers; there were hot tubs and whirlpools, foot baths and sound baths. There was a clay mask made of bentonite that claimed to have healing powers. There were smudge sticks and palo santo, there were makers of handcrafted amulets. There were alarm clocks that, instead of making sound, would slowly give off light, simulating the effects of the sun. There were white noise machines and whale noise machines and even machines that played the sounds of freeway traffic, flowing like a river. There were SAD lamps that promised euphoria and bumper stickers saying FOLLOW YOUR BLISS. There were yoga DVDs, Pilates DVDs, meditation DVDs with names like *Calming the Turbulent Waters* and *Cultivating Equanimity.*

I paused at a booth with the sign MEET YOUR MIND.

"Have you ever experienced sensory deprivation?" the man at the booth asked. He wore very small glasses, perched low on his nose.

"Sensory deprivation?" I said. The words conjured up space-age pods and claustrophobia, visions of the future. "No, I haven't."

"Would you like to? Free for conferencegoers at our facility here in LA. Off-site. It'll take about three hours round trip."

He handed me a pamphlet with the words *Float Free* across the front. Inside was an image of a woman lying on her back in a small tank of water, a look of total peace on her face. Her presumably naked body was blurred. In the place where her body should have been was a list of words: *Relax. Renew. Restore. Heal. Escape. Float.*

Below that was a paragraph explaining how Float Free worked:

> The ultra-purified Epsom salt solution gives participants the opportunity to float effortlessly in a body-temperature solution devoid of light and sound. The original Float Free hygienic technology* allows total peace of mind, with an all-organic filtration system guaranteed to produce a 99.9% or greater disinfection rate.
>
> Experience weightlessness. Boost creativity and peace. Meet your mind.
>
> *Patent-pending

I looked around me at the infinite booths, all trying to sell something, to sell happiness. The sound of thousands of people talking, the sight of people, everywhere, the smell. Was it really possible to turn it all off? Here, I thought, was something I could tell Dr. Luce about.

"Sure," I said. "I'll try it."

✳

Float Free was housed in a basement in Venice. On the van ride over, me and the other would-be floaters—six of us in all—were given liability forms to sign. The form was relatively standard: releasing Float Free of all responsibility in case of accident, attesting that I was in good health and physically capable of entering and exiting the float tank without assistance, that I had no known heart conditions, open wounds, or infectious diseases. But at the very bottom, there was a line that seemed distinctly nonstandard: *I acknowledge that it is impossible to predict the outcome of mental release, and that Float Free, LLC, does not and cannot guarantee my mental safety for the duration of the float experience.* I almost laughed out loud, but the rest of the van was silent, dutifully reading their liability forms, preparing to connect with their innermost selves, their utmost selves, another promise the pamphlet had made. I had noticed that the Float Free language was careful to only promise the *opportunity* to connect with one's truest self; they did not guarantee connection. That part was up to us.

At the facility, we watched a short video and then were led to our float chambers. I slipped my shoes off and left them in the hall, then entered the room I had been assigned. It was a small space lined with white tile, and very clean. I pressed the button to lock the door behind me and undressed, stepping into the shower as I had been instructed, to wash away any impurities I might otherwise take with me into the float tank. When I was done, I toweled myself off and reviewed the instructions posted on the wall one last time. We were supposed to enter the tank completely nude, no jewelry, no hair elastics, nothing except the earplugs they had provided.

On the back wall of the room was a door that was not quite a door but was more like a cross between a porthole and the door of an airplane. It didn't come to the floor but was instead about a third of the

73

way up the wall. When I pulled on the handle, the door opened with a great slurping noise, the resistance of the suction surrounding it. Inside, all was dark. The video had told us that the room measured five feet wide by eight feet long by eight feet high: no way to hit your head. I lifted my leg up and over the edge of the door and climbed in.

My foot hit water: shallow and warm. I lifted the other leg in and pulled the door shut behind me. I waited a moment for my eyes to adjust to the darkness, but this was a darkness engineered to withstand the eye's adaptation. This was a pure darkness. I heard no sound except the rippling of the water when I moved my legs. I lowered my body down into a crouch, repositioning—as instructed—so that my feet faced the door. Then I lowered myself farther, feeling my body hit the slick bottom of the tank, but only for a split second before I bobbed back up to the surface like a cork. I could feel my neck tensing, trying instinctually to keep my face above water. Slowly, with intention, I released the muscles in my neck and shoulders, letting my head hang back. My body did not want to cooperate. My body was sure it was headed toward certain doom if it let my face—my nose, my mouth, my breathing apparatuses—come near the water. The water should not be able to support the weight. But the water held. My head floated. And I was aloft.

What was supposed to happen now? *Meet your mind.* I thought of the slogan, of the testimonials I had read on the back of the pamphlet, people saying they had lost track of all their physical boundaries, lost track of time and space, that this was what it must feel like to be back in the womb. It was warm, and it was dark, and my body was suspended in a slippery liquid, but I wasn't sure I would call it womblike. I lay there and waited for something interesting to happen, but my mind, perhaps, was just not that cooperative. Or not that interesting.

Was I doing something wrong? Was there something I was supposed to be doing to make this a Significant Experience? Was everyone else having a Significant Experience except me? Was there something wrong with me, that I was lying here, thinking these things, instead of embarking on a metaphysical journey through time and space, dissolving the boundaries of self and other, being filled with love and connection?

The pamphlet had advertised meeting your mind, but I had never been so aware of my own body. Instead of dissolving into the water, released from my own corporeality, I felt intensely conscious of the boundaries of my limbs, where they ended and this strange, buoying water began. I wiggled my body to the left; I wiggled my body to the right. It was almost exhilarating to move through that weightless world, the only sound the splash of water against my skin. I let my body lie still. I raised my arms above my head.

Maybe, I thought, I had already met my mind. All I did all day was live in my mind. But what about my body? I thought about my dissertation; I told myself not to think about my dissertation; I thought about it again. Maybe I had been too quick to discount the body. My forearms, I thought, were starting to feel warm. I raised them out of the water and lowered them back in. The heat was spreading throughout my body, but it didn't feel like the water was hot; it felt like something in my veins was warming me, surrounding me.

Was I having a Significant Experience?

And then I began to hear what sounded like a chime. The sound got louder and louder. Even with the earplugs, it felt piercing after such complete silence. The video, I remembered, had said that we would hear a chime at the end of the session. But how could it be the end of the session already? Hadn't I just gotten into the water?

I pulled myself up in the darkness and opened the portal back to my white cube. I blinked my eyes several times, letting my vision adjust to the sudden brightness, and then I stepped out of the water and onto the cool tile. I took a hot shower and put my clothes back on. I had not dried myself thoroughly enough, and my pants stuck to my skin as I tried to pull them on. Out in the lobby, the rest of the group would undoubtedly be discussing their Significant Experiences with each other. But before I joined them, I sat for a minute on the chair next to shower, trying to hold on to the sensation of weightlessness, to ingrain it in my body.

✳

I skipped the late-afternoon goat yoga, but I made it back down to the lobby for the #ChooseHappiness cocktail hour. The bar was packed. When I finally made it to the front, the bartender tried to sell me on the conference's special cocktail, the Kombucha Sunset: two kinds of kombucha, beet and mango, layered in the glass to produce a sunset effect. Tequila optional. All around me, people were holding up their cocktails in one hand, their phones in the other, snapping photos as the colors streamed together. The drink had clearly been designed to be maximally photographed, maximally shared, maximally liked, a sea of these photographs, all with the identical hashtag #ChooseHappiness.

I ordered a gin and tonic.

I stood in the middle of the crowd and wondered if I was missing something. All around me, I could hear people talking about how amazing their days had been, how much they had learned, how refreshed they felt, how they couldn't wait for day two. On the van ride back from the float lab, I had listened silently as the rest of the group discussed their out-of-body experiences. I did not feel refired or rewired. Was I doing something wrong?

"Don't let all this happiness get you down," a voice said. I turned around and there was Henry, holding a beer in one hand and two shots of tequila in the other, wedges of lime precariously balanced on their edges. He was looking at me with what I thought might be a flirtatious expression, but I wasn't sure; it had been a long time since I had flirted with anyone.

"I needed something a little stronger," he said, handing me one of the shot glasses. "I got one for you, too." I was going to say I couldn't, I had my panel tomorrow, it wasn't a good idea, but then Henry was already lifting his shot to his mouth, and what could one shot hurt? I hadn't had straight tequila since college. It tasted like rubber, and I hurried to press the lime between my teeth.

"Phew," Henry said, collecting my shot glass and putting it on the tray of a passing waiter. "Gonna need more of those tonight." He took a sip of his beer. "These things are always the same. Competitive happiness, I call it. Who can convince themselves that they're getting the most out of the conference, that they're going to go home a changed person, that now they'll be happy in a way that up until this life-changing weekend was not possible. They've lived thirty, forty, fifty years on this earth, but it's going to be this one weekend in this hotel in Redondo Beach that changes everything for them."

He was standing, I thought, a little closer to me than someone who was not flirting with me would stand.

"Aren't you supposed to be on board with this?" I asked. I picked up my gin and tonic again. "Selling your energy bars and all?"

"We need people to believe that by buying our energy bars, they are buying happiness. Think about it. How do you get people to choose your energy bar, out of all the bars in the now saturated energy bar market? Consciously, they think they're only buying an energy bar. Choosing a flavor. Carrot cake. Oatmeal raisin. Chocolate peanut butter. But subconsciously, what you're selling them is the belief that this energy bar will make them into a newer, better version of themselves, slimmer, stronger, more attractive, more productive, more efficient. This energy bar will save them from a life of mediocrity. This energy bar will make them into the person they've always wanted to be, the person they've always known they could be, the person they've always had inside them, buried deep down in the slog of PowerPoint presentations and parent-teacher conferences and permission slips and oil changes and groceries and budget spreadsheets and requisitions and authorizations and approvals. But you eat one of our energy bars and suddenly you are not this person, the person who is yelling at the kids to buckle their seat belts, the person who has to submit receipts to accounting for reimbursement, the person whose jeans are starting to feel a little too tight around the waist, tight in a way that can probably never be reversed, not even with diet and exercise, because they are getting tight in the way that is simply due to the spread of the body in middle age, the first step in the inexorable march toward death.

"You eat one of our energy bars and you are no longer this ordinary, run-of-the-mill person. You eat one of our energy bars and you could go rock climbing, you could go windsurfing, you could start training for a marathon. You could sell all your belongings and move to Wyoming to work on a horse ranch just like you dreamed of as a child. You probably won't, but you could, and that is the key thing, that is what you are buying when you buy one of our energy bars: possibility. Three hundred eighty calories, twelve grams of fat, eighteen grams of protein, and unlimited possibility."

"You really believe that?" I said.

"I get paid to believe it," he said. He took another sip of his beer. "What about you?"

"What about me?" I asked.

"I realized I don't know what brought you to this conference," he said. He was maintaining an almost unsettling level of eye contact. I felt an involuntary flutter in my chest. He really was very good-looking. "What do you get paid to believe?"

I laughed and told him I worked as a researcher for the third-most-popular internet company, and that we were also trying to break into the happiness market. It surprised me that I used the word *we* instead of *they*. I didn't tell him I had been studying philosophy, didn't tell him about my angle on the mind-body problem. I felt like I was trying on a new identity, as a person whose life was straightforward. A person whose life made sense to her.

"So do you believe in what you're selling?"

"I guess I don't know," I said. "I want to believe. I mean, who wouldn't? What if happiness was truly attainable, if you just used the right tools, the right algorithms? What if we really could help users be happier? It would be a miracle."

Henry nodded.

"But . . . ," he said, prompting me.

"But," I said, "everyone around me seems to believe, and they are such smart people. Really brilliant. So are they seeing something I don't see?"

"Maybe they're just seeing what they want to see," Henry said. "But maybe that's the way to actually be happy in life."

I told him he had a point.

I could feel the conversation dwindling down, narrowing to some inevitability. I had not mentioned Jamie. I didn't know why. He was not part of the identity I was trying on, even though he was the most straightforward aspect of my life.

"It's getting pretty crowded," Henry said. It was true—the #Choose-Happiness crowd was packed in. "My room has a pretty well-stocked mini bar. Do you want to check it out?"

I was pretty sure I knew what he was asking. Apparently the person I was pretending to be had sent him these signals. How far would this person go? I pictured her, nodding her head coyly, putting down her empty glass, weaving her way through the crowded bar. Following this man into the elevator, watching as he pressed the button for his floor, the numbers rising as the elevator ascended. Walking down the hallway, waiting as he fumbled for his key card, watching the light on the door flash green, going inside.

But the thing was, I wasn't that person.

"I can't," I said. "I have my panel in the morning."

Henry nodded. I put my glass down and took the elevator up to my room, alone.

TWELVE

The next morning, I woke up to a text from Jamie wishing me good luck on my panel, a formulation I had always found strange. I had prepared my notes, I had practiced. What did luck have to do with it? Still, I recognized that it was a thing people said—a nicety. I had not been raised on niceties; my father had not been a nicety person. I was pretty sure he still wasn't a nicety person, though I couldn't be sure about anything anymore when it came to him. If my father had said anything to me before a big test or a big presentation, it wouldn't have been *good luck*. It would have been *Perform to the best of the abilities that you have carefully cultivated* or *Make maximal use of your time-consuming and long-standing preparations.* They didn't roll off the tongue quite as well.

I texted back a heart emoji.

At breakfast, I went over my notes. The panel was called "What Is Happiness? A Philosophical Roundtable." The other three people on the panel were all philosophers: an older man who taught at a prestigious East Coast university, a middle-aged woman who taught at a prestigious public university on the West Coast, and a youngish man, close to my age, who taught at a school I had never heard of in the Southwest. They were, as I was coming to expect at this conference, all white.

The panel itself was being held in the KALAHARI room. It was the first panel of the day, and I was the first to arrive, fifteen minutes early. Two men who I recognized from their online photos as my fellow panelists entered within a few minutes, all of us sitting at different points in the room, waiting for someone to tell us to take our places onstage. Minutes passed. The room began to fill up. Four empty chairs sat at the front of the room, loosely arranged to face each other, like a salon. The panel was supposed to begin at ten, but when I looked down at my watch—ten a.m.—no one had arrived to direct us. I scanned the room for Dr. Luce and spotted her red hair in one of the back rows. My palms were getting sweaty. The audience had gone quiet, expectant, but still nothing was happening. The two men seemed unconcerned, scrolling through their phones.

Just then, a woman around my age came bustling in, holding a clipboard and wearing an earpiece.

"I'm afraid Professor DeLoughry's flight was canceled," she told the three of us, after she had collected us together. "We'll just have to soldier on without her, but she was supposed to be the panel moderator, so one of you will have to step in."

She waited for one of us to volunteer. The older man either was not paying attention or was putting on an excellent show of not paying attention, his gaze focused somewhere off in the far reaches of the room. The younger man and I looked at each other. I could tell that he wanted it, could see the CV bump from panelist to moderator turning in his head, but still, he held his palm out to me, as though offering me the position, a pantomime of scholarly grace. I shook my head decisively.

"I'll do it," he said, as though he were making a sacrifice.

We stepped onto the small stage. I sat down in my chair and waited for the younger man to start us off.

"So," the man said, drawing out a long pause. He leaned back in his chair and surveyed the audience with a self-satisfied expression. "What

is happiness? That's what we're all here to discuss, isn't it? For the next…"
He paused again to look down at his watch. "…forty-six minutes."

There was a long silence. Both the older man and I continued to look at the younger man. I was expecting another question, one of the questions the professor whose flight had been canceled had told us to prepare for.

Such as: Is happiness a moral good?

Such as: Is happiness dependent on faith in God or another higher power?

Such as: Is happiness correlated to virtue?

But it appeared that no such questions were forthcoming. The younger man looked at us expectantly. I looked out at the audience—now full, except for a couple of stray empty seats; they were also looking at us expectantly. I looked down at my notes. Despite my extensive preparation, I had not written any notes on "What is happiness." Why had I not written any notes on "What is happiness"? I scoured my mind for an answer, but all I could come up with was a blank.

The older man adjusted his sizeable body in his seat. The chairs were tufted black leather, low to the ground, classy. They looked like the kind of chairs that would appear in a one-story Palm Springs hideaway with glass walls and an infinity pool in the back. They gave the panel the feeling of a luxe intellectual salon, which, in some ways, it was.

"Well," he said, "I'm an Aristotelian by training, and in *The Nicomachean Ethics*—"

"Ah, yes," the younger man interrupted. "*The Nicomachean Ethics.*"

The older man looked at the younger man, waiting for him to say more, but the younger man was silent. It became immediately clear that the younger man had only wanted to register that he, too, knew of *The Nicomachean Ethics*, one of the most famous books in all philosophy.

"As I was saying," the older man continued, "in *The Nicomachean Ethics*, Aristotle writes about eudaimonia, which is a Greek term that we would translate as 'happiness,' but which actually has a much more complex meaning, hard to put into modern English. 'Human flourishing' might be more appropriate, or, if we were to look directly at the etymology, then it would be something like 'well spirit'—eudaimon. It is, at any rate, not a simple word, nor is it a simple concept.

"I could, of course, talk about eudaimonia alone for far longer than forty-six minutes, but for the sake of time, what I'll say is that even the ancient Greeks were sorely divided about what it meant to lead a worthwhile life, per se. Did it mean pursuing pleasure? Did it mean pursuing virtue? Could one live a worthwhile life and not even know it?

"For Aristotle, eudaimonia is the highest good. Everything else we as humans pursue—wealth, liberty, health, love, shelter, safety—is in service of it. Eudaimonia is the only thing in life that we seek for its own sake. And, according to Aristotle, the way we as humans achieve eudaimonia is by exploiting that which is distinct to us as a species: the gift of reason. Since humans are uniquely equipped to perform rational thought—"

"I just . . . ," the younger man interrupted again, then looked down, giving another one of his long, theatrical pauses.

"Yes?" the older man said.

The younger man looked up and out at the audience, clearly gauging how to make the maximum dramatic impact.

"I just don't buy any of it," he said.

"Excuse me?" the older man said, visibly irritated. Meanwhile, I still had not said a single thing. This, I thought, would be a good time for me to jump into the conversation. I couldn't see Dr. Luce's face, but I knew a lot was riding on me figuring out a way to jump in at some point. I did not jump in.

"My allegiance is with Nietzsche," the younger man said. He raised his voice, and spoke as though channeling Nietzsche: "'"We have discovered happiness," say the last men, and blink thereby.'" He gave yet another of his dramatic pauses and then let his voice go back to its normal, slightly nasal tone. "Happiness is a falsity, and making it one's ultimate goal makes one contemptible."

A few members of the audience shifted unhappily in their seats. We were, after all, at the world's premier happiness conference; no one wanted to hear that making happiness one's goal was a reason for contempt. The younger man, though, continued on, uncowed.

"The last man is comfortable, he is secure, he lives a life without struggle or pain. But he lives a life with no chaos, with no ambition. He lives a life that is unquestioning, that has become manageable and small. He is sure he is living a life in the present that is better than any life ever lived in the past.

"Are we not already living as the last man? With our computers and our delivery apps and our streaming television? We hardly need to do anything for ourselves anymore, hardly need to interact with another human. We may all be last men, but there is a place where this phenomenon is the worst, where they are actively indoctrinating us, to what purpose I don't know. Perhaps because they truly believe this is the better way, perhaps because they know there is only so much we can do to resist, and then, when our resistance is tapped, they will control every aspect of our lives, and we will thank them for it, will praise them for it, will pay them for it. I speak, of course, of Big Tech, those companies who live in your houses, your offices, your cars, your pockets and purses. They say that this is the best time to be alive, the easiest. But did humans not survive for thousands of years without food that is delivered at the push of a button? They are making last men of us all."

With that, the younger man sat back in his chair, signaling that he was finished. The room was silent for a long moment, the audience's bafflement palpable. A few people stood up and walked out, casting irate glances back at the stage.

I still hadn't said anything, and it was beginning to seem like I might never say anything, not just on this stage, on this panel, but possibly ever again. But Dr. Luce was in the audience. I knew what I had to do. This was my cue.

"I have to disagree on that last point," I heard myself say. The younger man turned to me with surprise, the older man with interest. "Tech isn't turning anyone into the last man. Yes, it makes life easier, but what we do with that more frictionless existence is up to each of us. Modern technologies may turn some of us into last men, but they also create room for others to do more, to have more ambition, to make a bigger life. Tech only provides the tools, and tools are—by definition—neutral entities. Humans decide how they use the tools that tech provides. If you think you are becoming one of the last men, it's your own responsibility to use the tools differently."

I didn't entirely believe this argument, but I had long training in espousing arguments that I didn't fully believe. My voice, I could tell, sounded confident and decisive. I could see the audience perking up. I tried to gauge Dr. Luce's reaction, but her face was blocked by the person in the row ahead of her.

The younger man looked temporarily stunned. Before he could rebut my point, the older man turned to me.

"That's a very excellent point, about the neutrality of the tool," he said. "Well argued. And who, then, do you find persuasive on the subject of happiness?"

I hesitated for a moment. I knew my answer, but I wasn't sure it was the answer I was supposed to give as a representative of the third-most-popular internet company. But hadn't Dr. Luce told me I was independent? Hadn't she told me to be true to my own theories?

"I would have to say Montaigne." I had read Montaigne in a graduate seminar years ago, and had revisited his work just a few weeks before. It hadn't made much of an impression on me the first time I read it, but now it seemed to me that he was speaking directly to our team's project, to the work of happiness.

"Montaigne?" the younger man said, his voice skeptical.

"Yes, Montaigne," I said, more firmly. "Montaigne believed there was such a diversity of humans in the world—humans with different needs, different wants, different ways of being, different ways of experiencing reality—that there must also be a diversity of happiness. That happiness was, in other words, subjective, not objective. There is no universal human nature, and so there is also no universal human happiness. There is only what we each find.

"This is the reason that Montaigne argues for a separation between public and private spheres—the subjective nature of happiness demands it. We each need space to try to achieve happiness privately, without interference from the public. Montaigne would be horrified, for example, at the proliferation of social media, where we take what should, in his view, be private and make it public. Not only is it obscene, it doesn't serve us. We obscure our own happiness from ourselves by trying to project it and articulate it and prove it to others. These sites, he would say, flatten and falsify happiness when they ask us to affirm each other's life choices through likes."

"Interesting," the younger man said.

I tried again to see Dr. Luce's face, but it was still hidden. I felt satisfied with my answer; even if I had taken some liberties, let some of my doubts about the happiness project show, I knew I had spoken well, and I felt a satisfaction I recognized from the semesters when I would teach undergrads, standing in front of the classroom as their guide through dense and unrelenting texts. It was a feeling—a sensation of mastery—that I had not felt very often, if ever, while working at the third-most-popular internet company. I wanted to hold on to the feeling, bottle it so that I could examine it later, but just then, the younger man leaned forward, as though about to broach an intimate subject, and the feeling dissipated.

"So far, we've been focusing entirely on Western philosophy," he said. "But Eastern philosophy has a very different orientation toward happiness that I, personally, find fascinating. In Buddhism, there's the notion of *sukha*—hard to translate, but meaning something like 'lasting well-being,' as opposed to *preya,* a transient pleasure." He looked very pleased with himself. It was a look I recognized from men telling me that they had spent a year teaching English in Japan.

I braced myself for a long lecture about East versus West, about suffering and acceptance and nirvana, but instead he turned to me.

"Do you want to weigh in on this?" he said.

I paused.

"Weigh in on what?" I said, even though I knew what he was asking, why he was asking it.

"I thought you might want to say a few words about Buddhism."

I could have played along. It wasn't like I didn't know anything about Buddhism; I had taken classes on Eastern philosophy.

"Why would I have something to say about Buddhism?"

The audience had gotten very quiet. The younger man looked visibly uncomfortable. It was not too late to rescue him, but I forced myself not to say anything else, to let my question hang in the silence.

"I don't know," he said, finally. "I just thought you might."

"I don't have anything to say about Buddhism," I said.

THIRTEEN

The next day, I woke to a knock on my door, early. Through the peephole, I could see that it was Dr. Luce, looking freshly showered and very awake. While I was standing there, staring at her, she raised her hand and knocked again, startling me. I was not sure what to do—I didn't want her to know I had been standing there, watching her. I waited a few beats—long enough for a person to theoretically rise from their bed and walk the short length of the hotel room—and then opened the door.

"Let's get out of here," she said.

She told me to bring all my things, that we would be gone for the day and then head directly to the airport for our evening flight. She did not, however, tell me where we were headed.

"Here," she said, handing me her phone once we got in the rental car. "You can plug in our destination." I clicked the navigation app.

"Where to?" I said.

"We're going to Anza-Borrego," she said. "My therapist says I should see the super bloom."

※

The super bloom, I learned from Dr. Luce, was a rare event in which heavy rains in Southern California cause the wildflowers to erupt, carpeting the hills and valleys and anywhere, really, that flowers can grow. January was very early for a super bloom, which usually came in March, or even April. Scientists took it as evidence of climate change; it was, apparently, spectacular. Dr. Luce was surprised I hadn't heard of it.

"Whenever they don't know what to talk about on the news, they just show photos of the super bloom," she said. "Not even their own photos, photos they've found on social media. Hashtag super bloom, hashtag bloom report. I can't stand it, when the news reports on social media. If I wanted to know what was going on in social media, I would look at social media. But then they save the money on sending their own reporter out there. Why do original reporting when you can just cull a bunch of posts?

"Anyway, it does look quite beautiful. It will be interesting to see it in person after seeing so many photos of it. I wonder if it will live up."

Anza-Borrego was supposed to be the best place to see the super bloom. Its official name was Anza-Borrego Desert State Park, and I pictured it in all caps above one of the hotel's conference rooms: ANZA-BORREGO. Possibly, I wasn't picturing it all, but remembering it. I wondered what was going on at the world's premier conference on happiness, but I didn't much care. I'd had enough.

The drive was supposed to take three hours, but with Dr. Luce driving in the far left lane the entire way, it was more like two and a half. As we left the freeway and approached the park, the speed limit began to drop, the road becoming a two-lane highway, desert scrub stretching out on either side, towns popping up and disappearing as we sped by. Every so often, we'd pass a truck parked by the side of the road, a painted sign propped against its wheels: DATES, ALMONDS, PISTACHIOS, FIREWOOD, JERKY.

Five miles from the entrance to the park, near an unincorporated community called Hellhole Palms, the traffic began to slow. The car's air-conditioning had been working full blast, but as our speed dwindled, so did its power. The temperature reading on the dashboard said 96°F. It was only ten in the morning, on a weekday, and by my estimation there were hundreds of cars already waiting to enter the park.

It felt like several hours passed as we inched forward, but I knew from the clock on the dashboard that barely forty-five minutes had gone by. I wanted to ask Dr. Luce why her therapist said she should see the super bloom, but it didn't seem like an appropriate question, so instead, we sat mostly in silence. When it was finally our turn, Dr. Luce handed the ranger the ten-dollar entry fee and he handed us a visitor's map.

"Be alert. Drink plenty of water. It's hot out there," he said. "And please respect the wildflowers." There had been widespread problems, Dr. Luce told me, with people trampling the flowers to get the best photo, of them standing in the flowers, of them lying in the flowers, of them sitting in the flowers, reclining with a thoughtful look on their faces, angled into the light just so. People were traveling hours to the desert just for a new profile picture, for the huge uptick in likes that was basically guaranteed by this limited-time-only backdrop.

As we drove into the park, something felt strangely familiar.

"I think I'm having déjà vu," I said as Dr. Luce edged the car along. The speed limit was fifteen, and the other cars were also crawling. We could see a smattering of yellows and pinks on the hillside, but nothing worth slowing down for, not yet. Still, it was like they were rubbernecking, only at flowers instead of a gruesome accident. No one wanted to miss a single petal.

"Déjà vu," Dr. Luce said. "French for already seen. Related to *déjà vécu*, the feeling of having already lived through an event. I've never actually experienced déjà vu." I looked at her with surprise. "Thirty percent of the population hasn't," she said. "I wish I could know what it feels like, but it seems that if I've made it this far in life without feeling it, I probably never will. Some people think it's a form of precognition, telepathy; others go with reincarnation—you were here in a past life. I've also heard arguments for déjà vu as prenatal consciousness—you're feeling your mother's memories, not your own. The scientific explanation is different, of course. Something about this place is simply stimulating a memory trace. It's a sign of good memory function.

"It would be interesting to study," she continued. "An avenue of neuroscience that is still not fully explained. The latest theory I read is that it's a temporary disorientation in the hippocampus. You just felt it?"

I nodded.

"Can you describe it to me? But none of that tingle-down-my-spine, out-of-body talk. That's what people always say."

That was basically what I had been about to say.

I thought about it again.

"It feels like watching a flip-book," I said. "Like a stutter in time."

Dr. Luce looked thoughtful. My description evidently passed muster.

"Have you ever heard of *jamais vu*?" she asked.

I shook my head.

"I think it must be experienced at much lower rates than déjà vu, since we hear about the one all the time and never the other. Of course, they're both the same to me. *Jamais vu*, French for 'never seen.' In some senses, the opposite of déjà vu. *Jamais vu* is when a situation is familiar to you and yet you feel that you are seeing it for the first time. In fact, many people have experienced *jamais vu*, they just don't know it. Think about if you ever write the same word over and over again, or if something breaks your concentration in the middle of writing a word. The word begins to look strange. You begin to question whether it is even a word at all. That feeling is the feeling of *jamais vu*. The more extreme version being when you suddenly don't recognize a person or a place that you should, rationally, know."

I thought about seeing my father and Kumiko washing dishes, about how my father had looked like a stranger to me—a true stranger.

"But if déjà vu is a sign of normal memory function, then what is *jamais vu*?" I asked.

Dr. Luce shrugged.

"It hasn't been studied enough," she said. "*Jamais vu* is normal, to a degree. Everyone will experience disorientation if they have to repeat a word enough times. But the other forms, those are more dangerous. Capgras syndrome, when a person holds the delusion that someone they know has been replaced by an identical impostor. Dissociation. Detachment from reality. But these are severe mental disorders. Very uncommon."

The car ahead of us inched forward. We inched forward behind it. I looked in the rearview mirror. A line of cars filled the road behind us, stretching back as far as I could see.

There was more that I wanted to ask her. Was dissociation really that uncommon? Did other people really not feel the way I did, sometimes, all the time, for at least a brief moment every single day, feeling that stutter-stop of the flip-book, jolting out of place? But before I could figure out how to ask, if I wanted to ask, she began to speak again.

"I wanted to talk to you about your panel yesterday, your thoughts on Montaigne," she said. "Tell me if I'm wrong, but it seems like you're not fully on board with what we're trying to do with the app."

At first, I thought her statement was rhetorical, but then I realized she was waiting for me to answer. Should I tell her that she had misunderstood, that I was completely on board with everything the company was trying to do? If I told her the truth, would I still have a job when we got back? But she didn't seem like the type of person who was interested in hollow reassurances.

"I guess I am a little skeptical," I said.

Dr. Luce nodded, as if she had expected that answer and it didn't bother her in the slightest.

"I think my question," I said, "is whether happiness can really be standardized, because people aren't standardized. My concern is that if we try to standardize happiness, to create a kind of uniform container for human experience, we run the risk of unintended consequences. That people will use what we're building and they themselves will become more standardized. And that can't be what we want, can it?"

Dr. Luce nodded, keeping her eyes focused on the road ahead of her, the slow-moving traffic.

"I'm used to skepticism," she said. "I remember how I felt when I was in your shoes, coming out of grad school and starting to work for a company. Everything felt monetized, optimized. But I stayed with it because I realized something. I realized that this company can get things done. If I stayed, I could make things happen. What if there was a way to know how a person was really feeling? What if we could test, objectively, how happy or unhappy a person was? We could revolutionize mental health, maybe even physical health. We could change people's lives. That's why this research is so important, Evelyn. This isn't just some frivolous app."

"You of course have independent leeway," she went on, as we turned, at last, into a parking lot and she found a space. "But your ideas about Montaigne are not really what we had in mind for this position."

She put the car in park and turned to look at me. "I'm not sure working here is the best fit for you if you feel this way, Evelyn. But I want you to stay with the team. I think you could be a major asset. What do you think? Can you get on board?"

I thought about going back to my advisor, telling her I had failed. I thought about my paycheck, the glass-walled office, my advisor, the organic grocery store, the rent, Jamie, my dad, Kumiko, even. "I can get on board," I said.

"Great," Dr. Luce said. Something in her voice made it clear that she had viewed my acquiescence as a foregone conclusion. "I'm happy to hear it."

She leaned over and pointed at the paper map in my lap.

"We're here," she said. And then she was out of the car, was pulling on her hat, was rubbing sunscreen into her face, was passing the bottle to me and insisting I put some on.

It was time to go look at the flowers.

※

Brittlebush, ocotillo, dandelions, golden poppy, lupine, wild Canterbury bells. Bigelow's monkey flower, Payson's jewelflower, Fremont's desert thorn, Coulter's lyrepod, Wright's buckwheat, Torrey's amaranth, Palmer's milkvetch. Desert trumpet, desert five spot, desert globemallow, desert star, desert mistletoe, desert sunflower, desert chicory, desert evening primrose, desert sand verbena, desert lily, desert lavender, desert apricot, desert holly, desert bluebells. The list of flowers one could, potentially, spot in just this section of the park went on and on. I had never heard of most of them, but someone—many someones, over the course of many years—had gone to the trouble of cataloging them, naming them, noting the distinguishing marks between, say, the heart-leaved primrose and the brown-eyed primrose, like the differences between anger and rage.

The parking lot was built in a dip, surrounded by dunes, and so when we got out of the car, there was little to see. Dr. Luce had packed water for us, and a pair of energy bars. I wasn't dressed for the desert— I only had the black leather flats I had been wearing at the conference.

I didn't have a hat. Dr. Luce had said we wouldn't have to walk far. I thought it would be okay.

Outside, free of the car's air-conditioning, the heat felt like it was working in surround sound: beating down from above, but also radiating back up from the black pavement of the parking lot, pressing in from all sides. There was only enough shade for a small lizard or a rodent under the branching spikes of the scattered cacti. No human-size shade. This was a place, I felt suddenly, where humans were not supposed to be. Even with all the people, with all the cars, with all the phones doing their best imitation of camera shutters, *click click click*, it felt very still, as though it were expressing a primordial calm. This was a place that would not answer to demands.

I followed Dr. Luce across the parking lot to a trail that cut through the dunes. The dirt was silty and hot and it quickly infiltrated my inappropriate footwear, catching between my toes with every step. I wondered if I should turn back.

But then, a few steps farther, we had broken free of the dunes and in front of us was a wide expanse of hillside, awash with color: reds and pinks and blues and yellows and oranges and purples, whites and browns, and, underlying it all, a faded, silvery green. A gust of wind swept through, the flowers on the hillside rippling in a great inhalation and exhalation. Was this what everyone was talking about, what everyone came here for? This feeling of overwhelm, in the face of all that the desert could do, this great abundance of life in such seemingly hostile territory.

And then I remembered—I had been here before, with my parents. Or at least I thought I had, here or some other desert that was much like this one. I could picture my mother, the dusty ground, the shimmering light. I was eight or nine and my father was with us, too, and they showed me how to sled down the dunes, the sand whooshing alongside as I careened down at speed, my mother whooping up at the top while my father took photo after photo. These were the kinds of things we used to do, when she was still around to do them.

Where had we been? Why had we gone? I tried to hold on to the memory, to expand it, but I felt it dissolve. Around me, the air smelled of sun and warmth and a faint perfume of flowers and must. It had rained the night before, and there was that smell, too, of the moisture baking off, being pulled from the silt. Sweat had already begun to soak through the collar of my shirt, the armpits. I could feel droplets forming at my hairline. Dr. Luce had gone up the path and was referring to a book she had pulled out of the trunk. Other people were scattered in groups of twos and threes and fours along the path. An older couple had set up a tripod at the far end of the field. They were wearing matching cargo shorts, matching hiking vests, near identical floppy hats, the waterproof kind with a chin-strap toggle.

A pair of teenage girls walked by me, wearing denim cutoffs and wide-brimmed hats, loose flowing shirts with flower prints. This, I believed, was what was known as "festival wear."

"It looked better in Chloe's pictures," one girl said to the other. She was of ambiguous ethnicity, the kind of ambiguous ethnicity that I often caught myself trying to decipher. It was not only white people who wanted to know, but maybe it was only white people who felt they had the right to ask.

"Yeah," the other girl, white, responded. "Still cool, though."

"Still cool."

They headed down the path, further into the flowers.

At my feet was a bed of fuchsia, the blooms tessellating across the desert floor. I crouched down to look more closely at a single flower, the wonder of its identical geometry. How could nature produce such uniform models, bloom after bloom after bloom? I pulled my phone out of my back pocket to text Jamie a photo. No service. I thought I would take the photo anyway, and text it later, but as I tried to focus the lens, I couldn't get what I was seeing to appear on the screen. It was there, of course, the flower. A lupine, I was pretty sure. But the lupine on my screen didn't look anything like the lupine that stood in front of me, growing out of this unfathomable earth. An impostor.

I took some photos anyway, and stood back up, but I must have stood too fast. Suddenly, the world pixelated. I tried to keep my balance, but things were starting to spin and blend into each other. I could see the two teenage girls nearby, taking photo after photo of themselves among the flowers. I was fighting to stay standing but I could feel something taking over—a looseness shimmering through my body. Maybe I should sit down, I thought, just for a second. I needed to drink some water. But then the looseness had reached my head, it was coming up my neck, up the back of my skull like electricity sweeping through me, the whole world going yellowgreen redblue—

❀

When I came to, the two teenage girls were standing over me, asking me if I was all right. A small crowd had gathered—a family, the matching couple. Dr. Luce made her way to the front. I told her I was fine, but she said we had to go to the nearest hospital. I told her it really wasn't necessary, but she insisted. Liability.

At the hospital, they ran many tests. Tests for things that seemed, to me, completely implausible.

When I got the news a few hours later, I reached for my phone. Jamie had texted me five times:

Can't wait to see you tonight!

I'll make dinner for us

Do you know if we have work sauce?

Worcester sauce?

Worcestershire sauce!

The latest text had been just a few minutes ago. I pictured Jamie rifling through the kitchen cabinets. I knew that if he didn't find it, he would go out and buy some, even if he had already been to the store that day. He would go back to the store, and he wouldn't mind at all, because that's the kind of person he was, someone who didn't mind the tedium of life, who could see the beauty in it, and the joy.

I'm pregnant, I wrote, but that didn't seem quite right.

I'm pregnant! I wrote, but that didn't seem right, either.

I'm pregnant!! I wrote, adding an emoji of a baby, an emoji of a fire-cracker, an emoji of a heart.

I deleted that, too.

It's in the cupboard to the right of the fridge, I wrote, and pressed send.

II

FOURTEEN

Jamie was the one who wanted the baby. It wasn't that I didn't want it, not exactly. But I didn't want it in the way he wanted it, in the way his face exploded with joy and certainty when I told him that night, after I came home from Los Angeles. In the way that it fit, perfectly, with his vision of his life, a vision he was ready to make reality. I felt joy, too—a lift in my chest that startled me with its potency. But I also felt something else, something that wasn't the seemingly pure joy I saw in my acquaintances' pregnancy announcements, the announcements I liked, even as I wondered how they could be so confident, so sure.

I was barely four weeks pregnant when they told me. Early enough not to have missed my period; early enough not to have noticed that something so elemental had shifted in my own body. I was not one of those women who knew they were pregnant before the test. Even when the doctor told me, my first reaction was that he had to be wrong. There had to be a mistake. For one thing, I had been on birth control since I was twenty; eleven years of little pink pills. But then I remembered. There had been a weekend when the pills had gone fuzzy for me, when I realized I had missed two days in a row.

A few of my friends had begun to have children, but they all lived in faraway cities. I'd sent them the requisite baby gifts: tiny moccasins, primary-colored onesies, plastic doodads that you hung from the stroller to keep the baby mentally stimulated. But I had yet to meet any of these babies in person. These friends of mine who had had babies all were married, all owned houses, all brought home hefty paychecks. I brought home a hefty paycheck now, too, but the feeling of financial security was still new to me, and I was unsure how long it would last. How much money did one need to raise a baby? I had no idea, but I knew it was a not insignificant amount.

I had always assumed, in a very abstract way, that I would have children at some point, or at least a child, but I had never really thought about the fact that in order to be a person with a child, I would have to actually *have* a child: to carry it, and birth it, and wake up in the middle of the night with it, to see it all the way through as it grew to a toddler and then a teenager and then an adult, the school drop-offs and pick-ups, the permission slips, the college applications, the heartbreaks, the rebellions. That there would be a small human in the world, depending on me for its safety, depending on me for love.

I told Jamie some of this. I told him I wasn't sure. He said nobody could ever be sure. I said he seemed pretty sure.

Men always say they're getting married because the woman wants to. Having babies because the woman wants to. I thought this was perhaps just a filmic trope, but then I reached the age of thirty and saw it enacted in more than one of my male friends. Could I talk about Jamie the way these men had talked about their girlfriends/fiancées/wives?

I wasn't sure I was ready, I'd say. *But he said he felt like the clock was ticking.*

I knew I could end the pregnancy. I was only thirty-one. Jamie and I talked about it. We could try again in a few years, he said, when I was ready. What I didn't tell him was that I wasn't sure I would ever be ready.

I spent a few days reading everything I could about making this decision: articles, blog posts, forums. There wasn't much in the way of philosophy; unsurprisingly, the great philosophers—almost all male—had not concerned themselves with matters they felt were predominately, if not wholly, female. In *The Second Sex,* de Beauvoir—who herself never had children—wrote that woman's "misfortune is to have been biologically destined to repeat Life," that pregnancy and motherhood made the body a passive instrument, that the woman had to sacrifice herself to the child. But, also, she wrote that there was a wondrous curiosity in every mother; that it was a "strange miracle" to hold a living being who had been formed in and emerged from one's self.

I wished I could talk to my mother, but that was, of course, impossible. I knew nothing about how she and my father had decided to have me. I thought about calling him, telling him, but something made me stop.

No one else, I realized, was going to give me the answer. This was not a question I could use logic to work my way through. I couldn't just read about it, and think about it, and analyze it, and write papers about it. If I wanted to experience the strange miracle, then I had to actually be the one to do it.

※

For our first appointment with the obstetrician, we went to a beige office building and rode the elevator to a beige hallway. In the waiting room, we filled out form after form. After the forms were filled out, Jamie scrolled through his phone and I picked up one of the magazines that was sitting on the low table, page after page of easy weeknight meals and organizational tips and ways to refresh your wardrobe for under fifty dollars. I was particularly fascinated by a full-page spread that offered ten ways to reuse a cardboard toilet paper tube: a knife sheath, a DIY birdfeeder, an extension cord holder.

Finally, my name was called, and we were led to an exam room. The exam room had a strong luau theme. Three of the four walls each had a poster of a multicolored sunset over a pristine beach—slightly different multicolored sunsets, slightly different beaches—overlayed with the name of the island, written in slanted cursive: *Maui, Kauai, Oahu*. I wondered if each doctor got to pick the decor for their exam room. Or was it the nurse? Who among the staff at the clinic we had so carefully chosen was the Hawaii fanatic?

Since the ADAPT ad for Hawaii, other advertisements for Hawaiian vacations had been appearing on my social media feeds. YOUR OWN PRIVATE GETAWAY, the ads said. ESCAPE TO PARADISE. The algorithm, it seemed, had decided that I should go to Hawaii, and once the algorithm decided something, it was unclear to me how to change its mind.

On the fourth wall, there was a poster that was meant to look handpainted but had, of course, been mass-manufactured. It said:

THINK POSITIVELY
BE HAPPY
LOOK UP
BE BOLD
CARPE DIEM
LITTLE THINGS
MEAN A LOT

I was studying this poster when the doctor knocked and entered, charts in hand. I had chosen her because she took my insurance and had very good reviews online, though it was hard to know how much to trust the kind of people who bothered to review their ob-gyn. Also, she was Asian; not Japanese, but Asian. I didn't know why this mattered to me, but it did.

She looked like she was about ten years older than me, maybe fifteen. She introduced herself and shook our hands, then immediately went to the sink to wash up. Her black hair was cut in a clean, utilitarian bob that she had pulled back with clips; she wore a white lab coat and sensible black clogs. Somehow, I already felt that she was trustworthy.

"And how are we feeling today?" Dr. Subramanian said. I noticed that everyone in this office, from receptionist to nurse to doctor, used this phrasing: How are *we* feeling? I was no longer singular. I had become plural.

"I'm fine," I said. "I'm tired, but fine."

She nodded, peering at me like I was a ripe fruit.

"Any nausea?"

"Some," I said. "Not terrible."

She nodded, then went on to ask me a series of questions about my family history, Jamie's family history, my health. She typed as we talked, occasionally nodding in what I took to be approval. The good student in me would not be quelled. I wanted my gold star.

She told me to lie back on the exam table for the ultrasound.

"Time to listen to your baby's heartbeat," she said.

I scooted around on the crinkling paper, putting my feet in the stirrups.

"Ready?" Dr. Subramanian said, positioning herself between my legs. I nodded.

She inserted the wand. On the video screen next to the table, an image appeared. It was in black and white, like a classic movie, except this movie was of the inside of my body. My organs, my tissues. A black orb, which she said was my uterus, came into view. And inside that, a small whitish blob, which she said was the fetus, a quarter of an inch long.

"The size of a blueberry," she said. "Measuring perfectly for seven weeks."

"Why aren't we hearing anything?" Jamie said. So far, there had only been a faraway swishing. "Is everything okay?"

"Everything's okay," she said. She looked at me. "Don't forget to breathe, Evelyn."

I hadn't noticed that I was holding my breath.

Dr. Subramanian moved the wand for a long moment, and suddenly, there it was, fast and rhythmic, the heartbeat. Online, people had said it sounded like a train going through a tunnel, or like a galloping horse. I did not hear a train going through a tunnel. I did not hear a galloping horse. Instead, it sounded like it was coming through a seashell, echoing underwater.

Then, I realized. I was the seashell.

"It's incredible," Jamie said, a wide smile on his face.

"Everything looks fine," Dr. Subramanian said. "Perfect heartbeat. Congratulations."

Every time she said that everything looked fine, I felt I had gotten away with something.

※

Back at home, Jamie said he would make dinner.

"You just put your feet up and relax," he said. I felt like we were re-enacting a movie about a pregnant woman and her caring husband. I wasn't nearly pregnant enough for my feet to be hurting yet, though I was more tired than usual.

"Do you want a drink?" he called from the kitchen. "I got a case of that sparkling lemonade you like."

"Sure," I called back.

A few seconds later, he returned to the living room, holding two cans. He gave one to me and opened the other for himself.

"Thanks," I said. I put my feet up on the couch, as he had suggested.

I opened the can of lemonade and took a sip. He leaned over to put a pillow behind my back. I felt immensely comfortable.

"So, I was thinking," Jamie said, "as long as you can't have alcohol—and sushi, and whatever else—then I won't have it, either."

"Okay," I said. I had heard of partners doing that—abstaining for the length of the pregnancy, in solidarity—but it didn't make sense to me. "I don't think you really have to do that."

"I want to be there for you," he said, smiling. "To know what it feels like."

I knew it was an innocuous comment, that, surely, Jamie didn't think giving up a few food and drink items would be the same as pregnancy, and yet I felt, immediately, extremely irritated.

"I don't think giving up alcohol and sushi is going to adequately simulate pregnancy," I said. My voice sounded sharp.

"You know that's not what I meant," he said.

"Well, that's what it sounded like," I said, doubling down. Even as I said it, I wasn't sure why this question of whether Jamie would also give up certain foods was so important to me, but it suddenly felt like a hill I was willing to die on. "Like the greatest hardship of pregnancy is giving up sushi and alcohol."

"Are we having a fight right now?" he said. This was something we said to each other to diffuse the situation. It was true, I did want a fight, and it was annoying that Jamie would not take the bait.

"You're not going to be a we-er about this, are you?" I said.

"A we-er?"

"One of those men who says 'we're pregnant.' It's not us who is pregnant. It's me."

"Okay," he said, putting his hands up as if in mock surrender. "I will drink lots of beers and eat lots of sushi, I will fill my body with alcohol and mercury. Is that better?"

"That's better," I said.

"Great," he said, smiling. "Now that we've got that resolved, I'm going to make dinner."

❋

I turned on the television. I flipped through the talking heads, the laugh tracks, the endless advertisements. I stopped, finally, when I heard a familiar voice. An episode of *Misfits!* had just started—as it happened, on the seahorse, one of the few species on Earth whose males give birth instead of the females. Others, the voice-over explained, included the leafy sea dragon and the pipefish, as well as the water bug and the Surinam toad.

Scientists were not sure what evolutionary advantage male pregnancy gave the seahorse. One theory was that it assured the father of his paternity; another was that it allowed for a shorter reproductive cycle by sharing the burdens of the reproductive process between two partners. While the male seahorse is bearing the young, the voice-over explained, the female can begin preparing the next batch of eggs. Some seahorses could give birth in the morning and be pregnant again by evening.

"When the seahorse is ready to breed," the voice-over said, "the male and female engage in the courtship ritual of a morning dance for several days in a row, interlocking their tails and moving through the water together." I watched as these two primeval creatures rotated around each other, the floating plankton and dark sea giving the impression of a romantic snowy night. Their bodies looked like human spines with snouts and eyes, their fins like delicate lace, wafting this way and that with the movement of the water.

"Eventually," the voice-over said, "they perform a true courtship dance, lasting approximately eight hours. During this time, the male seahorse pumps water through the egg pouch on his trunk, which expands and opens to demonstrate that it is empty and ready for the female's eggs."

I looked down at my stomach. It had been a strange few weeks, this period of secrecy, this time when something can still so easily go wrong. In the beginning, you weren't supposed to tell people you were pregnant, so that, the logic went, if the worst happened, you wouldn't have to tell people you were no longer pregnant. In Japan, I had read, they had a specific kind of statue for babies who were never born, small figures called Jizos that are attended by the parents, who leave snacks and toys for their child in the afterlife. In America, we just pretended that nothing had happened.

We had heard the heartbeat, and there was only a little more than a month to go until we made it to twelve weeks—to safety. Or at least, relative safety. Even after that point, there was still so much that could go wrong. It was nice, I knew, that Jamie had offered to give up alcohol, give up sushi. He wanted to do everything he could to support me. But the fact was, there was only so much he could do. It was my body that had to shelter and protect that heartbeat, to grow and expand with it, to deliver it safely into the world.

On the TV, the male seahorse was getting ready to give birth. Its breathing became faster, the gills on the sides of its snout puffing open and closed. Its body began to jerk from side to side—contractions, the voice-over said. In just a few seconds, it had changed color, from dark stony gray to mottled chartreuse. The female seahorse hovered nearby as the male seahorse's contractions became more and more violent, his body flipping right and left. And then, finally, the male arched his armored body back, sticking out his swollen stomach. He pushed his tail forward and, through an opening that emerged in his stomach, expelled the first tiny seahorse babies, a flutter of bright yellow bodies, wispy and light, twisting and turning in the currents of the water. He continued to shoot them out from his stomach, *poof,* *poof, poof,* like a pillow exploding.

Seahorses could give birth to up to 2,500 babies in one go, the voice-over said, but only .5 percent—five in one thousand—would survive to adulthood. The seahorse parents did nothing to nurture or protect their young, leaving the baby seahorses' delicate bodies vulnerable to predators and ocean currents and minute changes in temperature. It was enough to have birthed them, enough to have given them a sheltered place to grow from egg to a tiny being. The voice-over noted that they were actually fairly good parents, compared to other fish, who abandoned their eggs immediately after fertilization.

I watched as the male seahorse ejected the final stragglers. Exhausted, he fell to the bottom of the ocean amid a cloud of yellow.

"Need anything else in there?" Jamie yelled from the kitchen.

The female seahorse was already circling the male, ready to transfer a new batch of eggs to his once again empty stomach.

Jamie, I thought, would be so much better at this than me.

FIFTEEN

By the time I had my bat mitzvah, my mother was already sick. She didn't know it yet, but the cells were dividing and mutating inside her, chromosomes and chromatids and malignancies. On the day of my bat mitzvah, she wore a suit embroidered with fake pearls that looked nicer than it sounds. And she stood on the bimah, and she blessed me, her daughter, the Hebrew words flowing easily out of her mouth, a lifetime of synagogue and siddurim embedded in her tongue. There was an old VHS tape of the service that I'd watch from time to time in the years after she died, my mother in her pearl suit, so beautiful, so unaware, her body no longer her own. For years, when I would watch the tape, I would look for signs of what was to come, for any hint of vulnerability. And I would look at my face, the eager face of a thirteen-year-old just beginning to grow into her new body. I wore a matching blue velvet shirt-and-skirt combo that looked just as terrible as it sounds, but I felt beautiful in it, and that shows on the tape, too, in the way I walk up to the bimah, in the swish of my hips, a little swish I did not yet know how to do—that I never quite learned how to do—but that, in that moment, I was practicing. I was trying at adulthood.

Over the course of the following year, I watched my mother fade away. It was more violent than that at the time—my mother had the best doctors, the best care, but the cancer was powerful and fierce, and her body just couldn't fight it. But the way I remembered it was like a picture being slowly erased, only the smudges of the pencil lead left behind on the page, traces of her image, her eyes, her hands, her ears that were always too large for her head. We did not take any pictures during that year, no videos. But wasn't her sickness part of her life, too? It was one-fourteenth of the time I knew her; one-tenth or so of the time I was cognizant of knowing her. Weren't there times in that year worth remembering?

When I was in the second year of my PhD program, I had the VHS converted to DVD. For safekeeping. Is a DVD really safer than a VHS? They are both just objects, somehow imprinted with one's memories. I took the tape to one of those stores with the sign VHS TO DVD!! down on Geary. All the shop did was convert VHS to DVD, per the sign, and I wondered how large the market could possibly be for its services. Was there an army of people out there with these memories that they needed to save, that they needed to survive? I handed my VHS to a teenager who inspired little confidence, and five business days later, I no longer had only one copy of my most precious memory, but two.

Ever since Kumiko had first invited me to go with her to church, I had studiously avoided the subject. But finally, toward the end of February, my father emailed me a formal invitation, one that was impossible to avoid. It would have been easy enough to make an excuse. I was pregnant, after all. I'm too tired, I could have said. I'm too nauseated. But I couldn't use any of those excuses, because I hadn't told him I was pregnant.

It wasn't that I was keeping it a secret. Not exactly. It wouldn't be possible to keep it a secret, after a certain point, anyway. But I wasn't at that point yet, and so what was happening inside me remained hidden, known only to me, Jamie, and a select few medical professionals. And

Dr. Luce, of course. And Jamie's parents, whom he had called excitedly, immediately. So really, actually, the circle wasn't all that small.

There was never a good time. I wanted to tell my father in person, and I hadn't been down to visit since the end of December. Kumiko was always there, and I wanted to tell him alone. My list of excuses went on and on. I could tell I was avoiding telling him, but I couldn't decipher why. Was it because I was afraid of his censure, because Jamie and I weren't married yet? That didn't seem right. We weren't telling most people, not yet, but my father wasn't most people. I wished there were someone, or something, that could tell me what it was I felt about telling him. It was a secret I had hidden even from myself.

And so, with no ready excuse for declining, I said yes, I would go to church. On the agreed-upon Sunday morning in March, I drove down the freeway alone. Jamie had said he would come with me, but in a way that made it clear to me that he hoped I would say he did not have to come. It was a cool and rainy day; it had not rained yet, but it would. The sky was gray and misty, the kind of sky that doesn't change color all day. As I pulled into the parking lot, I noticed first one family of Asians, then another, then another. Asians streamed by me, not a single non-Asian face to be found. It was as if I had flipped into an alternate universe. Kumiko had not told me anything about the church; she had just given me the address, along with the elaborately detailed directions that had long ago been rendered obsolete by smartphones and GPS but that people who had not grown up with smartphones and GPS still tended to include with their invitations.

I got out of the car and saw the sign, bronze lettering running along the front of the building: JAPANESE FOR CHRIST CHURCH.

Now it made sense. I hadn't even known a niche like this existed. I had thought Japanese people were largely secular. Buddhist, maybe, in some kind of very vague, nonpracticing way that involved putting out mochi and mandarin oranges on New Year's. My father had certainly never indicated any Christian leanings, or any leanings whatsoever. But my father was the one who had wanted me to come. He had said it would mean a great deal to Kumiko. He did not say whether it would mean anything to him.

I was ten minutes early, but as I approached the church, I saw that Kumiko and my father were already standing outside waiting for me. It was Kumiko I spotted first, wearing one of her many floral-print dresses, her face bright and eager. My father stood next to her, wearing his churchgoing outfit of pleated khakis and a tucked-in polo shirt, his face much older than I remembered. He had been coming to church with Kumiko for months, but still he seemed out of place, and I wondered if he felt as uncomfortable as he looked. Of course, I would never ask him.

After exchanging our greetings, we walked up the wide stone steps and entered the church. As we moved down the aisle, I watched Kumiko greet her fellow churchgoers, nodding and smiling. She seemed to know everyone. My father hung back, like her shadow. I followed them down a pew, climbing over pantyhose- and khaki-clad legs to get to the empty seats. There were lots of other seats available, ones that didn't require climbing over pantyhose- and khaki-clad legs, but these, apparently, were the seats Kumiko wanted. She probably sat here every week.

People trickled in, veering off to their chosen spots like they were preprogrammed, radio-controlled. A girl in the pew ahead of us wore a lacy pink dress and black patent Mary Janes. Her feet didn't touch the floor, but stuck out straight ahead of her. I watched as she stared at the device in her hand, rapidly pressing buttons to make jewels—cartoon images of jewels—move left and right on her screen before they fell.

I didn't know how I had ended up here, sitting in a pew in the JAPA-NESE FOR CHRIST CHURCH, eleven weeks pregnant and yet not having told my own father that I was pregnant. The baby book I was reading said it was normal to feel uncertainty. Prenatal ambivalence, the book called it, just one of the many things to expect during the third month. Elevated blood pressure, vaginal discharge, forgetfulness, breathlessness, bleeding gums, nose bleeds, prenatal ambivalence. But how much prenatal ambivalence was the normal amount? The book didn't say.

I felt my phone vibrate. A text from Jamie:

How is it?

Fine, I wrote. I stared at the word on my phone. The letters began to get strange. I pressed send before the word lost all meaning. Next to me, Kumiko and my father whispered quietly about something. I pulled a Bible out from the pocket on the pew in front of me. It was printed in English on one side, in Japanese on the other, the incomprehensible characters trailing down the page. It was not unlike the siddurim at the temple I'd grown up in, printed in Hebrew and English. Except I had learned how to read Hebrew, had been sent to Hebrew school twice a week, three times a week. No one had taught me how to read these words, how to recognize these letters. The English, I could understand, but its meaning, the New Testament take on our place in the world, was almost as foreign to me as the Japanese characters.

"Are you comfortable?" Kumiko asked me, leaning over my father. I wondered for a second if she knew. I gave her what was probably a strangely startled look. But no, she was just being polite.

I said I was fine.

"It's a nice church, isn't it?" she said. "I've been coming here for . . ." She paused to think. ". . . sixteen years."

I said that was a long time.

"I guess it is," she said. "It's been the same priest the whole time. Though he's older now, like me. Wrinkled."

I opened my mouth to protest the mention of wrinkles, the way I knew I was supposed to, but she knew the protest was coming and waved it away. My father sat silently between us.

"I started coming here when I was right around your age, a few years older maybe. I had just turned thirty-four." Something in her voice seemed to flicker when she said that, and I thought she was going to say more, but just then the pastor entered and the chattering in the pews quieted down. He was an elderly Asian—Japanese—man, and I couldn't help but think he looked wise in the way that films had conditioned me to think elderly Asians looked wise. Elderly minorities of any kind, really. Repositories of wisdom.

I looked around at the pews, filled with expectant faces. I didn't think I'd ever been around this many Asians, let alone Japanese people specifically, before in my life. The pastor climbed the steps to the pulpit, and as I waited for him to begin, I wondered if maybe I would learn something about how to be, in this world, in this life. It had worked for all these other people.

Maybe I was about to have a revelation.

But when he began to speak, the words coming out of his mouth were incomprehensible to me. Around me, everyone else seemed to absorb the service with perfect clarity. Even the girl in the lacy pink dress sat with an unexpected attentiveness. As nonsensical as it was, my first instinct was to wonder, for a moment, if this was some strange and previously unrecorded side effect of pregnancy: language itself becoming unfamiliar. It took me a long moment to realize why I couldn't understand the words.

He was speaking Japanese.

✻

On the bat mitzvah tape, my father reads a prayer, too. I remember him practicing it night after night, struggling through the transliteration, trying to make his mouth make the *ch* sound of *chet*, of *challah* and *Chanukah*—but *ch* is a sound that comes from the throat, a deep rasping best taught in childhood. He was never going to be able to get it by moving his lips, and why were there so many h's, anyway, he would ask, when they were all silent? My mother liked to tell the story of my father's attempt to convert, how he had the bad luck to get a traditional rabbi, one set on the old custom of turning away a potential convert three times. My father didn't know and wouldn't accept my mother's explanation after the rabbi called to cancel their first meeting at the last minute. He never set up a second meeting, and certainly not a third.

And yet he was the one who picked me up at school and drove me to Hebrew school on Tuesday and Thursday afternoons, and picked me back up again at the temple at six, when classes let out, the two of us listening to NPR in silence. My mother was the one who insisted I go, but her schedule was not her own to control, whereas my father could arrange for one less tooth-cleaning, a few less cavities to fill. He never once came in, never attended services, only set foot in the synagogue the day of my bat mitzvah. My mother always took High Holidays off— that, at least, was allowed by her firm—and so it was she who would go with me, would sing the Shema and the V'ahavta, would stand beside me, rocking up onto the balls of her feet three times during the Amiduh, *kadosh kadosh kadosh, holy holy holy,* would press the corners of her tallit to the Torah scroll as it came around and then press them to her mouth in a sacred kiss, would hold her arm around my shoulders and show me how to do the same, urging me forward, into the heritage she felt was mine, by blood and by right, no matter that all the faces that looked back at us in the synagogue were white and my face was something else, not white, but not not-white, either.

That had been the deal, when the Kominsky family's only daughter had announced that she was marrying a Japanese man: that the little Japanese Jewish children would be brought up in the temple, would be bar and bat mitzvah'd. There had only been one child, but my parents had kept their end of the bargain. No matter how much I tried to get them to let me stay home, it was no use. I always found myself in the same plastic chair in the same makeshift classroom at the temple, reciting the same

Hebrew lines, trying to master the difficult melody of the haftarah, practicing my Torah portion over and over again, the vowelless words swimming in and out of comprehensibility on the scroll before me.

But somewhere along the way, the deal had been perverted, somehow my mother's body had misunderstood the terms. It seemed as though it had thought that once the little Japanese Jewish child was bat mitzvah'd, it was no longer needed. That its job was complete.

※

After the service, Kumiko and my father gathered outside with the other congregants, milling about on the sidewalk. I stood a little ways off, at the edge of the lawn, texting Jamie. I didn't have anything to say, really, but it was something to do, something to make it look like I had something to do. Jamie asked how I was feeling. He asked me this all the time. I suppose it wasn't fair. I was the one who got to be with the baby at all times. If Jamie could have, he would have traded places with me in a second.

I watched as two older women approached Kumiko. They chatted for a minute before Kumiko caught my eye and waved me over. I was hungry and my feet hurt and all I wanted was to go home and lie down. I knew that when I told Jamie the whole service was in Japanese, he would ask why they had even invited me. Kumiko knew I didn't speak Japanese, but maybe she didn't quite believe it. Maybe she thought my soul would be saved anyway, via osmosis.

"Is this your daughter?" one of the women asked Kumiko, in English.

"Oh, no, no," Kumiko said. She said something in Japanese, pointing at my father.

"Ah, ah," the women said, in unison.

They talked for a few more minutes, then said their goodbyes. I stood there, decoratively; no one asked me anything. Around us, families headed to the cars. I felt a few isolated drops of rain, barely discernible.

We were still standing in front of the church, but almost everyone else was gone. Kumiko turned to me and asked if I wanted to come over for lunch. I wondered if that would be a good opportunity to tell them—I had by then resigned myself to the impossibility of speaking to my father alone—but I did not want to go to the house. I did not want to go to the house that used to contain my mother but did not contain her anymore. I did not want to have this baby without my mother, who would not be able to see it, to hold it, to babysit and burp it.

I heard the grumbling of thunder in the distance. Soon the sky would open up. We began walking to my father's car—to their car. When we got there, we stood by the trunk. Kumiko thanked me for coming to church, my father nodding. I wondered if I was supposed to say I had enjoyed it, that I would come again. I did not say any of those things.

"I'm pregnant," I said instead.

I wanted to look at my father, but I was distracted by Kumiko, who clapped her hands together in delight. Then, just as quickly, her face changed.

"Are you going to get married?" she said, her voice taking on considerably more urgency than I had ever heard from her.

"I don't know," I said. I was not expecting this line of questioning, though perhaps I should have. "We've talked about it."

Kumiko looked at me, waiting for me to continue, waiting, perhaps, for an explanation that would make sense to her. I wanted to tell her that I didn't know why I wasn't getting married, that I didn't have to get married, that I wanted to keep my independence, that marriage was a fundamentally patriarchal institution, that I didn't understand Japanese and probably never would, that I hadn't wanted to come to the church, that I had done it as a favor to her, or, rather, to my father.

"I'm just not sure it's for me," I said, finally.

Kumiko opened her mouth to say something else, but my father put his hand on her arm, gently.

"This is wonderful news," he said. "Wonderful."

He asked me if I needed anything. He told me to be sure to tell him if I needed anything.

Kumiko asked again if I wanted to come to the house for lunch, but I told them I was tired and wanted to go home. I felt a few drops of rain on my arms. She reached out to hug me goodbye, as if our exchange about marriage hadn't even happened. She smelled like her usual smell of lotion or shampoo, mixed with the smell of the air, of the coming rain. She got in the passenger side of their car, and I saw my father lean over and say something to her. He closed her door and said he would walk me to my car, which was parked halfway across the lot. I wasn't sure what to say, so as we crossed the parking lot, I told him about the most recent scan, how far along I was, that we didn't know the sex yet and that we weren't sure if we wanted to know.

At the car, we paused. I unlocked the door and opened it.

"Kumiko means well," he said to me.

"I know," I said.

"She's a very different person than your mom," he said. He said this completely neutrally, with no implication that different meant better or worse.

I felt like I was holding my breath. He mentioned my mother so rarely; I waited to see if he would say anything else. He looked over at his car, where Kumiko was waiting.

"Anyway," he said. "You'll let me know if you need anything?"

"You just asked me that," I said.

"Did I?" he said, smiling a little. "Well, I must really mean it, then."

"Thanks," I said, lowering myself into the car. "I'll let you know."

We said goodbye, and I watched in the rearview mirror as he walked back to his car, as he turned the headlights on and backed out of the parking spot, as he and Kumiko headed off to the home they would soon share.

SIXTEEN

A few weeks later, I tried to go for a walk to Lands End. Jamie wanted to go with me, but I told him I wanted to go alone. It was a place my mother had liked to go, and I remembered driving up from our suburban cul-de-sac and walking the trails on the edge of the city with her, looking out at the endless horizon. It was a place, she said, where she could just be; these words stuck with me because she was otherwise such a go-go-go person, sweeping my father and me along with her through life like a swift current. I hadn't been there for many years.

At that moment, I was interested in just being. In not worrying, in not thinking.

But when I got to the parking lot, it was roped off, closed, apparently. A man was standing by the barricades handing out fliers. He looked like he was in his mid-sixties, tall and rangy, with white hair pulled back in a low ponytail and multiple piercings in one ear. He wore a pair of old jeans, brown leather cowboy boots, and a denim shirt that looked like it had been distressed the old-fashioned way—by actual wear.

"Excuse me," I said. "Do you know what's going on?"

"Parks department rented it to a big-shot media company. Filming a commercial," he said. He continued looking straight ahead, not making eye contact with me, and his voice lacked inflection. "BMW or Audi or some such."

Next to me, a group of Spanish tourists wearing what looked like high-end designer outfits murmured in disappointed-sounding tones. The man handed them a flier.

"Eleven thousand six hundred and fifty-two dollars. Six hours of filming," the man said, still not looking at me. "Closed two days. It's a matter of public record."

I saw something buzz by in the air, whirling like a miniature helicopter.

"What was that?" I asked.

"Drone," the man said. "FAA says bystanders have to stay back two hundred feet."

"Is that even allowed?" I asked, somehow only now noticing a police car parked behind me on the path.

"Eight thousand dollars to the parks department, one thousand to the film commission, two thousand six hundred and fifty-two to the police," he said. "Everything is for sale these days."

I took a flier. Across the top, in bold capital letters, it read DRONES = MURDER. Underneath that, a grainy black-and-white photo of a car crash, with a small blur in the upper right, a giant Photoshopped arrow pointing to the presumably not-Photoshopped blur.

Underneath that was a bullet-pointed list of the murders supposedly committed by drone since their introduction to US military strategy, extreme in its detail: a hit on a thirty-three-year-old investigative reporter whose cover story on a US Army general's misdeeds in Afghanistan had led to the general being relieved of his command and who was in the middle of writing a similar exposé of the NSA at the time of his four fifteen a.m. death on a small street in Los Angeles, a crash so bad that his body was not immediately identifiable; a many-layered thesis about a B-movie star who also died in a car crash, and who had ties to the Illuminati—such ties supposedly evidenced by a poster for one of the celebrity's action movies, in which he shows only one eye, the all-seeing eye symbol of the group—but was on his way to betray their recent experiments with a sterilization vaccine in an unnamed Southeast Asian country; a hit ordered by the president on two single-family homes in Huntsville, Alabama, belonging to aged former Nazi scientists whom the US had been sheltering for the past seventy years and whose plywood-sided houses had finally exploded in bursts of flame that authorities had erroneously attributed to an almost simultaneous meth lab accident and electrical fire, respectively; an attack ordered by a high-ranking-but-not-presidential government official to kill his pregnant mistress in Missouri, which authorities had supposedly traced to a gas leak, allowing the woman's family to collect a massive insurance payment.

"Surveillance," the man said. "They're always watching."

"Thanks," I said, lifting the flier in a half wave. The man nodded back solemnly but did not say anything more. I folded the flier and dropped it into my bag. As I walked back home, I thought about him. He looked like the kind of person I had grown up seeing everywhere on the streets of San Francisco, but who was now rare. Where had they all gone, those conspiracy theorists of my youth? They had once seemed so extreme to me, so untethered from reality, but the longer I worked at the third-most-popular internet company, the more I felt there might be a kernel of truth in what they preached.

That night, I brushed my teeth, staring at the image of myself in the mirror staring back at me. I edged closer to the mirror. I had read online that pregnant women's noses could get bigger due to increased estrogen. Was my nose growing wider?

Before I climbed into bed, I looked out the window at the night sky. All clear.

A few days later, I filed into the third-most-popular internet company's glass-walled conference room along with the rest of the happiness project team. Outside the window, a bird flew by. Not just any bird—this one was enormous, with a long, fanning tail and an enormous wingspan. I watched it glide through the air, wheeling around with a quick pivot and turning back toward us. It seemed to be headed straight for our conference room, as though it was indifferent to the glass that separated us, which would surely injure if not kill it upon impact, but at the last second, it lifted up, soaring above us and out of view.

"Peregrine falcon," Sabine said. She was sitting next to me, tapping on her phone. "They have a nest on the roof of a building nearby. The company set up a webcam—you can watch them lay their eggs and everything. I was really obsessed with it one year. Watched the eggs hatch, the parents feeding the babies, watched them grow, watched them take their first flight."

"I heard one of them was hit by a car out in Martinez," Josh said.

"Great, Josh," Sabine said. "That's just great. Thanks for ruining that beautiful experience of nature for me."

I asked him how he knew.

"The falcons are all tagged," he said. "The scientists know where they are at all times."

Sabine went back to tapping on her phone. I went back to waiting, doing nothing. I was very aware of my stomach, of the way it had begun to protrude. Of my coworkers, some of whom I had told and some of whom I hadn't, some of whom had learned from the ones I told, or the ones they told, and came to me to congratulate me, some of whom had not been told by anyone and looked at my stomach for a beat too long, confusedly, still unsure if I was simply gaining weight. I wondered if the falcons knew about the webcam, streaming their every move to an audience of thousands as they fed their babies, beak to beak. I wondered if they could feel the weight of the bands on their legs, if it chafed them as they soared high above the earth.

The door to the conference room swished open and closed. Dr.

Luce entered and took her seat at the head of the table. She and I had not spoken since the premier happiness conference in the world. I kept expecting to run into her in the hallway, in the elevator, for her to stop by my desk or email me, to ask how I was doing. She was the first person to know I was pregnant, after the doctors and the nurses. She knew before Jamie knew. I had assumed this had established some kind of intimacy between us, but it was clear that I was wrong.

She waited for her assistant to load the presentation onto the screen behind her. The image came into focus. JOYFULL, it said. A hush fell over the room.

"Our happiness app is ready," she announced. "We've assembled the beta testers and will begin testing today."

The app, she explained, combined all our disparate research over these past few months into one all-encompassing program designed to help the modern human with all the stressors of day-to-day life.

"It reminds you about your basic physical needs," she explained. "To drink enough water, to get enough sleep, to exercise. But it goes much further than that. It gives you various prompts throughout the day to help you develop aspects of happiness: gratitude, serenity, generosity. It gives you a place to track your mood, and also uses various biofeedback methods to measure your affective state. Then every week it will aggregate the data to show you where and when you're happiest."

She flipped through the slides, showing us a mock-up of the tracking, the line graph shooting up and down with this hypothetical user's happiness, recorded minute by minute. The next set of slides showed the questions the app would ask for the preliminary self-assessment—the questions, supposedly, that Sabine and Josh and I had generated. Except the questions on the screen were not our questions. I didn't recognize a single one.

"The research isn't ready," Sabine said, interrupting. In theory, it was fine for her to interrupt; the third-most-popular internet company's rhetoric was all about democratization, against hierarchies. In practice, interrupting was something that very few people other than Sabine would consider doing. Dr. Luce looked not so much annoyed as perplexed.

"We don't know enough about how this will affect people," Sabine went on. "Will there be negative feedback to seeing a low score? Will this become a self-fulfilling prophecy? We don't know."

"That's what the beta testing is for," Dr. Luce said.

"It's not even ready for beta testing," Sabine said, looking around the room for support. The room was quiet. "Evelyn," she said, turning to me, "what do you think?"

Everyone in the room turned to look at me. Dr. Luce stood patiently at the front of the room, holding her laser pointer in one hand.

"Yes, Evelyn," Dr. Luce said. "Better for us to know now if there's a problem."

"I'm not sure," I said. My six-month trial was about to come to an end; my contract was about to be reevaluated. I could see Sabine shaking her head out of the corner of my eye. "Those aren't the questions we submitted," I managed.

"Oh, right," Dr. Luce said. "The questions. We had to change those to make them a little more user-friendly. Not so academic." She paused, looking over the room. "Any other concerns?"

No one said anything for a long minute.

"Okay," Dr. Luce said. "In the absence of other critique, we are going to move forward. And in addition to the beta testers, we'd like to invite anyone on the team to also try out JOYFULL. Strictly voluntarily, of course. But we do hope that many of you will be willing to participate, as your feedback will be the most valuable."

She explained how to sign up for the app, the happiness intake survey we would take to establish our baseline. She told us that we were an integral part of the third-most-popular internet company's success. She told us that they—the higher-ups—had big plans for JOYFULL. They were hoping to make the testing go quickly, to be first on the market.

We had been told that participating was voluntary, but when I looked around the table, I knew that everyone would leave the meeting and immediately sign up for the app—not because they felt like they had to, but because they wanted to, because they believed in the third-most-popular internet company, in the team, in the product, in the mission.

They—we—were going to revolutionize happiness.

Back at my desk, I watched as the first page of the happiness intake loaded on my phone. All around me, the other members of the team were also getting ready to be measured. Who would be the happiest among us? Who would be the least happy? I hoped it wasn't me. I was about to have a baby. It couldn't be me. Or if it was, I supposed, I would have a ready-made excuse. The hormones. The fatigue.

I selected my age bracket, my sex. I said whether I smoked, whether I drank, whether I used illegal drugs, whether I used legal drugs. I input how often I exercised, what type of exercise. My income bracket. My level of education, my parents' level of education. Whether or not I had siblings. Their level of education.

It asked me for my relationship status, but the options were only: single or married. I held my finger over MARRIED, but it did not seem right. I clicked SINGLE.

The app was quickly learning most everything there was to know about me—on paper, at least. I wondered if it would be wrong to lie. I was tempted. I wanted to keep some things to myself. But probably the third-most-popular internet company would find out. Probably the third-most-popular internet company already knew, even though I still used the first-most-popular internet company most of the time.

I scrolled down the page to the next question.

RACE

○ WHITE (CAUCASIAN)
○ AFRICAN AMERICAN
○ LATINO/A
○ ASIAN
○ NATIVE AMERICAN/PACIFIC ISLANDER
○ OTHER

I hovered my finger over ASIAN. I hovered my finger over WHITE (CAUCASIAN). I clicked OTHER and stared at it. I clicked ASIAN, which made the check next to OTHER disappear. I clicked OTHER again, which made the check next to ASIAN disappear.

I pressed the forward arrow and moved on to the next page. As the next question loaded, I wondered if I should go back and change my answer to ASIAN.

WHEN WAS THE LAST TIME YOU MARVELED AT
THE WORLD?

I clicked the bracket for WITHIN THE LAST WEEK, which seemed not as happy as TODAY but considerably happier than NEVER.

I moved on to the next question.

DO YOU AGREE OR DISAGREE WITH THIS
STATEMENT: I FEEL LIKE I AM FLOURISHING

○ STRONGLY AGREE
○ SOMEWHAT AGREE

○ SOMEWHAT DISAGREE

○ STRONGLY DISAGREE

Was I flourishing?

I clicked SOMEWHAT AGREE, then switched it to SOME-WHAT DISAGREE. They felt, to me, exactly the same. I wondered if Dr. Luce would be reviewing our results. I wondered if it was better to start with a higher baseline or a lower one, to show more improvement or less need to improve.

I changed it back to SOMEWHAT AGREE.

I answered more questions, about whether I felt purposeful in my life, about whether people said I had a good sense of humor, about how many people I interacted with on a given day, how many people I felt I could trust. About whether I saw projects through to the very end no matter what obstacles got in my way, whether I saw life as rewarding, whether I thought people were fundamentally good or fundamentally evil, whether I thought most people cheated on their taxes, whether I thought the world was a good place, whether I was optimistic about the future, whether I felt I could rely on other people, whether I mostly kept my problems to myself, whether I had a cheerful effect on others, whether I thought I was likable or unlikable.

A few of the questions that Sabine, Josh, and I had developed had made it into the questionnaire, but most of the questions were new to me. I tried to click the buttons instinctively, which was what the instructions had said to do.

Was I likable? I clicked SOMEWHAT AGREE.

I paused.

I changed it to SOMEWHAT DISAGREE.

On the next screen, instead of a question, there was an image of an eye and instructions to hold my device up to my face. I lifted my phone and watched as my face appeared on the screen, and then as the image zoomed in on my right eye. A small wheel at the bottom of the screen rotated.

SCANNING. SCANNING. SCANNING.
SCANNING COMPLETE.

I lowered my phone and clicked the big blue button at the bottom of the test that said GET MY SCORE.

I watched the wheel turn again as the app plugged my answers into its algorithm. The algorithm that I had, in a way, helped design.

The next screen loaded.

7.1 OUT OF 10, it said. Neither happy nor unhappy. The average, it said, was 7.2. I was .1 happiness units away from average. That did not seem like the right score for a pregnant woman. Wasn't bringing new life into the world supposed to be the pinnacle of joy? Was this, I wondered, something to be concerned about?

THIS IS NOT SOMETHING TO BE CONCERNED ABOUT, the next screen said. It said that happiness was a process, that I should come back tomorrow for a new activity to help build my emotional fitness.

I looked up from my screen. Most of the other strategists were still bent over their phones. I wished there were a way for me to know what they were answering. I wanted to know their scores.

This is not a competition, I told myself.

I thought back to the philosophy roundtable. Montaigne would say it was fine to be a 7.1. That it didn't matter what anyone else was scoring; that the only thing that mattered was my individual experience of my individual happiness.

It's okay to be a 7.1, I told myself.

My computer pinged: a new email. From Dr. Luce. The subject: "Renewing Contract." The email was short and to the point. It said that the third-most-popular internet company was happy with my work so far, but they were not sure about making my position permanent. Instead, they would be extending my contract for another six months. I was supposed to go to HR to sign the paperwork ASAP.

Soon after the fall in the desert, the hospital, the news, Jamie and I had spent several evenings conferring, running numbers for our new life as three people instead of two. We had been counting on my going permanent. At the third-most-popular internet company, contractors still received health insurance and parental leave, so that would be fine. My leave wouldn't count toward the six months of the contract; I'd have a job to come back to, at least for a few more months. Still, I needed the job to go permanent, if not now, then the next time the contract came up for renewal. I wondered what I had or hadn't done, what I did or didn't need to do. The email did not say.

I looked back at JOYFULL, at my 7.1.

I would have to redouble my efforts.

SEVENTEEN

At the ultrasound facility, they spread a cold gel on my belly and I imagined all the things that could go wrong. It was mid-May, time for the twenty-week anatomy scan, and we had changed our minds: we were going to find out the sex of the baby.

The ultrasound tech pressed the wand against my stomach and started moving it around. Jamie and I watched as the black-and-white picture on the screen went in and out of focus, something that looked like a head, something that looked like legs, something that looked like a foot, appearing and disappearing.

Jamie watched the screen, completely enthralled, turning to me with an enormous grin on his face each time the tech confirmed the presence of a body part. I nodded my head, but I was having a hard time keeping up. Every time the tech said, "There's the left arm," or "There are the lungs," I felt like I had when I was a child and my friends would look at those Magic Eye books. They would squeal with delight at finding the image, but I could never see it, no matter how hard I tried.

What I did see, though, was a spot on what looked like the baby's chest, rising up and down, quick, quick, quick. What was this? Why could I see it? I hadn't seen it in any of the videos, hadn't read about it in any of the books. It did not look right. I felt myself beginning to panic, just a little.

"And there's the heart," the tech said.

I felt my own heart constrict.

"Sounds great," the tech said as we listened to the heartbeat. "Strong heart."

She began poking and prodding again. "Are you ready for the sex?" she asked. We nodded. Jamie squeezed my hand. We had both said that the sex didn't matter to us. Jamie, probably, was telling the truth, but I wanted a girl. It didn't feel safe to admit, not until we knew, possibly not even then. Would I love the child less if it was not a girl? It seemed unlikely, but I didn't know how to argue with the feeling, which came from somewhere deep inside me, a place I could not name.

The tech was still fiddling around with the wand, pushing it this way and that, trying to get a better angle. I imagined the sound waves pulsing through my stomach and refracting off the baby's body, like a whale navigating the deep sea, sending out its calls and waiting for the echo to bounce back.

The tech turned to us with a smile. "It's a girl."

It was no longer an it. Now it was a she.

Dr. Subramanian had said walking was good for the baby, and so I began walking home from work, taking a longer-than-necessary route through Golden Gate Park, watching the Frisbee players and the joggers, the squirrels and the pigeons darting underfoot. Every day, I passed a hunched old woman sitting surrounded by pigeons, tossing out seed from a battered plastic bag. Each time I passed her, I worried for her, wondering if she had somewhere to go home to. But still, I didn't say hello, I didn't ask if she was all right. Who was I to say that she was not all right? And, as it turned out, one day I left work a little later, and I came upon her, not feeding the pigeons, but with her arm looped through the arm of a man who looked just the right age to be her son. I watched from a distance as he helped her into a car, opening the door for her and helping her lift one beige-stockinged leg at a time into the passenger seat. It was clear, somehow, from the way they interacted that this was a daily routine, and I felt absolved.

I rarely interacted with anyone on these walks, and this was something I enjoyed about them, the feeling of moving through the world unnoticed. The park was full of noises—the yelps of children, the motors of cars, the swoosh of bicyclists—but I felt like I was ensconced in a bubble of quiet. Increasingly, wherever I went, people wanted to touch my stomach, wanted to give me their seat, wanted to know how far along I was, how I was feeling, wanted to tell me how many children they had, how long their labor had been, that I looked beautiful, that I was glowing, that the baby was high, and that meant it would be a girl, or that the baby was low, and that meant it would be a boy. But in the park, I was allowed thirty minutes each day to simply exist. Maybe that was why the old woman came, too, and feeding the pigeons was secondary.

So I was a little bit startled when, one afternoon, about two weeks after the ultrasound, a woman interrupted my walk and asked if she could draw me.

She was Asian. She looked like she was in her early or mid-twenties, an art student, she told me, working on her thesis project. She wore the signifiers of artistic identity: glasses with clear plastic frames; black Doc Martens, lightly scuffed; faded black jeans; a worn T-shirt with small holes at the collar and hem, which had either been earned through hours in the studio and many trips through the washing machine or, possibly, purchased at a vintage store. She wore no makeup and was thin in a severe way; later, when she turned from me, I saw a pack of cigarettes lodged in her back pocket.

"It's a series called Facial Recognition," she explained. "I'm making drawings of half-Asian women. The idea is that the drawings are like self-portraits, but refracted through another person. A self-portrait of a person who is not me."

I asked how she knew I was half Asian.

"I just did," she said, shrugging. "You are, aren't you?"

I replied in the affirmative.

"Good," she said. "I am, too, obviously. Chinese Dutch."

It had not been obvious to me.

She looked at me, waiting for me to give my self-identification. I told her I was Japanese Jewish.

"That's what I thought," she said.

She continued, explaining that the drawing was not actually the final product; after she made the drawing, she would take a photograph of me holding the drawing. The photograph was the final product.

"Kind of like a selfie," she said. "But also not a selfie."

As if she sensed my hesitation, she told me the drawing would be mine to keep. That, too, was part of the project.

A few minutes later, I was sitting on one of the park benches, trying to keep still. She had said it would only take a few minutes, and I could see that she was working quickly, her hand making fast strokes in her sketchbook.

I didn't know if I was allowed to talk—if that would make the muscles in my face move too much—but I asked her how she had come up with the project.

"I don't know if you used this app when it came out a few years ago, but there was this thing where you could take a selfie and upload it and then the app would match your face to a work of art?"

I nodded slightly. I did remember something like that.

"When I saw that, I thought it was so cool and—I'm embarrassed to say this now, but I was excited about it. All my friends were posting their results, and they were getting these beautiful images—Klimt and

Rembrandt, the lady in gold, portrait of a young woman—and they were just flooding my feed. I couldn't wait to find out which painting it thought I looked like, and to post it, of course. And then I took a selfie and uploaded it and all I got was this image of a baby, and I realized I had gotten it because it was one of the only images in the database with cheeks as wide as mine, and also with black hair. I tried a few more times, and the results were even worse: a geisha, a Chinese man working on the railroad. I tried again and again, with different angles, different lighting, different facial expressions, but I kept getting the same three results: the baby, the Chinese man, the geisha. I felt like I shouldn't be upset by it—it was just this stupid app—but honestly, I felt like I had been hit by a truck. It was all the worse because I was so unprepared for it. You know, I expect that shit when I open a fashion magazine or something, but I hadn't been expecting it at all with that app."

She paused and looked up at me, then down at the drawing, then up at me. Then she began to attack the drawing again.

"So this series is in conversation with that. Don't worry, I'm not posting the photos online. I thought about it—like, you know, citizen action, creating a database of my own as part of the piece. But then I was like, screw that, the tech companies will eventually just find any photos I post and mine them for their own uses. Of course, I know there are much bigger problems with facial recognition—authoritarianism, the police state. I haven't quite worked the whole project out yet, we'll see where it goes."

A moment later, she lifted her hand from the drawing and said it was done. She ripped it carefully from her sketchbook, then stood up and presented it to me. I took the paper from her, my own face looking back at me. It seemed to be a good likeness, a flattering one, but I didn't have time to study it; she was already setting up for the photo. She told me to hold the paper closer to my face—she wanted to zoom in as close as possible. I wasn't sure whether to smile or not smile. I decided not to smile. Then she snapped the camera several times in quick succession, recording the microchanges in my expression. After a minute of shooting, she looked down at the camera's screen and clicked through the photos.

"We're done," she said, thanking me. She didn't offer to show me the photos and I didn't ask, even though I wanted to see them, to see what she had registered of me.

※

At home, I sat on the bed and pulled the drawing out of my bag. I had pressed it between the pages of a book to protect it. The corners of the paper had gotten slightly frayed where they stuck out a bit past the book's cover, but otherwise it had survived intact.

I turned on my phone and downloaded the app the art student had been talking about. I gave the app access to my camera and held my phone away from my face. I hesitated, and then I took the photo. I watched my face, frozen on the screen, little pinpoints of light flickering across my cheekbones, my nose, my temples—the app's signal to me that it was scanning my face. And then my match appeared, a late-nineteenth-century painting called *Madam X*, by a Turkish artist, Halil Pasha. The woman was not unattractive, but she was far from beautiful; she had a plain, soft face and was almost entirely covered up, wearing a high-necked dress and gloves. I was curious to know more about her, but when I typed "Madam X" into the search window of the first-most-popular internet company, the results loaded instead with image after image of a painting called *Portrait of Madame X* by John Singer Sargent. Here was an image that was clearly meant to be one of beauty, of ravishment: the woman presented in stark profile, her white skin illuminated against a dark background, wearing a plunging black gown made of a luxurious fabric. I looked through several pages of results, but it was like my *Madam X* hardly existed, a bare shadow of Sargent's famous beauty.

While I was still looking at the screen, my phone pinged:

DO YOU FEEL LIKE YOU BELONG?

1   2   3   4   5   6   7   8   9   10

I hovered my finger over the number six, which seemed like an acceptable, if not quite ideal, response. I pressed the number three.

DO YOU WANT TO BELONG?

1   2   3   4   5   6   7   8   9   10

I put my phone down without answering.

I could hear Jamie moving around the kitchen, pots clanging. He had been wearing his blue-and-white-striped apron when I got home, and he had pressed his ear to my belly—a new habit of his that annoyed me, but that I didn't think I could tell him annoyed me, given that he was simply performing what he felt was a true and sincere act of fatherly love. Nothing was even happening yet; it was too early for the baby to be kicking. *Should I leave the two of you alone?* I sometimes wanted to say, though, of course, that was impossible.

I put the drawing in the drawer of my nightstand and went out to join him.

read online that an orca up in Canada was mourning her dead calf by carrying it with her through the water. The whale, named G32 by researchers, had given birth a few days before, but the calf had lived for less than an hour. The article said she had been carrying the baby ever since, balancing it on her rostrum—the area of the head right behind the nose—and diving deep to recover it when it fell. She had been carrying it for three days already, her pod staying close. Orcas, one of the quoted researchers said, had a seventeen-month gestation period. The mother had carried the baby for almost a year and a half, to see it alive for only a precious few minutes. The researchers said they were concerned about her health: swimming with the extra weight and making these deep dives would be taking a toll on her physically. It was unclear if she was eating, since there would be no way for her to catch food while also maintaining control of the body. Possibly, the researchers said, other whales in the pod were feeding her.

Humans, of course, were to blame. The orcas relied on salmon as their primary food; overharvesting and hydroelectric power had caused a massive decline in the wild salmon population. The pregnant orcas were not getting enough to eat, which meant that even if they could carry their babies to term, the babies died shortly after birth. Researchers did not know exactly what had happened to G32's baby—not yet. But they were watching her and her pod around the clock. To be very clear, one of them said in the article, no one would ever take the baby away from G32 while she was still carrying it. But if she left the calf and moved away for an extended period of time, they would attempt to recover the calf's body, in an effort to understand what had happened.

No, an expert said in response to the reporter's question, there was no way that G32 didn't understand that the calf was dead.

Grief and love, said the expert, don't belong only to us.

In mid-June, when I was twenty-four weeks pregnant, Dr. Luce called me into her office to have what she called a one-on-one. Her office was in a far corner, an actual office, rather than an open workspace. Still, the office had glass walls, as though to give the effect of transparency. Standing outside the glass door, I could see Dr. Luce at her desk, staring at something on her computer screen. She was facing me, but she didn't see me. I knocked on the glass and watched the recognition appear on her face. She waved me in, and I opened the door.

"Just give me one second," she said, holding up her index finger. I stood, waiting, just inside. The office had floor-to-ceiling exterior windows that covered almost the entire back wall, so it truly was like floating in a glass cube. Out the window was a view of another skyscraper, which almost certainly housed another tech company, or possibly something having to do with money: a bank, a venture capital firm, a hedge fund. I could see bodies moving across the way, but I could not make out their faces, and I wondered what it was they did in our doppelgänger building, whether it was possible that at this very moment, their VP of research was sitting down to a meeting in a glass-walled room just like this one.

I was still standing just inside the glass door when Dr. Luce finished whatever it was she was doing with an audible *click*. She stood up and came around from behind the desk to two large leather club chairs that faced each other at slightly askew angles.

"Here, take a seat." She gestured at the chairs. I lowered myself into one. It smelled like butter and money. She sat, facing me. "How are you feeling?"

I wasn't sure if she was asking how I was feeling as an individual person or how I was feeling as a pregnant woman. I told her I was fine.

"Pregnancy is hard," she said. "Or at least, I assume it is, from everything you hear. I've never been pregnant myself. That ship has sailed. Although you do hear about these celebrities these days, the technology, it's amazing. But I never really wanted kids. Not for me. Wouldn't know what to do with one. I'd say I've got no maternal instinct, but I'm not sure I buy that. What is maternal instinct except a way to shame women and condition them to believe that they are the ones responsible for the baby's well-being? Where is paternal instinct? Maybe if paternal instinct existed in our world, I would be more interested in having a baby."

She paused for a second, as though digesting her own thought, and then went on.

"Anyway, enough about that. I'm going to cut right to the chase," she said. "The analytics team is concerned about your JOYFULL results. Your happiness levels are far behind the other testers—not just your baseline, but your improvement, too.

"I should be clear," she said. "It's not your results I'm concerned about. It's the app. They say that you're an outlier in the data. But I think the data itself might not be accurate. I mean, what is the app doing right now? It asks you to self-assess, does a little biometrics. That's not nearly enough for a reliable picture. It's so frustrating, to have this vision of what could be possible and not know how to make it a reality. I'm not an engineer. They tell me my ideas are too complex for the system. So build a more complex system! But they tell me it's not possible. What they mean is, it's not possible within the product time frame. We're working to build a more intelligent system, but the question is, do people want a more intelligent system? I think they do. Why wouldn't they? But the product team thinks that people don't actually want a more complex system. They think that people want to just push a couple of buttons and be told that they're happy and go on with their lives. What do you think?"

She leaned back in the enormous leather chair. She looked through me, past me, so that I wasn't sure if I was supposed to answer or not. I was still thinking about what she'd said about my results—that my happiness levels were behind the other testers. Was I unhappy? I didn't think so, but JOYFULL said I was. I hardly thought a computer knew more about me than I did, but it was unnerving all the same. If I wasn't unhappy, then why were my results so low?

Then, suddenly, she seemed to jolt back into the present moment. She looked at me expectantly. I wondered if there was an answer I was supposed to give, an answer that would secure the elusive permanent position. Probably there was, but I didn't know what it was. I was tired of trying to predict what it was that the third-most-popular internet company wanted me to say.

"I think that pushing a couple of buttons and being told that you're happy would be satisfying at first, and even fun, but also it would quickly wear off," I said. "You'd think that people want to be told that they're happy, but really, I think what people want even more is to feel understood. People are much more complex than they're willing to show. A simple system will never be enough. We have to ask more complex questions, questions that account for the whole range of human experience, and then recalibrate the scales so that the app gives more complicated answers. I'd suggest starting by getting rid of happiness as the only determination."

"You want us to get rid of happiness," she said. The way she said it was not quite a question.

"That's what I'm suggesting, yes," I said. For once, I was able to hold her gaze.

She nodded. A long moment passed as she looked out the window at the doppelgänger building. She looked back at me with even more intensity than usual.

"Here is something not many people know about me," she said. "I was twelve the first time my mother tried to kill herself. I was the one who found her, passed out in the car with the engine running. I had gotten home from school and she wasn't there. There was a bunch of bananas on the counter, I remember. I was headed up to my room when I thought I heard something from the garage. I opened the door and I smelled the gas, and I didn't know what to do. Through the haze I saw my mother in the driver's seat and I ran to her. She hadn't locked the door, thank God, or the garage door, either. Maybe at that point she still wanted to be saved. I opened the door and I turned the car off and I held her by the shoulders and I shook her, but I couldn't wake her. And I tried dragging her out of the car, but I wasn't strong enough. And so there she was, her body hanging out of the car as far as I'd managed to get it, the room still filled with fumes, and I was coughing and coughing and my eyes were starting to water, my lungs starting to burn, and then finally, I remember it so well, I saw the garage door clicker. The mind is a funny thing, the way it narrows. I had all but forgotten a world existed outside that garage. But I saw the clicker on the dashboard, and I reached over her body and grabbed for it, and then the door started to rise, and it was rising so slowly, so terribly slowly, creaking up inch by inch, but still, the light from outside was coming in, and the gas was finding its way out, and the air inside was clearing. And she was still unconscious, but I started to shake her again, and eventually, that time, it worked. She opened her eyes. She came to.

"She asked me if it could be our secret. Told me there must have been a problem with the car, but she didn't want my father to worry, she'd fix it on her own. I think I knew even then that that was a lie, but I wanted to believe it.

"Then, when I was fourteen, my older brother found her in bed, unconscious. Pills. I was at soccer practice, after school, but when I came home the ambulance was there. He'd called 9-1-1. It wasn't a secret anymore. After that, we thought for a time it would get better. My father knew. My father would fix it. That's what I thought. I still thought, then, that it was something that could be fixed.

"The last time, when I was sixteen, my father found her in the bathtub. My brother was gone by then, a freshman in college. I was home, but he wouldn't let me look, he forbade me from going in there, not while we were waiting for the ambulance, not after.

"My father passed away a few years ago. Never remarried."

She paused for a moment, looking out the window. Then she turned back to me. Something in her face had changed in that moment, hardened back up.

"This is why I got into my doctoral work. Back when I was twelve, I couldn't do anything to help my mother. She was good at hiding. Good at pretending. And not just to us, but to herself. But if emotions had physical locations, then there must be a way to monitor them, to measure them. That's what my thought process was.

"The point is, I understand what you're saying, but I don't know if I can sell getting rid of happiness. That's the hook for the whole project, and it's a major priority for the company right now. But it's going somewhere larger, I can assure you of that."

I knew I should say something, but I didn't know what to say. In everything I had read about her when I had been preparing for my interview months before, I had never encountered even a trace of her family history. I wondered why she had told me, if there was some way she knew I had lost my mother, too—under very different circumstances but around the same age. I murmured some words about how sorry I was, how hard that must have been, but they sounded hollow, insufficient. These were things she was obviously used to hearing; these were things people had said to me. If there was anything that wouldn't sound hollow and insufficient, I wished I knew what it was.

✺

Back at my desk, I had an email from my advisor. She said she hoped that everything at the third-most-popular internet company was going well. She was putting together a panel about careers outside of academia in the fall. If I was interested, maybe I could participate? But really, the reason she was emailing me was business: my leave of absence would expire at the end of the summer. That was still several months away, but she wanted to be sure the deadline was on my radar. I had to let the university know whether I would be coming back or leaving the PhD program for good.

I closed it without replying and another email appeared. This one was from JOYFULL, saying that I had missed my daily happiness check-in. I opened the app on my phone.

HOW HAPPY ARE YOU TODAY?

1   2   3   4   5   6   7   8   9   10

I did not want to answer, but I knew I had to. The analytics team was watching. I held my finger over 8. I clicked 9.

WHAT IS BOTHERING YOU RIGHT NOW?

○ STRESS

○ LONELINESS

○ BITTERNESS

○ SADNESS

○ ANGER

○ OTHER

There was no drop-down option for the feeling that you had lost control of your life.

I chose OTHER and then held my phone up to my eye. I waited as it did its scan.

8.2 OUT OF 10, it said.

I was beginning to wonder if JOYFULL was programmed to keep the numbers artificially low, to keep the user—in this case, me— wanting more. Wanting to be happier, to be better. Or was it possible that JOYFULL knew something I didn't know?

LET'S FIND SOMETHING TO BOOST YOUR MOOD, the app said. A whirring circle appeared to signify that the app was thinking.

A new screen loaded, with what looked like an embedded video.

CLICK HERE, it said.

I looked around the office. Everyone else was absorbed in their own screens. I wondered what kind of happiness scores they were report- ing, the numbers my scores were, apparently, so far behind. Was every- one else really so happy? Or were we really all bundles of raw meat inside, walking around pretending the world didn't affect us? Would a one-minute-and-forty-eight-second video really be able to boost my mood? It seemed unlikely.

I put my headphones in and clicked play.

It began with a pair of gladiolas, two tall stalks of brilliant green, white buds crosshatching them, alternating up the stalk. As a piano played lightly in the background, the buds began to open, white flowers unfurling almost in unison. When they were not quite open, the video cut to another flower, a Peruvian lily, which looked like a simple pink on the outside but flipped open to reveal a leopard-spotted center. On to a hibiscus, whose magnificently red petals popped open all at once to reveal a frizzled yellow stamen that rustled back and forth as if caught in a gentle underwater current. As the music picked up, I watched irises and peonies and a flower the small type at the bottom of the screen identified as nigella damask, their petals curling open, pushing toward sun and light, toward the insects that would help them to propagate. In the video, the flowers looked incredibly, undeniably alive, and they were, of course, I knew that, but as I watched a dandelion bloom, its frothy white spikes arcing out to fill my screen, it seemed to me almost suspenseful, the music swelling into crescendo, the flowers bursting unstoppably into life.

When the video ended, I was surprised to find myself sitting at my desk. The caption on the video said that it had taken nine months and fifty thousand photographs to make. I had been at this job for nearly nine months, and I couldn't say I had accomplished nearly as much.

My phone pinged, reminding me that I was not done.

HOW HAPPY ARE YOU NOW?

1   2   3   4   5   6   7   8   9   10

My finger hovered over 10. I clicked 9 again. I let the phone scan my eye.

8.8 OUT OF 10, the app said.

EXCELLENT, the app said.

It felt like a benediction.

NINETEEN

When I pulled up to my father's house, he was outside, standing in the middle of the front yard, watering the succulents. This, I assumed, was a rare moment of hydrotherapy. They were, after all, supposed to be drought-resistant; the whole point was that they did not require any care. It was a quiet day on the street—it was always a quiet day there—but he seemed not to notice the sound of my car, its arrival at the curb.

I sat in the car for a minute, listening to the end of a story about the orca, G32. She was still holding on to her baby; she had carried it with her for more than five hundred miles. It was the tenth day, and the researchers were worried about how much longer she could survive.

I stepped out of the car. At the sound of the car door slamming, my father finally looked up. For a second, I thought he might not recognize me; his face looked completely blank, as though I were a solicitor or a door-to-door salesman hawking vacuum tubes or encyclopedias.

The blank look passed from his face to one of daughter-recognition, and he raised his non-watering arm in greeting, still spraying the hose with his other hand. We had never had a hugging relationship, and that had not changed now that I was pregnant. There was no reason for it to change, but something in me had thought it might.

"Everything's coming in nicely," he said when I got a little closer. "When I planted them, I wasn't sure how they'd do in this climate, but they've been doing fine."

I told him they looked like they were doing better than fine.

"These were suffering for a while," he said, pointing the hose at a cluster of plants that looked like blooming artichokes. "They were in the shade of the house—not enough sun. But I moved them here and they seem to have bounced back."

He took me around the yard, naming each plant as he sprayed it with the hose. The sunburst aeonium, with radiating pink-tinged leaves of yellow; the echeveria bombycina, which were covered with tiny white hairs that looked like they'd feel nice against my face; agave, dasylirion, and a sprawling plant that resembled an explosive coral in both shape and color, that he said was called sticks on fire. At each plant, he would stop and stoop over, carefully squeezing a leaf or two, sometimes sticking his fingers into the dirt next to the plant to check how far the water had saturated, cupping the leaves to lift them and peer at their delicate undersides. At a patch of jade plants, I watched him bend over and tenderly clasp one of the green nuggets between his fingers, cinching it off the plant. He held it close to his face to inspect it. He made a satisfied nod and let the nugget drop to the ground, then turned to me.

"How are you doing?" he asked, with what felt to me like sudden intensity. "Do you need anything?"

I told him I was doing fine, that the baby was healthy.

"I'll get you whatever you need," he said, his voice insistent, "you just have to tell me."

I looked at a plant he had not named, one with powdery violet leaves. What looked like another plant entirely was springing out of its base, shooting off bold pink rosettes. I bent down to touch it, convinced that the pink plant must be growing immediately next to the other. But they were connected; one grew out of the other.

What I wanted to say was: Since when do you know what kind of plant needs sun and what kind of plant needs shade?

What I said was: "Well, we still haven't bought a stroller."

On my way back from my father's, I stopped by Sharky's apartment. He had just come back from a trend-forecasting trip to South Korea, and he wanted me to come see some of the things he had discovered, things he believed would soon become ubiquitous in the US. Sharky had lived in a one-bedroom in the Outer Sunset for almost five years. He was there pre-gentrification, or had he been part of the gentrifying force? It was like a Zen koan: Did an Asian moving into an Asian neighborhood count as a gentrifier? He lived in a garden apartment, so when I got there, I bypassed the buzzers and went straight to his door, but no one answered my knock. I waited. I knocked again. Still no answer.

My phone pinged. I raised it to my face and the screen came to life.

**HOW WOULD YOU DESCRIBE YOUR
RELATIONSHIP WITH YOUR PARENT(S)?**

- O   LOVING
- O   STRESSFUL
- O   ANTAGONISTIC
- O   NONEXISTENT
- O   SUPPORTIVE
- O   DISTANCED
- O   OTHER

Did JOYFULL know I had just been to see my father? But how could it? It said PARENT(S), not PARENT, which meant it didn't know everything about me, at least not yet. I didn't know how I would describe my relationship with my one parent. I held my finger over DISTANCED, but even though that seemed mostly right, it didn't seem entirely right. I clicked OTHER.

DO YOU THINK YOUR PARENT(S) ARE PROUD OF YOU?

○ YES
○ NO
○ DON'T KNOW
○ N/A

I really did not know the answer to this question, but I didn't know if the correct answer was DON'T KNOW—because I didn't know—or N/A—because one of my parents, the parent I felt more sure would be proud of me, was no longer applicable.

My finger was still hovering over the two options—DON'T KNOW and N/A—when a woman who looked to be in her eighties came down the building's front stairs. She was slightly stooped and wore a pair of thick-soled orthopedic shoes.

"Hello?" the woman said, peering over the banister. She had a heavy Eastern European accent, to match her substantial shoes.

I told her I was waiting for Sharky—Sharukh Teitelbaum.

"The little Indian man?" she said.

It seemed easiest to just say yes.

She told me he'd gone out a few minutes earlier; she had seen him leave from her window.

"He looked like he was in a hurry," she said, making her way down the steps, "but he always looks that way. Hurry, hurry, hurry. That's how everyone is these days. Do this, do that. Not me." I watched as she placed one foot on a step, then lowered the other foot down onto the same step. "I'm ninety-two years old," she said. "You know how you get to be this old? You take it slow. I've lived in this apartment for forty-five years. I inherited it, from my parents." She lowered one foot onto the next step, then the other foot. "I get out every day. I go for a walk. I have a coffee or I go to the library or I go get one of those good sweet buns the Chinese make," she said. She looked closer at my face, as though trying to discern whether I was one of those Chinese who made the good sweet buns. I knew she would be interested to know that I was not Chinese. I knew she would be interested to know what I was, that this was the question lying behind her look.

Before she could ask, I spotted Sharky bustling back down the block, holding a pink cardboard box.

"It was nice to meet you," I said, ending the conversation. A not insignificant part of me took pleasure in having remained, at least for the moment, unclassifiable.

Sharky's apartment looked like an advertisement for a certain Swedish furniture company. Everything was white or gray or an otherwise muted tone, giving the space a minimalist and vaguely futuristic air. Sharky kept the place immaculate; there was no dust to be seen, even though he had been away for a multiweek trip. Even the rugs felt good underfoot, like ours did right after Jamie vacuumed them. Jamie always did the vacuuming. Vacuuming rugs was a part of adult life that I understood intellectually but had yet to physically incorporate into my day-to-day.

As Sharky made tea, I wandered around the apartment. There was always something new. This time, it was a plant, five feet tall or so, with broad leaves. I rubbed my fingers on one of them. It felt so sturdy, it almost seemed fake.

"You haven't seen that before? I got that one months ago," Sharky said, coming back into the living room. He was carrying a large teapot and two delicate teacups on a lacquered tray. Next to the teapot was a plate stacked high with what were presumably the same buns his neighbor had been telling me about. "Everyone's trying to predict the next big indoor plant. For a while I thought it might be ferns, but then I got one to try it out and they die too easily."

"You mean you killed it."

"I mean they die too easily," he said, putting the tray down on the modular coffee table.

"What kind of plant is this?" I asked.

"Fiddle-leaf fig," he said. "It was the hot plant last year, but they say it's over now. I'm thinking of getting rid of it, but I don't know. I still like it. But then, if someone comes over, and they see that I have it, are they going to think I'm not good at my job? Because I have last year's plant? I think the rubber plant might be the next it plant, but I haven't been able to find one. I might order it online."

How, I wondered, could a plant be over?

"I got this tea in Korea," he said, waving me over to the sofa. "I thought you might want to try it, for your research. They call it Dragon's Milk. It's supposed to boost happiness."

On the box, there was an image of a red dragon; its mouth was open, but no fire was coming out. I asked him how a tea could possibly make someone happier.

"You know, Ev," he said. "Ancient Asian secrets." He filled the cups. "Anyway, it tastes good. Cinnamon-y."

As we sat on the sofa and drank the tea, Sharky told me about the trends he had spotted on his trip. He was particularly excited about a drink he had found in a vending machine for just a thousand won—a US dollar or so. It came out of the can not as a liquid but as a gel, but was still, amazingly, carbonated. He brought out a can to show me but said he couldn't open it—he hadn't been able to fit that many in his suitcase and he needed to save them for his boss. He could see it being big here.

I didn't think it would be as big as kale, but I didn't say anything.

"This is the one I wanted your opinion on," he said, pulling out a white tube covered with Korean writing, surrounding a cartoon image of a woman's smiling face.

I unscrewed the cap and gave it a sniff. It smelled like nothing. "What does it do?"

"Go ahead," Sharky said. "Try it." I hesitated. "It's totally safe," he added. "Would I give you something that hadn't been tested?"

I squeezed out a tiny dollop and rubbed it in a circle on my forearm.

"It's a brightening cream," he said. "Do you know what that means?"

"It makes your skin brighter?"

Sharky laughed and poured us some more tea. The happiness tea was, in fact, very good.

"Brighter, yes," he said. "But also lighter."

I must have looked at him with confusion.

"*Whiter,*" he said, almost in a whisper. "It makes your skin whiter. Saying it's a 'brightening' cream is just code. These creams are huge in Asia and Africa, but they haven't really made it in the US. Everyone in Korea knows what 'brightening cream' means, but I'm not sure if people here do. Asians probably know."

"I'm Asian," I said.

"You don't count," he said, then looked at me. "No offense."

I shrugged. If anyone other than Sharky had said something like that, I would have been offended. But because it was Sharky, it was okay.

"What does the package say?" I asked.

"Let's see," he said, pulling out his phone. "I wrote down what the translator told me. Here it is: 'Chrysanthemum Brightening Cream. Radiant skin overnight. Healthy! Stimulating for the body.'"

"What does 'stimulating for the body' mean?"

He shrugged. He was less interested in the copy than what he'd learned about the world's biggest K-pop bands, how they, too, were lightening their faces—both physically, via skin peels and pills and keeping them, at all costs, out of the sun, but also technologically, with photo editors tweaking every press shot, advertisement, and album cover. They didn't even look white in the photos, Sharky said, they just looked like ghosts.

I looked down at the quarter-size circle on my forearm. Maybe it would get lighter and lighter and lighter, until it was like I had a tiny piece of an all-white person on my arm.

"So what do you think?" Sharky asked.

"I mean," I said, "it doesn't really seem like the kind of thing you should be promoting."

"Right," he said. "Of course. But do you think it would sell?"

I wished I could say that it wouldn't, but I had to say I didn't know. My phone pinged.

DO YOU THINK YOUR PARENT(S) ARE PROUD
OF YOU?

I still hadn't answered. The app was much more insistent than I had anticipated.

Sitting next to me on the couch, Sharky looked at my screen.

"Is that JOYFULL?" he asked. I nodded. I pressed a button, turning the screen black. "I've been hearing some stuff about it."

I asked him what he'd been hearing.

"I don't know," Sharky said. He was being strangely evasive. I pressed him. "To be honest, the trend forecasters are all saying that people aren't going to want this kind of invasive technology anymore. The upcoming trend is simplicity."

I had thought simplicity was already a trend, ushered in by a Japanese woman who people liked to compare to a pixie, a fairy, an elf, anything that was cute and fantastical and not quite human.

"Are you sure you really want to be a part of this?" he went on. "I mean, far be it for me to be advising you, as I sit here contemplating skin-whitening cream. But it's not like you don't have other options. You could go back to grad school. Finish your PhD."

He leaned forward to pour us each another cup of happiness tea. I picked up my cup and blew on the hot liquid before taking a sip.

"I know the money's better," he said. "But you loved graduate school, remember? When you started, it was all you could talk about—the books you were reading, the papers you were writing, the classes you were teaching. That could be your life, if you can just get through another year or two. I've seen you get the fellowships, the awards, the publications. You're just having a little setback in finishing your dissertation. Doesn't that happen to everyone?"

"I don't know," I said. "Probably."

"So I'm just saying," he continued, absently rubbing some skin-lightening cream onto the top of his hand as he spoke, "why not do that?"

I put my cup back down on the coffee table and leaned back into the corner of the sofa.

"I don't know," I said. "Sometimes it just feels so removed. It feels like everyone else is a part of the world, and I'm not. But I don't know if that was grad school or if that was just me."

My phone pinged.

WHAT DO YOU WANT?

I held the button, silencing it.

TWENTY

Every morning, while I rode the bus to work, I read updates about the orca mother, G32. Eleven days, twelve days, fourteen days, fifteen days, sixteen days. On the sixteenth day, she was still carrying her baby through the water. The body, the researchers said, was beginning to decompose. She had carried it for more than one thousand miles, pushing its weight—hundreds of pounds—through the currents. The scientists monitoring the situation could not get close enough to her to see her physical condition; they still feared she was undernourished, as she was putting all her energy into mourning her child instead of foraging and feeding. But there were hopes, too, that her blubber had become extra-fortified during her pregnancy, and that she was living off that, the fortification that would have gone into feeding her child feeding her instead.

An orca of G32's size, the articles said, could normally go for a month without eating and survive. Would she push on, I wondered, for a whole month? Newspapers around the world were reporting her movements every day. So much, they said, was still unknown.

I looked down at my stomach. The baby had just started kicking the week before. I had read that the first time the baby kicked, it would feel like popcorn popping, or a butterfly's wings fluttering. But to me, it mostly felt like a sensation I could not be sure I was feeling, like someone had just opened a soda can in my stomach, maybe, the foam hissing and fizzing against my internal organs.

I wondered if my body, too, was fortifying itself.

※

Later that day, we got an email for a meeting to update us on the progress of JOYFULL. I had been logging in every day, often several times a day, plugging in my numbers and answering the requisite questions. The email said we would be looking at case studies of JOYFULL users.

"Doesn't that mean us?" I messaged Sabine.

"Not me," she messaged back.

"???" I wrote.

"I'm not participating," she wrote. "My brain is proprietary."

I felt something ping in my mind. I hurried to find a piece of paper on my largely paperless desk.

I wrote: *Can a brain be proprietary?*

I thought for a second, then added: *Do we own our cognitive processes? Do we own our thoughts, our feelings? And if our online selves are an extension of our consciousness, then who owns the part of our consciousness that resides online? Can we sign our thoughts and feelings away, or do they remain intrinsically our own?*

I looked down at the words I had written. This felt, I thought, the way my advisor had always said coming up with an idea—a real idea, one of my own—would feel.

"What about you?" Sabine wrote in a new text bubble. "Are you winning at happiness?"

I wrote back with an emoji of a person shrugging. On the main emoji menu, the person shrugging looked like a white woman with blond hair wearing a purple turtleneck, but if you clicked and held the emoji there were other options: an Asian woman wearing a purple turtleneck, a light-brown woman wearing a purple turtleneck, a medium-brown woman wearing a purple turtleneck, a black woman wearing a purple turtleneck. There was also a woman who was more clearly a white woman with blond hair wearing a purple turtleneck; the woman on the main menu had yellow skin, whereas this woman's skin was actually white. I hesitated over the shrugging Asian woman, but the fact that they had tried to make her look more real made her seem even more cartoonish to me. I clicked on the yellow-skinned yellow-haired shrugging woman and pressed send. I hadn't realized that not participating was an option, but of course Sabine had. Though Sabine, unlike me, had a permanent position.

A few minutes later, I followed the rest of the team as they filed into the conference room. Out on the bay, it was the same scene as before, sailboats skimming across the water. It felt not quite like déjà vu, but not quite like reality, either. Was there a word for not-quite-déjà-vu?

The low buzz of conversation died away when Dr. Luce entered the conference room. We waited in silence for her presentation to load. I watched as a bird circled outside the window. This one was not a falcon; it was much smaller, with short, wide wings that didn't look built to fly at this height. How had it made it all the way up here? Office buildings were notorious bird killers, the floors of glass windows looking—to birds' eyes—like wide-open sky. I watched as the bird glided toward the window and away, carried by a gust of wind. I stared at it, willing it to fly away, to retreat back to safety.

On the screen were the words CASE STUDY #1.

❋

Three case studies later, there was no longer any sign of the bird that wasn't a falcon. In the past forty-five minutes, we had heard about a white man in his early thirties, married with one child, whose happiness had risen from an average 7.8 to an average 8.6 after three months of using JOYFULL; a white man in his late twenties, with a perfect BMI, perfect blood pressure, perfect cholesterol, perfect eyesight, perfect hearing, and raging anxiety that kept him up until three or four o'clock in the morning most nights, anxiety so powerful that even sleep meds were helpless against it, whose happiness had risen from an average 8.4 to 9.2 since beginning JOYFULL and, perhaps more important, whose body had been logging a consistent 1.2 hours more rest each night, which the app had determined by tracking his heart rate; a white woman in her late forties, with two teenage children and a long-term partner, whose happiness had risen from an average 6.8 to an amazing 9.7, but whom the analysts suspected of inflating the numbers, though they counted it as a victory for JOYFULL nonetheless.

After each case study, Sabine would pass me a note with a name and a department, her guesses at the subject's identity. If anyone could figure out who they were, it would be Sabine. But it was impossible to know. When I looked around the room, every face that looked back at me—with the exception of Sabine's—was a white face. They were not all early-thirties men or late-twenties-perfectionist-insomniac men or early-forties women. But there were enough of them clustered around each description that there was no way to know which person it was, or if it was any of them at all. They could, of course, be the beta testers outside of the company. Dr. Luce had also said they had changed some of the pertinent data for the presentation, fictionalized it.

I felt my head bob forward. I forced it back up, pulled my eyes open. I had slept badly the night before. A nightmare: I was at the hospital to give birth to the baby. I was lying on the hospital bed, wearing the hospital gown. I was ready to do what I had been trained to do: to breathe, to push, to stay calm. But instead my stomach kept growing bigger and bigger, steadily expanding upward toward the ceiling like a giant balloon. The doctors were afraid I was going to pop.

What was the dream trying to tell me? I wondered. Did other women have dreams like this? I had gotten out of bed in the middle of the night and typed "nightmares during pregnancy" into the search bar of the first-most-popular internet company. Pregnant women, an article said, reported 2.5 times more bad dreams than nonpregnant women. I found a list called "Nine Bizarre (But Common) Pregnancy Dreams, and What They Really Mean," which I read all the way through. Dreams about giving birth in public; dreams about giving birth to a litter of kittens; dreams about being trapped underwater, which the article said was a way for the mother to identify with the baby, which is itself trapped in her womb.

I read an article about how to avoid nightmares while pregnant, which said to think of something that makes you happy before you go to bed. For example, it said, you can picture yourself in an imaginary world, dancing with trees and animals in the forest.

This did not seem like very helpful advice.

I watched as Dr. Luce loaded what she said would be the final case study, CASE STUDY #4. I felt my head bob forward again, my body's uncontrollable urge to rest. For a moment, I seemed to be somewhere else entirely, and then I was back in my ergonomically friendly chair in the ergonomically friendly conference room.

"This one is one that concerns us," Dr. Luce was saying. "Really, it's the reason the team wanted to bring us all here now, to ask ourselves, how can we better serve a user like this one? Because that's what JOY-FULL is here for, to serve our users."

She advanced the slide.

"A half-Asian female in her early thirties. Pregnant, financially secure, has a stable partner. Her happiness began at 7.1, and it has only risen to 7.9 after two months of using JOYFULL. Now, that's around the same increase as our other case studies, we know, which means JOYFULL has done its job. But what concerns us is that females of comparable age and socioeconomic class, on average, show a score of 9.2 in the first trimester, 8.8 in the second, and 9.0 in the third. This opens a whole new batch of ethics questions for us. What might we conclude from this data? This subject appears to not want to have a child and, possibly, to be unfit to be a mother. But what do we do with those conclusions? Do we alert the subject? Alert the subject's partner?"

Dr. Luce was still talking, but I had ceased to hear what she was saying.

I was the only pregnant woman in the room. I was not the only pregnant woman at the third-most-popular internet company, but as far as I could tell, I was the only half-Asian pregnant woman.

That, and I knew my scores.

A few people looked my way, then a few more, trying not to let me see that they were looking at me.

I knew my scores, but I hadn't thought they were that bad.

I knew my scores, but I thought everyone felt the way I felt.

I knew my scores, but I didn't think they disqualified me from motherhood.

"That's not right," I heard myself say. The people sitting around me looked at me, but no one else seemed to have heard. There was still time to pretend I hadn't said anything, to let Dr. Luce finish, to keep the same placid look on my face, betraying no recognition at all of the person being described, this unfit mother who already didn't love her child enough, who might never love her child enough. I could do that, and I could file out of the meeting, and we—me and everyone else in the room—could pretend we had never seen that presentation, never suspected that I was CASE STUDY #4, and then, soon enough, it would no longer feel like we were pretending. It would feel like what we were pretending was the truth.

"That's not right," I said again, louder. "I don't feel that way."

This time, everyone heard. Dr. Luce paused, her laser pointer resting on one of the hundreds of data points I had not realized they were collecting.

"That's me," I said. "I know that's me. Those are my numbers, but those are not the right conclusions. I want this baby. I am not unfit. You need to go back and change the algorithm. The algorithm isn't correct!" My voice was rising. I was getting what some people might have described as hysterical, but I would describe as impassioned. "I'm not unfit!" I shouted. "I am very fit! I am a fit mother, this will be a fit child!" I saw that the people around me looked alarmed. Dr. Luce appeared to be mouthing something at someone, but I couldn't decipher what she was saying. I felt a hand on my elbow, warm and fleshy. I was standing up. When had I stood up?

"Evelyn," a voice said. I turned toward the voice, which appeared to belong to the hand on my elbow, which appeared to belong to Sabine. She was speaking in a way that I could tell was meant to be deliberately soothing, like one would talk to a child or a wild animal. "Evelyn," the voice said again, "no one is talking about you, Evelyn."

I looked at the screen. Dr. Luce still stood in front of it, still holding the laser pointer. The slide appeared to be focusing on some kind of marketing strategy, represented as a bar graph.

"I think you fell asleep," Sabine said. "Whatever it was you were thinking, it was just a dream."

"But that's not what was on the slide," I said.

I looked around at the faces, looking at me. I was no longer so sure.

"Is that what was always on the slide?" I said, looking at Sabine.

"You're just exhausted," Sabine said. "She's just exhausted," she said again, this time for the benefit of the room. All the white men nodded their heads. There were a few sympathetic murmurs, about wives and babies and how tiring it all was.

I let the hand on my elbow guide my body out of the room.

TWENTY-ONE

On the seventeenth day, G32 finally let her child's body go. That was the way all the articles I read put it—finally, as though we had all been waiting for this moment, as if letting go of the body was the only logical conclusion. But if I had been G32, wouldn't I, too, have carried my child's body for as long as I could? A thousand-mile funeral procession, witnessed by the entire world, reported across international media. And yet the articles I read sounded relieved; now G32 could go back to normal orca activities. She appeared to be healthy, researchers said, feeding and frolicking with her pod. Now, as the baby whale's body sank to the bottom of the Salish Sea, we could be absolved. No more daily news articles reminding us how we had failed this species so spectacularly.

Now we could forget. But, I wondered, would G32 remember? Would her body always know what it had been like to carry that weight inside her? Would she still feel the shape of her child's body beside her face, like a phantom limb? I wished there were a way to explain to G32 what had happened. But even if she understood our language, what was there to understand about a child being alive and then not being alive? That was a thing that was not understandable in any language.

❋

The day after the meeting, I got an email from Dr. Luce calling me up to her office for another one-on-one. As I neared her office, I could see that something was different. She was standing still and yet appeared to be moving. As I got closer, I could see the full treadmill, the rubber conveyor belt moving beneath her feet.

I knocked on the glass door and she gestured me in, but did not stop walking.

"Evelyn," she said, "Come in. I'm almost at four miles. You don't mind, do you? I got this thing so I won't die an early death. You know, you've seen the reports, I'm sure."

I had seen the reports. I had tried standing at my desk for a few days in the pre-pregnancy era, but found it excruciating. It was hard to tell if an hour of standing was worth the hours of time I was supposedly adding to my life.

She gestured for me to sit down in one of the leather chairs. I sank into it, feeling its soft luxury wrap around my body.

"We care about you here," she said. "I care about you, especially, and, of course, about your child. After all, wasn't I one of the first to know?" She had known even before Jamie, when the doctor in that hospital in the desert came to talk to me, holding a clipboard.

"We want you to be happy, we want you to be safe. Our first priority, always, is the well-being of our employees."

The treadmill beeped at her and she pressed a couple of buttons that did not seem to change anything about what the treadmill was doing.

"You haven't used nearly all of your vacation time. You should take some time off," she said, "get some rest."

I began to protest, to tell her that I was fine, really, that I hadn't slept well the night before the presentation, that was all, but she held a hand up to stop me.

"There are exciting things coming up for JOYFULL, Evelyn. It's developing at a rapid pace. That's partially thanks to you, thanks to your input. You're a valued member of this team. We need you to take care of yourself."

She paused for a second to adjust something on the treadmill, but again there was no perceptible change.

"Also, we'd like you to see your doctor. Just for a checkup. We've made an appointment for you for this afternoon."

I asked how she knew who my doctor was; that was not something I had ever told anyone at the third-most-popular internet company. It had never come up.

"What's important," Dr. Luce said, "is that we make sure you're getting the absolute best in care."

She hadn't answered my question.

"The data that I thought I saw yesterday," I said. "You do have that data, don't you?"

"Unfortunately, I can't share that information," she said. She pressed a button on the treadmill, began walking a fraction of a mile per hour faster. Before, it had been practically silent, but now I could hear a steady mechanical buzz.

"But you have some data," I said. "I know you must have some. You know what other pregnant women are feeling."

What I meant, but didn't say, was: Am I alone? Am I the only one? Don't you know the answer to that?

What I meant was: Did I make a mistake?

"The only thing is," she said, ignoring my question, "we would like you to keep using JOYFULL while you're out. You don't mind, do you? It's strictly voluntary, of course, but the data will help all of us know if you're doing better—to know that you're doing better. Win-win."

I opened my mouth to protest, but before I could say anything, she told me she had to get on a call. It was easier to acquiesce.

"We're all set, then, right?" Dr. Luce asked. I could tell she was ready to be done with this meeting. There had been a problem—the problem had been me—and the problem had been solved.

I said we were all set.

"Excellent," she said.

As I left the office, I could see her through the glass walls, her face full of focus as she pushed buttons on the treadmill, the conveyor belt below her moving faster and faster, going nowhere.

※

At the doctor, they tested my urine, took my blood pressure, checked the fetal heartbeat, and measured and palpated the outside of my stomach to check on the size of the baby.

"She's exactly where she's supposed to be," Dr. Subramanian said when she was done. I felt like a ripe melon. "Everything is looking on track," she said, scrolling through my data. They always entered everything into the computer; the only piece of paper I had seen was the one I signed at the very beginning, guaranteeing payment.

I told her about my dream. She told me dreams like that were completely normal.

"So everything is okay?" I said.

She asked me if I was experiencing any pain, any bleeding, any unusual discharge.

She asked me about dizziness, fatigue, shortness of breath, nausea, achiness.

She asked me about leg cramps, heartburn, constipation.

I answered her questions, and with each answer, she clicked a box on her computer that I assumed meant normal: *click, click, click.*

She asked me about stress.

I told her I was pretty stressed. What I didn't tell her was that I was worried that JOYFULL—my dream about JOYFULL—was right, that I didn't feel the way I should feel, that something was wrong with me.

"On a scale of one to ten, how stressed would you say you are?" she said.

I hesitated for a second.

"Nine," I said. I wanted to leave a little wiggle room.

She looked up from the computer screen, concerned.

"Stress isn't good for the baby," she said.

I told her I knew that.

"We have to find a way to help you relax," she said. I wanted to say that what would really help me relax would be if someone else carried the baby. "A lot of people go on babymoons—have you thought about a babymoon? If you can take the time off of work, it would do you a lot of good."

I wondered if it was possible that Dr. Luce had been in touch with her. I asked her if it was still safe for me to travel.

"Of course, of course," she said. "My husband and I went to Hawaii when I was seven and a half months, in fact." She pointed at the curling posters on the walls. *Maui, Kauai, Oahu.* So they were her posters, then. I tried to picture her in the middle of one of those tourist shops that also sells shot glasses and personalized key chains and souvenir spoons, carefully flipping through hundreds of posters of ever-so-slightly differing beach scenes, ever-so-slightly differing ocean sunsets and sunrises. It was hard to imagine.

"That was several years ago now," she said, wistfully. "I had just started my practice, and then we found out I was pregnant. My husband thought that it was too much, that I should give up the practice. Talk about stress!" For a moment, it was as if she had forgotten that I was in a paper gown, that she had a stethoscope around her neck. Usually, Dr. Subramanian was all business. "But obviously I stuck it out, and here we both are. Rahul is six now, almost seven." She nodded at a framed photo tucked away in the corner. The photo was of a smiling boy who might have been half Indian; as usual, I couldn't tell.

I felt this small intimacy hang in the air between us. I didn't want to be the one to shatter it.

"Anyway," she said, resuming her brisk tone. "Have you ever been to Hawaii?"

We never would have been able to afford a trip to Hawaii, not even on my new salary, not with the baby coming and all the extra costs that accompanied it, but Jamie told his parents that Dr. Subramanian had said I should go, and they offered to take care of it. He didn't tell them it was basically an enforced vacation. He didn't want them to worry. Had I done something that other people needed to worry about? Jamie seemed worried, asking me constantly how I was doing, how I was feeling. Planning a last-minute trip to Hawaii at least gave Jamie something to do, gave him a sense of efficacy as he pored over reviews of all-inclusive resorts. He and his mother worked together to use his father's excess air miles and hotel points to cover the babymoon—which was also the subject line of the email she sent to both of us only a few days after my meeting with Dr. Luce, an excla-mation point added: BABYMOON!

Jamie's father was a higher-up at a big insurance company—one of the top three—and traveled a great deal for work, even now that he was in his late sixties. His mother had been a stay-at-home mom when Jamie and his brother were growing up; now she busied herself with a mix of volunteer work and a series of hobbies that she picked up and dropped: photography, ceramics, Scrabble. We didn't see them often—Jamie didn't get a lot of time off, and I didn't much care one way or the other—but I knew more about their day-to-day lives than I knew about my father's, who lived only an hour away. Jamie's younger brother had moved to Florida, where he taught phys ed and coached a high school basketball team that was the best in the state, or the region, or maybe even in its entire conference, if that was the right word. His wife taught special ed in the same school system. They had two children already, boys, four and six. Andrew was three years younger than Jamie.

I didn't know what Jamie's parents thought of me, of the fact that Jamie and I were still not married. Theirs was a supremely normal family. Normal and white, with all the kinds of easy normalcy that whiteness provides. But ever since Jamie had let them know I was pregnant, they had begun emailing me. Jamie's mom, Lynne, mostly sent me links to products she wanted to buy for the baby, along with choice quotes from reviews she had read about why this was the best baby carrier, the best crib, the best bottle warmer. I would say okay, and two days later, the item would show up on our doorstep in a brown cardboard box. The emails were only ever sent to me, never to both of us, as though I alone was the keeper of the hoard.

Jamie's father, Tom, would send me articles about foods that pregnant women shouldn't eat—though of course I'd been over all that with my doctor long before. No note, just the article. Tom followed an impressive number of news sources, and the list was long: deli meats, smoked seafood, soft cheeses, unpasteurized milk, unpasteurized juice, pâté, salads from salad bars and also prepared salads, high-mercury fish. Every few days, he emailed me a new article on whether pregnant women could drink caffeine: sometimes yes, sometimes no, sometimes yes, in moderation. Everything seemed designed to hurt a pregnant woman; the list of things that could go wrong was long, sushi or no sushi: preeclampsia, low amniotic fluid, gestational diabetes, placenta previa, iron-deficiency anemia, meconium staining. And that was only while the baby was in utero. We would have eighteen years, at least, with this baby in our house, a lifetime of years with this baby in our lives. A lot of things can go wrong in a lifetime.

In fact, the night before the BABYMOON! email, I'd found myself going down a deep rabbit hole, researching what would happen if the baby was breech. I watched video after video of doctors massaging women's stomachs, trying to urge the babies into the correct position. I watched the mothers as they tightened their lips, trying not to show their discomfort as hands pushed and prodded at them like they were fine Wagyu cattle. On one of the forums, a woman had written that the pain of the procedure was indescribable. There was no reason to think our baby would be breech—it was too soon to know. And yet I stayed up for hours more that night, lying in bed, staring at the darkened ceiling, wondering what I would do if, at our next appointment, the nurse said something had changed. I wondered if there were exercises I could do now to ensure the baby would move into the correct position, exercises that every other mother-to-be, I thought, probably already knew.

And so, even though the all-inclusive resort, the very word "baby-moon," were things that normally would not appeal to me, things I would ordinarily actively resist, when I got the email proposing not just an all-paid but also all-planned trip, I simply said sure, let's go.

The resort picked us up at the airport in a fleet of white minivans, us and all the rest of the guests, families spilling in and out of the automatic sliding doors, suitcases and backpacks and duffel bags and golf bags, all the things one would need for a week in paradise. I sat in our van and waited for the driver to finish arranging the unbelievable amount of luggage in the trunk so that we could depart. More white minivans were parked along the curb, identical except for the logos of different resorts emblazoned upon their sides. I watched as a family of four approached each one in turn, the father peering at the logos, trying to determine which was the one he and his wife had committed to, which would shepherd them to their hard-earned vacation. Both children, a girl in her early teens and a boy who looked about eight or nine, were deeply immersed in their devices, and they straggled behind, lost in their digital worlds, as their mother, pushing their luggage cart, near overflowing, kept turning back and yelling something at them that I couldn't hear, the sound muted by the window of the van that stood between us. I could tell from the determined expression on her face that she had decided long ago that this was going to be a fun vacation, a memorable family experience.

As we sat waiting for the driver to finish loading the luggage, my phone pinged.

DO YOU FEEL TRAPPED?

○ YES

○ NO

○ NOT SURE

I put my phone away without answering and then heard it ping again almost immediately. What did JOYFULL want now? But it was a text from Sharky: *Happy babymoon!*

I sent back a series of nonsensical emojis that nonetheless communicated tropical enthusiasm and clicked off my phone.

The driver started the van, and I turned forward, losing sight of the family. What I wanted, for a few days, was to forget about life back at home and just do whatever it was that people did on babymoons in

Hawaii. Even the air in Hawaii smelled more fragrant, more alive, thick with paradise. Traditional Hawaiian music streamed out of the van's sound system, or at least what seemed to be traditional Hawaiian music, a thrumming of ukuleles that would have been grating any- where else but here seemed just one more part of the fantasy we were now living. Out the window, the scenery was unmistakably beautiful, awash with pink sky and the swaying green fronds of the palm trees that lined the streets, a sliver of sparkling blue ocean beyond. As we coasted along, the ocean on one side, the mountains rising up on the other, Jamie put his arm around me, and I leaned my head back against it, feeling the warmth of his body, smelling its familiar smell, returning to him now after the sterility of the airplane.

The resort itself was an enormous pair of buildings, one that was thirty-three stories tall and the other twenty-five stories; I had read that it held 1,300 rooms, plus another 250 condos for sale, if you wanted to live the Hawaiian resort life full time. The land all around was flat and green, sprinkled here and there with the occasional palm tree, and as the van turned off the main road and approached the re- sort, I watched the building rise up, monolithic. An ornate gate arced over the road, with a sign that announced we had entered the resort's grounds. The building was still far off, almost doll-size. To our left was a manicured golf course, the grass even greener than the grass outside the gates, as though it had been saturated with dye. On our right were a series of man-made pools, carefully landscaped with waterfalls and rock formations that, similarly, were filled with a water that looked bluer than blue, a water that somehow seemed more immediately en- ticing than even the perfect blue of the ocean, just ahead. I had looked up the resort online, so I knew that behind the hotel building— between the building and the beach—was a much larger swimming pool, complete with waterslide and lazy river.

"I read online that this place had to suspend construction during the recession," I said to Jamie. "The owners were on the verge of declaring bankruptcy."

Jamie raised his eyebrows at me in a way that I knew meant he didn't think I should be talking about this in a van full of strangers, all embarking on their merry holidays. We were entering a place untouched by time, history, reality. What I had said might spoil the mood.

I looked out the window, picturing the half-finished shells of buildings, the partially dug-out pools, their edges drying and cracking, waiting to be filled.

Our room was done in a style I would call *Hawaiian mystic*, relying heavily on pinks and golden browns the color of sand and sunsets. A few black-and-white photos of the ocean hung on the walls, nondescript and tasteful. I assumed that identical photos were hung in every room, with identical placement, though it was, of course, possible that the resort had an infinite supply of black-and-white ocean photographs, varying minutely from print to print.

The focal point of the room, though, was the bed, king-size, whose pristine white sheets were replaced every day. The comforter, also, was a perfect white, with no sign of ever having touched another person's skin. This was the mark of luxury: untrammeled whiteness, never allowed to dull. I lay down on the bed. Was it my imagination, or did these sheets feel better than the ones we slept on at home?

Jamie sat in the corner in a pineapple-printed chair and busied himself looking through the abundant gift basket that had greeted us, holding up each item in turn: dark-chocolate-covered macadamia nuts; macadamia-nut-flavored Kona coffee; macadamia nut butter toffee; a bar of milk chocolate with, unsurprisingly, macadamia nuts. There was also a tube of SPF 50 sunscreen and a bottle of aloe vera, the resort making advance preparations for the inevitable crisping of our bodies.

I had to pee again. I heaved myself off the bed and went to the bathroom, where barely a trickle came out. There was another gift basket in the bathroom, this one containing miniature bottles of every coconut bath product imaginable: coconut milk shampoo and conditioner, coconut moisturizing body lotion, coconut exfoliating sugar scrub, coconut restorative face cream, coconut oil foaming bath. I wondered if the resort had made a deal with the coconut lobby, the macadamia nut lobby, if such lobbies existed. I squeezed a little bit of the face cream onto my finger and dabbed it on my cheek. I could use some restoration.

I carried the miniature bottle of coconut body lotion with me back into the room and returned to my position on the bed. Jamie had moved on from the gift basket and was looking intensely at his phone.

"Look at this," he said, turning the screen toward me. On it was a photo of a little blond boy sitting on the ground in a barren landscape, playing with what looked like an animal skeleton. The scene looked more than slightly postapocalyptic. "They just released a new climate change report," Jamie said. "It says we're going to be feeling severe effects by 2040," Jamie said. "Intensified drought, wildfires, global food shortages . . ." He trailed off.

I had pulled up my shirt and squirted some of the lotion on my belly, but had not yet begun to rub it in.

"It's not for certain," he said, looking at me. "There's still time to reverse it."

He went on, saying what needed to be done, how we needed to raise taxes on carbon dioxide emissions, to invest in renewable energy, to convince our fellow nations to forgo the benefits of industrialization in order to reverse the damage we had done. I put my fingers in the lotion and began to spread it on my stomach. In there, I thought, was a person who was going to live longer than me. In there was a person who was going to, someday, be alone in the world without me.

＊

Dinner was a welcome luau, the dining area ringed with tiki torches. Jamie had changed into a Hawaiian shirt—red with pink flowers—that I didn't know he owned. When I asked him about it, it turned out he had bought it for the trip.

"You know," he said. "To get in the spirit."

I had packed one black dress. I thought it would travel well, wouldn't show stains, was unlikely to wrinkle.

According to the resort's schedule, every night seemed to feature a luau of some kind—the under-the-sea luau, the sailing-away-to-paradise luau, the ancient Hawaii luau—so I wasn't sure what distinguished the welcome-night one, but it did feature a whole roast pig, one that had been buried among hot coals in a pit in the earth and was only now being dug up, fifteen hours later, by a crew of shirtless native-Hawaiian-appearing men. I had also read that many of the people who staffed these resorts were not, in fact, native Hawaiian, but Filipino, often with families back in the Philippines to whom they sent the majority of their comparatively hefty American paychecks. The resorts hired Filipinos because they looked enough like native Hawaiians but, not being American citizens, could be asked to work considerably more hours for considerably less money.

A line of native-Hawaiian-appearing women greeted us as we arrived, a woman wearing a string bikini top and a grass skirt placing a lei of purple flowers around my neck. Her hair hung down to the crevice at the base of her spine. All the greeters were dressed this way; their hair all hung down to the crevices at the base of their spines. I wondered if the ad for whatever you might call this job specified hair this length, if women who wanted this job waited for months, if not years, to apply.

"Ho'omaika'i," the woman said, looking down at the bulge in my stomach. "That is Hawaiian for 'congratulations.'"

We got a pair of daiquiris—alcoholic for Jamie, virgin for me—and joined the buffet line. Ahead of us, scores of red-faced men and women piled their plates high with slices of roast pork, glistening cubes of raw tuna. I looked down at my forearm. Still very pale. I wondered if the spot where I had applied the skin-lightening cream was even whiter than the rest of me. In this light, it was hard to tell. The men wore Hawaiian shirts like Jamie's, the women low-cut cotton sundresses with patterns of starfish and orchids and other tropical things. I did not own anything like this, nor would it have occurred to me to bring it along if I had.

The line shuffled forward, and we moved incrementally closer to the buffet table. The sun was beginning to set, casting a burnished glow over everything: the bare-chested men carving up the pig; the scantily clad ladies beginning to sway their grass-skirted hips to the omnipresent strums of a ukulele; a group of children chasing each other around the tiki torches, which did not look like they were entirely securely planted in the ground; their parents and the other red-faced guests drinking drinks that had been paid for long ago and eating food that had also been paid for long ago, so that it now seemed as though the meal was simply an abundant feast supplied by the natives or, at least, our native-appearing hosts.

The luau was held on a bluff that overlooked a white-sand beach. Green-fronded palm trees were scattered here and there, completing the image of tropical revelry. It was an image I had seen before, I realized, as the buffet line moved infinitesimally forward. ADAPT. But this view was not just like that ad from the billboard; it was the exact image from the ad. It was as though the camera had been stationed right where I now stood, had panned the exact landscape I now surveyed with my own eyes.

Could that be? Could ADAPT have known that these many months later, I would be standing here, on a vacation chosen not even by me but by my not-quite-mother-and-father-in-law, two-thirds of the living grandparents of the baby in my belly?

I turned to say something to Jamie, but just then, we finally reached the buffet table. Plates were pressed into our hands, food loaded onto our plates. I let myself be shepherded along the buffet, let myself be led to a table, let my water be refilled, let my virgin daiquiri be replaced, let Jamie go to the table to get me more suckling pig. I was tired.

You can only be vigilant for so long.

TWENTY-THREE

t took less than twenty-four hours for me to melt into the routine of the resort. I spent the second day lying next to a fake lagoon, under the shade of a palm tree that was real but had nevertheless been carefully placed next to said lagoon, one of an assortment of native-appearing trees that were arranged so as to look random and natural. The sound of a fake waterfall flowed soothingly in the background, somehow obscuring the noise of the multitude of children who dunked and dove and splashed about, presumably under parental supervision, though their parents were invisible to me. From where I lay, I could see the ocean, but there seemed to be no reason to get any closer to it. There was a buffet table set up alongside the lagoon, and there were people who would fetch us drinks. The people fetching us drinks were very good at their jobs; I never got to the bottom of my virgin cocktail before it was refilled afresh. Still, as good as they were at their jobs, they were not allowed to accept tips—no one at the resort was. There were subtle reminders of this all over: printed in small type at the bottom of the menus, etched into a gold placard that sat on the bureau in our room. GRATUITIES NOT ACCEPTED.

We spent the morning of the third day much like we had the second, lying by the ocean-adjacent fake lagoon. After the buffet lunch, I retreated to our room, leaving Jamie asleep on his lounge chair. Outside, it was all cool ocean breezes, though I was not entirely convinced that the hotel didn't somehow manufacture those, too, with unseen, industrial-strength fans. Inside, the air was still, the very low hum of the air-conditioning barely discernible. I lowered my body onto the high-thread-count sheets and turned on the television, clicking about until, to my surprise, I found an episode of *Misfits!*, just starting, on the anglerfish.

The anglerfish, the voice-over explained, lived in the furthest depths of the ocean, so far down that they had rarely been seen alive by humans. Because it was so hard to find a mate that deep, the anglerfish had adapted an unusual mating ritual, in which the much-smaller male bites onto the female's stomach and doesn't let go. It hangs there, parasitic, fed by the nutrients from her blood. But not forever; the male's body begins to be absorbed by the female's. First its lips dissolve into the female's body, then its eyes, then its fins, then many of its internal organs.

Eventually, the male's body will almost completely fuse with the female's, the voice-over explained; when mating is complete, all that is left of the male are his testes, which protrude from the female where the male first attached himself to her body, giving her a ready supply of sperm whenever she is ready to reproduce.

I watched as a female anglerfish drifted through the pitch-black water. Her entire body was dominated by a gaping mouth filled with pointed teeth that varied in length, curving out and back like a fearsome metal hunting trap. She was made to be a predator, evolved with all sorts of adaptations that allowed her not only to feed herself, but to capture enough nutrients to produce her eggs, to propagate her species. A bioluminescent rod protruded from her head—the inspiration for the species' name, luring her prey with its light; her distended jaw and extendible stomach allowed her to eat prey bigger than herself. All around her body, more bioluminescent strands shimmered—spines, the voice-over said, that helped her sense her prey.

Close up, the female had a gruesome face, but with the bioluminescent strands drifting off from her body, she looked, from the camera's far-off view, like she was enveloped in an angelic undersea halo.

The female, the voice-over said, could mate multiple times; scientists had found one female anglerfish with eight sets of testes fused to her body.

The male, the voice-over said, could, of course, mate only once.

As the credits rolled, I heard Jamie putting his key card into the door. I turned off the television and leaned back on the pillows. Such fluffy pillows. How was it possible that the pillows at this resort were so much more comfortable than the pillows at home?

Jamie kicked off his flip-flops and dropped onto the bed. I told him that he shouldn't lie on the bed; it was clean and he was dirty, from the beach-adjacent lagoon. He said I was dirty, too. I said I was pregnant, and therefore could do whatever I wanted, as long as I wasn't consuming alcohol or raw fish or unpasteurized cheese.

He rolled toward me, pressing his body against mine, rubbing his head against my chest.

"How about now?" he said, his tone light and playful. He was careful to avoid my protruding stomach. It was not possible for him to squash the baby, but somehow it felt completely possible, at any moment.

"Still dirty," I said, trying to keep my face serious. Jamie looked at me, raising an eyebrow. He pretended he was about to dive-bomb my body, kneeling above me, arms raised, making a sound like a fighter plane. I turned toward the pillow, laughing. He lowered his body as though he were going to dive onto me but stopped short, reaching his hands out to tickle the spot on my thigh, not quite behind my knee, that through much trial and error he had located as my particular weak point.

"Okay," he said, lifting himself back up from the bed. "Shower time."

While he was in the shower, I heard my phone ping. I reached out for it, but it wasn't on the nightstand. I couldn't remember where I had put it. I pulled myself out of the bed and searched for it—in my bag, in the pockets of the pants I had worn and dropped onto the floor, in the folds of the sheets. Finally, I found it in the cushions of the pineapple-printed armchair. By the time I pulled it out, the screen had gone dark and I pressed the button to illuminate it.

DO YOU EVER FEEL LIKE YOU ARE ALL ALONE?

○ YES

○ NO

○ NOT SURE

I was still staring at the screen when Jamie emerged from the bathroom. His hair was wet and the lower half of his body was wrapped in a plush white towel.

"What does JOYFULL want to know now?" he said, pointing at my phone. I had been showing Jamie JOYFULL's questions all along, for the most part. A few I had kept to myself.

I showed him the screen.

"Huh," he said.

He laid his now clean body on the high-thread-count sheets and I laid my body, still dirty, next to his.

"What are you going to say?" he said.

"What?"

"To the JOYFULL question," he said. "What are you going to say?"

"I don't know," I said. I turned off the phone without answering and put it on the nightstand. We laid next to each other in silence for a minute or two.

"Sometimes," he said, "I can't believe this is happening."

I asked him what he meant.

"This," he said. He kept his eyes staring straight up at the ceiling while he spoke. I watched him as he talked. "All of this. I was watching all those people down at the pool, and, you know, some of these people are our age, and they have, like, four kids. Four! I can barely take care of myself some days, how am I going to take care of one kid, let alone four kids? But they don't seem to think that at all. They just know what to do. And I just can't believe it. That I'm going to be a parent, that I'm going to be responsible for another human's life, that this is my life. Sometimes everything feels like it just stops for a second and I'm like, oh shit, what is this life I've gotten myself into? And it has nothing to do with you, I love you, but sometimes when everything stops like that, I wonder if it's too late to move to a mountain hut where I tend goats or something? You know, where everything is clear and simple, where I wake up in the morning and know what the tasks are that I have to do that day, and they are finite, and then they are over, and I can sit by the fire in my mountain hut and eat my porridge and go to sleep without any weight on my mind. A life where every problem has a solution."

I had always thought Jamie did not think these things. I had always thought that I alone thought these things.

"But I guess," he went on, turning to look at me, "even the guy in the mountain hut must have problems that he takes to bed with him at night: a goat that's gone off its feed, a feud with the neighbor in the hut on the next mountain."

I told him about the anglerfish, about the male's lips dissolving. Jamie leaned down toward my stomach, suctioned his lips onto my belly with a loud squelch.

"I don't think it's working," he said.

I pictured the female anglerfish drifting along the ocean bottom. I wondered what it felt like when the male bit her, when his body began to merge into her own.

Ever since Jamie first brought up marriage, I had been thinking about something Nietzsche had written in *On the Genealogy of Morals*—that humans are animals with the ability to make promises. But to make a promise requires not only that one be able to remember the promise (no small task for a forgetful animal), but also that one has some degree of confidence in being able to keep that promise in the future. In order to be confident enough in the future to make a promise, Nietzsche wrote, a human must first be someone predictable—predictable even to one's self—so that she is able to make promises about her future behavior. According to Nietzsche, that is society's role: to make the human predictable, through what he calls the social straitjacket. But while the majority of humans make promises and keep them because they are beholden to society's conditioning, there exists the possibility of becoming a truly free human—a sovereign individual—one who makes promises and keeps them not because she is so societally well-conditioned but because she is in possession of a truly free will. The sovereign individual knows she is strong enough to withstand misfortune; the sovereign individual knows she has power over herself and her fate.

Part of me wished I could go on not deciding about marriage; that we could hang, forever, suspended in a world where we were not yet married but soon might be, where I was not yet a mother but soon would be. I had spent so much of my life thinking I didn't need anyone, wanting no one to need me. I had needed my mother, but I couldn't have her, and so I had adapted. But now I had this. A further adaptation.

"When do you want to get married?" I said.

Jamie lifted his eyebrows.

"Aren't you worried I'm going to suck all the nutrients out of you and fuse to your body?" He grinned.

I was worried about that, in a manner of speaking. It was true.

But what was also true was that I loved Jamie, that he was my ticknest person.

"Maybe I'll be the one to suck all the nutrients out of you," I said. "Have you ever thought about that?"

Jamie grinned and pointed to his bare stomach, puffing it out so that it inflated like a balloon.

"I'm ready," he said.

TWENTY-FOUR

On the fourth day, we decided to go snorkeling. I had asked Dr. Subramanian about it ahead of time; she said it would be okay. She told me to stay at the surface, not to hold my breath. She told me not to dive, which was fine, because even if I wasn't pregnant I would not be interested in diving.

We went out on the resort's glass-bottomed boat, and I watched the reeds sway under the surface as we passed, the fish shimmy this way and that. The water was shockingly blue, so blue that it seemed possible someone had taken an enormous vat of dye and unleashed it into the sea. Our guides were a man and a woman in their early twenties, both white, who seemed to know each other well, and as the boat chugged out to our snorkeling destination, I constructed an elaborate narrative for them, in which they had been college sweethearts and decided after graduation to come out to Hawaii for this seasonal job. Low pay, but easy labor while they figured out what they wanted to do next. She wanted to be an archaeologist, had majored in anthropology; he was a musician, the kind who carried an acoustic guitar around with him everywhere. But now that they had made it to paradise, my story went, the relationship was no longer working. He didn't like the long hours; she was itching to apply to graduate school, beginning to suspect that he was holding her back.

I had noticed that while the majority of the resort staff were either native Hawaiian or Fillipino, the people who the resort hired to interact with the guests were all white. The front desk staff, the concierge, the activities manager we had spoken to that morning about snorkeling. These two early-twentysomethings. Why was it, I wondered, that my mind had come up with this narrative for these two white people, when it had neglected to do so for any of the many native-appearing staff I had encountered so far on this trip? Was it just because I was bored and becoming vaguely seasick? Or was it because I, too, was complicit in the reflexive notion that white people deserved stories to be written about them, backstories imagined for them, and non-white people did not?

The boat glided to a stop and the male guide dropped the anchor.

"Right," he said, clapping his hands to get our attention. There were twelve of us in all: two sets of parents with two children each, and another youngish couple like us. "It's very calm today, very safe out there. All we ask is that you stay within sight of the boat, and stay with your buddy."

I watched as the other guests crowded around the guide to get what were called snorkel vests—inflatable nylon vests that looked like life vests but without the bulky foam. The guides were very clear that they were not the same as personal flotation devices, and that they would help us float but could not be counted on in an emergency. When it was my turn, I nestled mine around my shoulders and blew into a tube to inflate it, letting it cradle my neck.

"Buddy?" Jamie said to me.

"Buddy," I said.

᠅

The water was still and calm, just as the guide had said it would be. Everyone else had entered the water by a daring-looking two-step method, plunging off the side of the boat, but because of my pregnant stomach, the guides insisted that I do a far less glamorous squat-and-roll from the steps that led into the water. No matter. It was the same water, and we all got there, one way or another.

The other snorkelers headed one way, so Jamie pointed in the opposite direction, and I followed. I had not been snorkeling since I was a child, and I found it difficult at first to relax into the mechanics of the breathing tube, the slightly constricted airflow. The body I carried was a tense body. I had noticed this before, with doctors and massage therapists and even hairstylists, who told me to relax, relax as they lowered my head back into their shampooing basin, into their massage chair, the muscles in my neck resisting their hands even as my mind tried to send signals to my body that all was okay, that we were safe.

I wondered at the guide's instructions. Staying in sight of the boat allowed for an immense distance, stretching far out over the open water. Surely, I thought, he should have been more specific.

But once I mastered the breathing, I began to enjoy myself, the sensation of weightlessness as I floated, aided by my snorkel vest, at the surface of the water, peering into this other world. On land, my back had begun to hurt and a vein in my leg was often throbbing, but here in the water, I was able to move my increasingly large body without pain. Below us, a school of yellow-striped fishes fluttered by, their mouths puckered as if they were blowing miniature kisses at everyone they saw. Orange-and-white clown fish darted among the rocks and reeds as though playing hide-and-seek. A larger fish, solo, burbled along, opening and closing its wide jaw. Even the rocks below were like something from a distant planet, covered with fuzzing algae in shades of purple and green, bursts of red and orange where starfish and anemone clung to their surface. Fronds of pink seaweed swayed hypnotically, the whole ocean a burst of Technicolor. I had known it would be magnificent, but I had not expected this. Maybe, I thought, there was a reason everyone went to Hawaii.

We made our way to the far end of the reef, away from the children who, I assumed, were disregarding the guide's rules about not touching the coral. But who knew? Maybe this generation of children were wildly, rigorously respectful. Maybe they would be the ones to save the coral, the fish, all of this. And I had to admit, it was more difficult to not touch the coral than I had thought it would be, the current constantly pushing us toward it as we fought to stay away, to avoid infecting the reef with our human oils.

Jamie seemed to be having an easier time than I was, his body hanging almost motionless in the water, the barest movement of his flippers keeping him stationary.

"I think I'm going to dive," he said, doggy-paddling over to my side. He deflated his vest the way the guides had shown us, until the neon fabric was drooping around his neck. I continued to slowly tread water, watching as he dove down, his body moving through the water with purpose. Seconds later, he was excitedly pointing at something in the reef. His finger was jabbing at an opening, but that was all it was, a dark hole. He stayed down there, waiting for something, holding his breath for longer than I would have thought possible. I doubted I'd be able to make out whatever it was we were waiting for, anyway.

But then I saw it: the head of an eel, like a miniature dragon, with a grasping jaw and rows of impossibly sharp teeth. Jamie was pointing at it and pointing at it, and I was trying to signal to him that I had seen it, that he could stop pointing, that his finger was far too close to the eel's primordial mouth, to its body, weaving like a ribbon through the holes in the reef.

At last, Jamie must have run out of breath, and he swam to the surface, leaving the eel behind as it watched his retreating body protectively from its lair. He stuck his head above the water and took his mask off, breathing in great gulps of air. I watched as he breathed into the tube on the vest, reinflating it. Next to him, I treaded water. I told him that I wished he wouldn't get so close, that the eel might have bitten him, that I was worried.

"You worry too much," he said, but as he said it I could hear a growing roar in the distance, the sound of a motorboat, a motorboat that was not supposed to be there, I didn't think.

The boat was getting closer, its wake frothing white. Too close. It passed by with a roar and I could feel the change in the water, feel my body beginning to bob up and down when before it had been still and straight. Jamie turned to say something to me, but before either of us could do anything, a much larger wave suddenly came crashing over our heads, knocking me under and back. I felt the water filling my mouth, heaving up my nostrils. My feet were searching for the bottom but couldn't find it. I could see it, but I couldn't touch it, couldn't make my way to solid ground, to solid air. My mouth was full of water and I was not thinking of myself, drowning, but of the baby, drowning. I would not drown, I knew that even as I thrashed about, fighting the mask and the seawater, waiting for the vest I was wearing to buoy me back up, but who knew what was happening inside me, how these seconds without air would affect the thing growing within my body.

And then I could feel Jamie's hands around my waist, lifting me up, holding me so my head was above the waves and I was spitting out the salty water, but I felt like I would never suck in enough air, like I would never get the taste of salt out of my mouth.

And then, as suddenly as it had been kicked up, the water was quiet again, the motorboat off to a different part of the coast, knowing nothing of the disturbance it had caused. The water was still and calm, and I could breathe, and I paddled slowly back to our little glass-bottomed boat, Jamie swimming by my side, to rest.

❋

Back in the room, we spent a frantic few hours trying to get in touch with Dr. Subramanian. We had gotten back from snorkeling in the midafternoon, but it was several hours later on the mainland, and her office was already closed. We pushed the button to signal that our voicemail was an emergency. We waited. We called again and left another voicemail and again pushed the button to indicate that our voicemail was an emergency, deserving of a higher priority than any other call. We waited again. I monitored my body for signs of anything amiss. My ears were still full of water, but otherwise I felt the same.

When Dr. Subramanian finally called back, she said she understood why we thought our call was an emergency, but that she had listened to our message and it was not an emergency. She said the baby would be fine, everything would be fine. She sounded, I thought, a little bit impatient. I heard a child in the background yelling something about pizza. We asked questions and she provided reassuring answers, but it was hard to let go of the feeling that I had done irreparable harm.

At dinner that night, we were seated with a trio of couples. Dinner was always that way—communal seating. Something about the festive atmosphere, I think. It was, of course, another luau, although this one featured roast fish instead of suckling pig. A change. Otherwise, the setting was much the same: tiki torches, buffet table, green-fronded palm trees swaying in the evening breeze.

I did not feel festive. I was tired, but also extremely alert, keyed into any sign that things in my body were not the way they used to be. I let Jamie go through the buffet on my behalf. Two of the couples came back to the table, plates piled high as was the custom. I sat on the opposite side of the table from them. We nodded politely all around, and then I watched as they fell into conversation. They were all four in their early fifties. Everyone at the table was white, except for me. I drank my ice water. I picked at a roll from the bread basket.

The other couple sat down next to me, the woman to my immediate left. They were around our age, mine and Jamie's, both of them also white, both of them blond. Jamie returned then, and placed a plate in front of me.

"Barramundi," he said.

"What?" I said.

"The fish," he said, nodding at my plate. "Barramundi. Soy and sesame marinated."

We might have kept talking, but the man on Jamie's right introduced himself, asked him something about golf. Jamie did not play golf, but he was a ready conversationalist. I focused on the barramundi.

"The key at these things," came a voice from my left, "is to not get distracted by any of the cheap stuff." The voice was coming from the blond woman, I realized. She was talking to me. "No potatoes, no bread, definitely none of that rice pilaf that they put at the beginning of the buffet line, trying to get you to accidentally fill up." She eyed my plate. In addition to the barramundi, there were a couple of cooked shrimp and a piece of red meat. "Your husband did a good job," she said. "Big-ticket items."

"I'm Cindy," she said, sticking out her hand before I had a chance to correct her about Jamie, how he was not yet my husband but soon would be.

"Evelyn," I said. Her hand was small but surprisingly strong, like a little bear paw.

"This is Lucas," she said, gesturing her fork at the blond man next to her. He smiled and lifted his fork in greeting before going back to plowing through his plate. Lucas looked like he was used to letting Cindy do the talking.

"We come here every year," Cindy went on. "I'm a lawyer and Lucas is in real estate, we need the break. Leave the kids at home with Lucas's mom. Three kids. Can you believe that? I'm thirty-eight, a partner in a law firm, and I have three kids. But we get it all done. Forget their names sometimes, but we get it all done." She laughed and looked at her husband. It wasn't clear if he was listening. Jamie was still talking

to the man beside him. I could hear something about golf courses in
Scotland. I did not want to talk about golf courses in Scotland, but I
nonetheless resented that Jamie got to talk about golf courses in Scotland while I, inevitably, had to talk to this woman about her children.

"What about you?" Cindy said, finally reaching for her fork.

"Babymoon," I said, looking down at my stomach. "A gift from his
parents. First time in Hawaii."

"Ohhhhhhh," she said. "Lucky you. First baby?"

I nodded. She took a bite of fish and surveyed me while she chewed.
After she swallowed, she leaned toward me, as though she had something to say in confidence.

"If you don't mind my saying so," she said, her voice lowered, "that's
going to be a very commercially viable kid." I didn't know what I had been
expecting her to say, but it wasn't that. She began to tell me about her kids'
modeling careers, about how they were doing well, but really, the ethni-
cally ambiguous baby was the look of the future. To my relief, she was interrupted by an announcement, a voice cutting in over the loudspeaker.
Due to popular demand, it said, they were bringing out a suckling pig.

"Anyway, you're what, half Asian?" She peered into my face. "I'm
not sure—"

I was so surprised by the veer in the conversation's direction that I
simply nodded.

"Asian and what?"

"Jewish," I said.

"Jewish," she repeated. "Perfect."

I didn't know why that was perfect.

"And he's what?" she said, nodding her chin at Jamie.

"I don't know."

She waited expectantly. I considered not saying anything more, but
we would be sitting at this table next to them for the entire night.

"I think a long time back, the family came from Norway," I said. I had vague memories of a certain kind of Christmas cookie his mother made. "I just think of him as being from Michigan."

"Ah," she said. "Corn fed."

"I suppose," I said.

"Well, I want to get to the buffet table before all the good parts of the pig are gone. But give me your phone."

I didn't know why she was asking for my phone, but I handed it to her. She took it from me and held it to her phone, like the two phones were embracing. I wondered what she considered the good parts of the pig.

"Now you have my contact info," she said. "When you have that baby, get in touch."

She stood up and her husband followed, leaving their dirtied plates behind. That was buffet etiquette. Every time you went up to the buffet, you got a new plate, as though you were starting afresh, with a whole new appetite. As though the version of you who had already eaten a plate of food, two plates of food, had been forgotten, or had never even existed. I watched Cindy and her husband blend into the buffet line.

I felt the baby kicking.

"How are things in there?" I whispered. No one was around to notice. I closed my eyes and waited for the popping in my stomach to subside. "We had a little scare today," I said, "but you seem to be just fine." The kicking felt the same as it always felt.

Just then, my phone pinged.

**DO YOU FEEL THAT YOU ARE IN CHARGE OF
YOUR OWN LIFE?**

I clicked it off without answering. I looked back to the empty seats where Cindy and her husband had been. Their dirty plates were gone, swooped away. My plate was still full of big-ticket items, but everything had gone cold.

TWENTY-FIVE

For our second-to-last day at the resort, Jamie's mother had pre-booked us a package tour: a trip to the historic leper colony on the nearby island of Molokai. The package involved driving from our resort to the airport and taking a twenty-minute plane ride; we would land at a small airport in what was now a national historical park. For me, snorkeling had been enough of an activity. Lying next to the beach-adjacent lagoon and drinking red-colored drinks had not exhausted its potential. But Lynne had already paid for the trip, or used Tom's points for it, and so I woke up at six thirty in the morning with a minimum of resentment. I could be a person who said yes more often, I thought. Leper tourism, yes.

We rode in one of the resort's white vans to the airport and then were somehow allowed to bypass security and walk straight onto the runway, where an exceedingly small plane was waiting. A few other families were with us in the van, and the rest of them boarded without a moment of hesitation. I looked at Jamie; he squeezed my hand. But when we approached the stairs to climb into the plane, the attendant looked at my stomach and said we'd have to distribute the weight. She led me to one side of the tiny plane and Jamie to another. Before I could say anything, she had seated another man next to me. He didn't seem noticeably bigger or smaller than Jamie, but I was terrible at estimating weight. Anyway, Jamie was, of course, already busy chatting with the woman sitting next to him, a blond woman in her early sixties who looked about the same size as me, with the obvious difference that I was pregnant.

The man sitting next to me introduced himself—he was named Paul. He looked like he was either Asian or possibly native Hawaiian. I guessed he was in his mid-forties, though it was hard to tell; his skin had the deep wrinkles of having spent many years in the sun. Paul, it turned out, was not part of our tour. He ran a business breeding mules on Molokai, but he worked part time at the resort to make ends meet. He was hitching a ride back to the island, he said; there had been a seat free and he knew the pilot.

The activities manager at the resort had told us that the other option for getting to the leper colony was to fly to the main airport on the island and then ride a mule down the mountainside to the park. But because I was pregnant, I couldn't do the mule ride part, and so we were flying directly. I asked Paul if he supplied the mules for the tour, and he nodded affirmatively, but added that the real money was—or at least, used to be—in selling mules to the mainland.

"It's not a good market in mules these days," he told me as the plane readied for takeoff. "Everyone wants horses, no one wants a half-breed."

"A half-breed?" I said.

"Sure," he said. "Mule's a cross between a donkey and a horse. Didn't you know that? Better than both, if you ask me. Tougher and surer-footed than horses, a hell of a lot smarter than donkeys. Hybrid vigor, they call it."

"Hybrid vigor," I repeated.

"That's right," Paul said. "Like me. Half native, half Japanese. I've got hybrid vigor, too, that's what I always say."

I nodded.

"What about you?" he asked, looking over at me. "You look like you've got some hybrid vigor in you."

I told him he was right, that I was half Japanese. Paul nodded affirmatively, pleased with having sussed me out.

"No point in not talking about it. What, we live in a post-race era now or something? That's what people were saying for a while, but I always knew we weren't post-race. That's a white-person delusion. Because if it's post-race, they don't have to feel bad about anything anymore. Post-race means post-white-people-feeling-bad. But the thing is, we were never in the white-people-feeling-bad stage of things. Or not for nearly long enough, I say. So how can we be post?

"Here," he went on, "at least we don't pretend. I tell my kids, mainland is different. You go to college on the mainland, move to the mainland someday, people are going to act real different about you, about the color of your skin. They won't understand there, not like they do here."

This seemed like the moment I was supposed to ask how many kids he had. I asked how many kids he had. As he talked about his kids three of them, the oldest a soccer star, high hopes for a scholarship—I thought about the mules. I had more questions: What is the market for mules? How do you transport them to the continental US? But it seemed there was no way to go back, at least not without revealing myself to be someone who cared more about mules than I did about children, or at least someone who would rather talk about mules than talk about children.

As we began to coast down the runway, I waited for a lull in the conversation, a chance for me to bring it back to the mules. I had one question I really wanted to ask.

"So if a mule is half horse and half donkey," I said, "what does a mule breed with? Other mules?"

"You really don't know anything about mules, huh?" Paul said, chuckling to himself. "Mules are sterile. Wrong number of chromo-somes. Every once in a while, you get a mule mare who can mate with a purebred, but that's real rare."

The plane began to pull up into the air and Paul leaned back in his seat.

"Here we go," he said. "We'll be there in a jiff."

※

What I knew about leprosy was minimal. Open sores, windows through to the flesh. Was Mother Teresa involved in some way? Probably. Some-one had told me that they had heard Mother Teresa was actually not so nice. Now that I was remembering it, it seemed ridiculous, "not so nice," like a piece of elementary school gossip. Nice—what a loaded word. That neuterer of women the world over.

As if you had to be nice to be a saint.

The first stop on our tour was the leprosy museum, a low white-washed building with uneven wooden floors that gave me a mildly sea-sick feeling, like everything had been turned slightly askew. This had been the home of the priest who ministered to the lepers, our guide said. He figured prominently in the black-and-white photos that lined the museum's walls, a white man standing a whole head taller than the Hawaiians who surrounded him, cast out of their homes and forced to live in this place.

Behind me, the guide was talking about the mistaken belief that leprosy was highly contagious. The need to isolate the disease. The establishment of leper colonies. In fact, he said, leprosy was very diffi-cult to transmit. My back was turned, but still, I could somehow tell that the rest of the group was gathered around him, listening; that I, too, was meant to gather.

Instead, I stared purposely at the photo in front of me. A formal photo, posed figures, in black and white. Everyone wearing their best clothes: the men in dress shirts buttoned up to the collar, the women in long-sleeved dresses with lace at the wrists and high necks. Not a single smile. Not a single indication of whether they had begun to adapt to life in the colony, whether they had begun to accept that this was the life they would lead until their deaths. Perhaps because of the clothing, I could make out no gaping wounds in the photos, no ruptures in the skin.

After a minute or two, I felt a body approaching my body. A body standing so close to my body that it had to be a body I knew.

"Hey," Jamie said. I turned. "Is everything all right?"

"Everything's fine," I said. The word "fine" felt strange in my mouth.

"Good." He lowered his voice to a whisper. "Why don't you come join the group? I think the guide is kind of anxious for you to listen to his spiel. He keeps glancing over here."

I followed him back to the group. The guide was talking about modern-day treatments for leprosy, but I kept thinking about the horror of this disease, wondering what it would feel like to have your skin, the boundary between your body and the world, begin to break down, to have your insides exposed. Maybe the uninfected really believed it was highly contagious—or maybe they simply did not want to see into another person in that way, that they preferred that what was inside to remain hidden.

After many years ministering to the lepers, the priest who lived with them eventually contracted leprosy himself, the guide said.

No body is impermeable.

✻

For lunch, we sat in a loose circle in the grass and ate chicken sandwiches and snack-size bags of potato chips that had been packed for us in paper sacks. Jamie made small talk with some of the other people, but I mostly focused on my sandwich. The wind was picking up. The palm trees shivered overhead, creaking as they swayed from side to side, the dried bottom fronds threatening to drop.

A voice rose out of the low chatter. A man in his mid-forties, with brown hair and wire-rimmed glasses and a wide, confident face. He had something to say, and he wanted the whole group to hear it.

"I was surprised," he said, "that the guide gave so little background on leprosy as a medical condition." He acted as though he was only talking to the woman next to him, presumably his wife, and then looked up, with seeming shock, to find the whole group waiting for his next words. The guide was off tending to the mules, so the man could slander him without repercussions.

"I studied leprosy in medical school," he continued. "And the real danger with leprosy isn't the sores, per se. It's that you stop feeling the infected parts of your body—they go numb. The fingers, the hands, the feet. Your extremities. That's when the trouble really starts. You touch a hot kettle and don't feel it. The burn, otherwise easily treatable, festers into another kind of infection entirely, and the finger ultimately has to be removed. You cut your hand on a knife or a thorn or a needle. You stub your toe or drop something on your foot. Seemingly innocuous stuff. But the problem is, you no longer feel that part of your body at all. You know it's there, you know it's physically connected to you, but you can't incorporate it into your sense of self."

Incorporate, I thought. A good choice of words. To make part of the body. To give bodily form.

"It's really quite fascinating," the man went on. "The role of pain. We need pain to survive. Without pain, we can't know that a part of us is suffering, that a part of us needs to be looked after. We all shy away from pain, we'll do anything to avoid it. But pain is the body's way of saying, stop, take care. Pay attention."

He was still talking, but I had stopped listening. I was thinking about the baby. I was thinking about my hybrid vigor. Jamie was sitting next to me, and when I looked over at him, he raised his hand and placed it on the back of my neck, like I was a pup.

※

After lunch, we toured the facilities. The living quarters, the mess hall, which had the look of an old summer camp, albeit one that you could never leave. I had hated sleepaway camp. My parents had sent me to a Jewish sleepaway camp one summer, but I was so miserable I asked to be picked up early—that was me, the one person every summer who needs to be picked up early.

The rest of the group began to make their way back to the plane for the return trip. I told Jamie that I'd be ready in a minute, I just had to use the bathroom. Pregnancy meant using the bathroom all the time. This was something I had known before I was pregnant, but I had not been quite prepared for the magnitude. Everywhere I went, I located the bathroom first, like a spy checking on her escape route.

At the former leper colony, the bathroom was small and antiquated, with an old porcelain toilet and a flush chain. A sign taped to the back of the bathroom door read PLEASE DO NOT FLUSH ANYTHING DOWN THE TOILET OTHER THAN TOILET PAPER!! ☺, a sign familiar to me from women's bathrooms everywhere.

I turned the lock on the door and sat down on the seat. But then, instead of the hot stream of urine I expected, I felt something else come out of my body, something thinner and slimier, something that, instead of being expelled by me in a controllable flow, fell out of me all at once. I scooted back on the toilet seat and looked down between my legs. The liquid in the bowl was clear, but it had a shimmer that water did not have, a texture like strands of gelatin. I was debating whether to reach my hand in and check—I could always wash it and wash it and wash it again—when I felt a sudden onrush of hot pain, a bloom of warmth in my stomach, no, lower than my stomach, warmth that felt like it was burning me from the inside out. I'd had bad period cramps before, the kind that felt like someone had stuck a wrench up inside me and scraped it around. This was like that but times a hundred, times a thousand, times an unquantifiable number. I closed my eyes and waited for the pain to pass, the way it always did. I closed my eyes, but the pain subsisted, a level of pain that I did not know could subsist, that I did not know I could survive.

I opened my eyes again and looked down. In those brief moments, the toilet bowl had filled with blood. Even diluted by the gallons of water, it was a bright, pure red. The pain was still searing through me, but my body had somehow acclimated to it, so it had retreated to a dull roar. The blood-water was dotted with clumps that were black and thick, like magma.

Where was all this blood coming from?

I reached my hand down and touched my body.

The blood was coming from me.

TWENTY-SIX

I remember being loaded into the helicopter and feeling like my insides were dropping out of me. I remember concentrating hard, thinking that if I concentrated hard, I could keep them inside of me, where they belonged. I remember Jamie's face, which flashed to pure terror when I staggered out of the bathroom but quickly transformed into a look of resolve that made me think, even then, that this was why I loved him, that he would be a good father.

I remember the voice of the doctor who had been talking about leprosy, saying there was nothing he could do, they had to get me to a hospital right away, they would have to airlift me out.

I don't remember taking off, I don't remember the medics onboard, I don't remember being shifted from the back of the helicopter, surely now covered in blood, to a gurney.

I remember the feeling of slickness on my thighs.

I remember being raced through the corridors of the hospital, everything white and sterile, the hallways, the ceilings, the gowns of the orderlies and nurses who were pushing me, but we were going too fast for Jamie, we were leaving him behind—where was he?—and then everything was white and I don't remember anything more.

＊

When I woke up, I was in a hospital room, and no one was there. Wasn't someone supposed to be there when you woke up? That's how it always was in the movies. But my room was empty, the chair next to my bed, empty. Out the window, a palm tree swayed in the breeze. I watched it go back and forth, back and forth. My mind felt thick and foggy. I was in the hospital. Why was I in the hospital? I lifted the sheet and looked down. No no no no no no, I thought. Where was everyone? I needed to see someone. Wasn't there a button I could push? Tubes ran from my arms to an IV next to the bed. There had to be a button somewhere.

＊

The next time I woke up, Jamie was there, and a nurse. The nurse wanted to take my vitals, but I wouldn't let her until they told me what had happened.

You're okay, Jamie said, squeezing my hand. You're okay.

I know I'm okay! I said, with surprising force. It felt strange to hear my voice. I was having a hard time modulating its volume.

I can tell that I'm okay, I said, trying to speak more normally. What about the baby.

Jamie squeezed my hand again.

We don't know yet about the baby.

＊

I drifted in and out of wakefulness. They had put me on a lot of drugs. For the pain, they said. I felt no pain, none at all. I wondered what the pain would feel like, when I did feel it.

The baby is in the NICU, Jamie said, on a different floor. That's where he had been the first time I woke up.

She is very small, he said.

She looks like a fighter, he said.

How can a baby look like a fighter? I thought. Doesn't it just look like a baby? But I wanted to believe him, so I did.

※

The next time I woke up, my father was in the chair. He was reading a newspaper. *USA Today.*

Dad? I said.

He looked up, as though I'd startled him. He put the newspaper down and came to the side of my bed. He looked like he was debating whether or not to touch me. He didn't know what to do.

How are you feeling? he said.

I feel better, I said. It was true. What about the baby?

My father's mouth closed into a flat line.

No change. But no change is better than bad news. That's what the doctors told us.

Who's us?

Me and Kumiko. We came as soon as Jamie called us.

How long have I been here?

It's only been a day since you were admitted. Twenty-six hours. We got here five hours ago.

He reached out and put his hand on my shoulder.

They said they might not know about the baby for several days. We just have to wait.

Placental abruption, the doctor said. The placenta separates from the inner wall of the uterus. No way to predict it. No, you didn't do anything wrong. No, it wasn't the snorkeling, or the wave. No, it wasn't the plane ride to the leper colony. How many pregnancies are affected? One in 100. A 1 percent chance. The primary indications are drinking and cocaine use. You haven't engaged in any drug use while pregnant? No, I didn't think so.

I know it can be hard to accept, the doctor said. But we really don't know what causes it to happen.

At first they said I couldn't see the baby. I was too weak, they said. I had lost a lot of blood. I was still recovering from the C-section. But somewhere around thirty-six hours, I started to feel very lucid, as if a heavy blanket had been pulled off my body.

I can do it, I told Jamie.

I can do it, I told the doctor.

Jamie pushed me in a wheelchair to an elevator that took us two floors up. Two floors up, the hallway looked exactly the same, the same linoleum floor, the same sterile, white corridors. When they brought the baby here, I had still been in the OR, or unconscious in my room. She had been all alone. Had Jamie been with her? That was no way to enter the world, all alone.

Jamie squeezed my shoulder, his hand warm and firm through the flimsy material of the hospital gown.

The room was filled with babies. Seeing it was something of a shock. I had been thinking of only our baby, but here were rows and rows of them, some in worse condition than ours. Instead of lying in cribs, they were each in their own clear plastic box, a contraption that made it look like they might shoot off into space at any moment. We passed baby after baby after baby, until finally we got to a clear plastic box with the nameplate BABY KUMAMOTO-PETERSON.

She was so small. I knew she would be small, but she was so much smaller than I had imagined, than I had ever thought possible. I looked at her fingers, her toes, her tiny rib cage, moving microscopically up and down with each breath. She wore a diaper and a pink knit hat, plus the tube that was attached to her nose, the sensors attached to her chest. Her eyes were shut, and yet her face still looked prematurely fretful, as though she had been born to carry the weight of the world.

I felt frozen. I looked to Jamie. He had been here before. He smiled at me.

That's our baby, he said.

You can hold her, if you like, the nurse said.

They rolled me over to the sink, where Jamie and I soaped up with scalding water. They rolled me back to her space cube.

You go first, I said to Jamie.

Are you sure? he said.

I nodded.

He stuck his hands in two arm-size circles cut into the side of the space cube. He placed his pinkie next to the baby's hand. Her hand opened and closed back down around it, his smallest finger larger even than her fist.

See, he said, looking at me. Look how strong she is.

I nodded. I thought probably I would start to cry.

Jamie waited until the baby let go of his finger on her own, then he retracted his arms through the arm-size holes.

Your turn, he said.

I put my arms in the space capsule.

I put my finger next to the baby's other fist and waited for her to grab hold.

I put my other hand on her chest.

I waited to feel the beat of her heart.

※

They still didn't know about the baby, they told us. They might not know for several more days.

The baby, the baby. We had not wanted to name her until she was born. And now she had been born, and she had no name. She had had no name for days now.

※

The nurse helped me to the shower. I undressed, standing on my own again, if a little unsteadily. I felt the water come down over my shoulders, my breasts, my stomach. Above my pubic bone was a long horizontal gash, stitched closed with thread that looked like dental floss. The nurse had said to let the water wash over it, to keep it clean so it wouldn't get infected.

I had been having a thought that I had not yet spoken out loud, that I might never speak out loud. I had been pushing this thought away for the past forty-two hours, but standing under the shower, alone, it came at me with full force.

If the baby didn't survive, it would be my fault.

Somehow, my body had known I was not sure about the baby. My body had acted, unilaterally.

I looked down at my newly heavy breasts, my softly protruding stomach, the C-section incision, its edges red and angry.

Whose body was this?

※

We decided to name the baby. Charlotte. That was her name.

TWENTY-SEVEN

t started to rain. Fat, thick drops exploded against the windowpane like miniature water balloons. I lay in the hospital bed and clicked from local news channel to local news channel, all the weathermen and weatherwomen seeming equally surprised by the sudden storm. It came out of nowhere, said Channel Four. Usually we see these weather patterns developing days, if not weeks, ahead, said Channel Seven. There was a high chance it would be upgraded to a tropical storm, said Channel Five.

The rain held steady for a day and a night. On the second day of rain, my fourth day in the hospital, the doctor came to see me. The doctor said that they were ready to discharge me, but that they would have to keep the baby for observation.

"Her name is Charlotte," I said. I told the doctor her full name, even though Jamie and I had already begun to call her Lotte. "We named her."

"I see," the doctor said. "We'll need to keep Charlotte here for observation."

"How can I be ready to leave if she isn't ready to leave?"

The doctor explained that this was how it sometimes worked. That Lotte was still having trouble breathing on her own. That her heartbeat was very weak. My body, on the other hand, was doing fine. I had a little bit of pain, but it was not, the doctors said, abnormal. The C-section scar was looking good. I would not even need to come back to have the stitches removed. They would dissolve into my body.

"But she's going to be okay?" I said. The doctor did not immediately say anything. "Is she going to be okay?"

The doctor said they still didn't know, that it might be several more days before they knew anything. The doctor said I was welcome to visit as much as I wanted, but that it was also important that I get some rest. My body, he said, had been through a lot.

I nodded. After the tests, the monitoring, the imaging, the Dopplers, the books, the websites, the videos, the rules on what to eat and what not to eat, what to drink and what not to drink, how much to sleep, which vitamins to take, it turned out it had not mattered what I put into my body or what I kept away from it, what the doctors saw inside me and how often they had checked.

It did not seem to me that he knew very much about my body at all.

✻

My father and Kumiko had been staying in a condo a half mile from the hospital. It had two bedrooms and two bathrooms, and when Jamie wasn't camped in the chair next to my hospital bed, he would go back there, too, to shower, to lie down for a few minutes. It was a nice place, he said. Very comfortable.

When they came to pick me up, my father and Kumiko were both wearing enormous plastic ponchos, the clear kind that allow you to see the body underneath. Jamie wore one, too. Under his arm, he carried another, still folded in its packaging.

"This one's for you," Kumiko said. She had gone to a superstore nearby to buy them once the rain started. "This is the best kind. Strong and cheap. It will keep you completely dry. We've got extras back at the condo."

I let her help me into the poncho, pulling the plastic over my arms, over my hips, down past my knees. I told the nurse I was fine to walk out of the hospital on my own, but she said I had to get in a wheelchair. Hospital policy. I let the nurse wheel me down the corridor, into the elevator, down three floors, along another corridor to the exit. How was it possible that I was exiting, when Lotte was still inside? We stopped in front of the sliding doors. My father was pulling the car around. Where had the car come from? They had rented a car, Kumiko told me. There hadn't been many options left, she said.

"Someone has to stay with her," I said.

"What?" Jamie said.

"We can't all leave," I said. "She'll be all alone. You have to stay with her."

Jamie looked very tired. I had not noticed it before, in my room. I wondered if he had slept at all, these past few days.

A gold convertible pulled up to the curb, my father behind the wheel.

"All right," Jamie said. "I'll stay."

❀

The condo was pristine and virtually empty. It had bare white walls and a big sectional couch.

"How did you find this place?" I asked.

"It belongs to a friend of mine from church," Kumiko said. She looked at my father. "A friend of ours. We were staying in a hotel, but when she heard what happened, she called and said it was empty, that we should use it."

There was a kitchenette to the right, a loaf of sandwich bread on the counter. Kumiko asked if I was hungry. She could make me something, she said. But all I wanted to do was sleep. Had I slept at all at the hospital? That was more or less all I had done for five days, between visits from doctors to me, visits from me to Lotte. And yet I felt like I hadn't slept in weeks.

Kumiko pointed me toward one of the bedrooms, and I crawled into bed.

When I woke up, it was still raining. I could hear it on the roof, on the windows. A digital clock on the nightstand said it was four p.m., but it was dark outside. Either the clock was wrong, or the outside was wrong. One of the two.

I could hear someone rustling out in the living room. Kumiko, surely. My father wasn't a rustler. I looked for my phone on the nightstand, but I hadn't brought it into the bedroom with me. It was out in the living room with the rest of my things—my things from the hospital and the things that Jamie had retrieved from the resort. If there was any news, the news would be on my phone. If there was any news, the news would be outside, with Kumiko.

I pulled off the covers and swung my legs onto the floor. My body felt creaky and weak, like I could sleep for another several days straight. My body seemed to think the worst was over, that now it could finally relax, recover. But the worst isn't over, I told myself. I was still dressed in the clothes they had brought me when I was discharged. I looked down at my stomach. I couldn't bring myself to lift the shirt, to look at the stitched flesh. It was enough to look at this deflated space, space where there had been something and now there was nothing.

But there wasn't nothing. There was something. There was Lotte.

※

Kumiko seemed startled to see me. She was sitting on the sectional with a cup of tea and a magazine.

I emerged from the bedroom and immediately began to look for my phone, but when I found it, the screen was dark. It was dead.

"No news?" I said to Kumiko. She had put the magazine down and was watching me.

"No news," she said. Her voice was gentle. I had never heard her voice this gentle before.

I rustled through my bag to find a charger and plugged the phone in. I waited, willing the screen to light up with a call from the hospital. But of course, if there had been news, Jamie wouldn't have just given up at the sound of my voicemail—he would have called Kumiko, and she would have already told me. When the phone finally came back to life, there were no missed calls. No news.

"Do you want some tea?" she asked.

I shook my head. I sat on the edge of the sectional. It was so enormous, curving around the small room, that I was still a good ten feet away from her.

"Where's my dad?"

"He went to pick up Jamie. The doctor said that Lotte needed some rest."

"Meaning Jamie needs some rest."

Kumiko nodded.

"You know," she started, then hesitated. Something in her face resolved, and she continued. "It may not be my place, but I wanted you to know that I understand. I can imagine what you might be feeling."

I didn't say anything. I could hear the rain, still pounding on the windows, on the roof. As far as I knew, it had not let up for two days.

"I was married before," Kumiko went on. "When I was twenty-four. My college sweetheart, just like your parents." Something about this was shocking to me. Not that Kumiko had already been married, but to hear the story of my parents, those words—*your parents*—coming out of her mouth.

"His name was Daichi," she said. "He had been born in Japan, like me, and come over when he was young. He was a civil engineer. After graduation, we moved to Gardena, near the Toyota factory. There were lots of Japanese down there then. He made a good salary. We bought a small house, one story. I had my degree, but I didn't work. Daichi didn't want me to, but not in that way like you think. It's hard to explain, but at the time it seemed like the right thing. I worked on setting up the house, keeping the garden. I made friends in the neighborhood, other wives. Daichi came home every night at six and we ate dinner together in the dining room, at the table. I was only twenty-four and I had a dining room and a dining-room table! That was all I had ever wanted, truly." She looked at me. "I know that may be hard for you to understand. You're a modern woman. I am, too. Now I am. But then, I was happy.

"After about a year, I became pregnant. A son. We named him Timothy. A good American name. He was nine pounds, two ounces. Enormous. An enormous head. I thought he was going to break me, coming out. But he was a healthy baby. He was healthy for a long time. A strong, big-headed boy.

"You could tell, even that young, that he was going to grow up to be a good man. I know every parent probably thinks that about their child, but with him it was really true. I watched him, I knew. Other children would sometimes have these moments of casual cruelty, moments I'm sure most of them would grow out of, but they had them, nonetheless. When they would push another child or grab the toy they wanted without thinking, or when they would leave another child out of their games, already playing at hierarchies. Timothy wasn't like that.

"When he was four, he started to seem different. Still a happy child, but pale. Low energy. We took him to the doctor after he got a bruise playing baseball and it just wouldn't go away. His body wasn't healing itself. Turned out it was leukemia.

"We did everything we could, we did everything we were supposed to do. I have photos of Timothy, somewhere. Daichi wanted to take the photos. So that we could show Timothy later, what he had been through.

I haven't looked at them in twenty years, but I can still picture them. Timothy, smiling, with that bald head. Child leukemia has a very high survival rate, you know. It's higher now than it was back then, but even then it was a good chance. That's what the doctors kept telling us. Good chance, good chance. Then they stopped telling us anything.

"I started going to church soon after. One of my friends from the neighborhood brought me, and it helped. Daichi wouldn't go, though. He handled his grief differently. He didn't start drinking or anything like that. But he got even quieter, even more internal, as though he could pretend that the outside world didn't exist, hadn't betrayed us in this way. After a year passed, I wanted to try again, but he didn't. I was thirty-three. We could still have had another child. But he said he couldn't.

"I lost touch with him after the divorce, but I heard he moved back to Japan. His parents were still there, and his sister. She already had two children when we got married, it's possible she might have had more. I sometimes think about trying to find him now, it probably wouldn't be too hard with these social networks. But I haven't even searched for him. I prefer it this way, I think."

I thought that she might go on, but she stopped there.

"Why didn't my father tell me any of this?" I asked. Once the words were out of my mouth, it seemed like a wildly insufficient thing to say.

"I'm sure he thought it was my story to tell, if I wished to tell it," Kumiko said.

I nodded.

"You know, your father canceled everything the second he got the call from Jamie. All his patients. He told his secretary to cancel them indefinitely. He got us on the next flight here, and he got us the hotel, and he's the one who arranged for this condo with my friend from church because he thought you'd be more comfortable here—"

Kumiko broke off at the sound of steps in the hall, the sound of a key in the door. Jamie and my father came in, one after the other, their clear ponchos dripping wet, so it looked like they were translucent ghosts come to us from the other side. I watched as Jamie struggled to get his poncho off, as he revealed his body, dry and safe underneath.

I looked at him and I knew that the look on my face was a look of hope.

He shook his head.

Still nothing.

※

Days passed. They still knew nothing. They told us she was hanging on, that they would let us know right away if there was any change. We went to the hospital every day and sat by the space capsule and I felt for the beat of Lotte's heart. I told Jamie that I thought she was getting stronger, but he just smiled grimly and squeezed my shoulder. She was getting stronger, though, I was sure of it.

Every three hours or so, I attached a breast pump to my chest, letting it pull and tug at my nipples until the milk began to flow. Sitting next to Lotte at the NICU, sitting in the car between the condo and the NICU, sitting in the condo. It seemed like I was pumping constantly, producing milk for my baby so she could continue being a fighter. I didn't understand how it was possible that this was all I could do, but at least I could do something. If I kept pumping, then Lotte would have to keep taking the milk, would have to keep growing stronger.

I pumped and pumped.

My phone pinged every couple of hours, but none of it was news from the hospital, news about Lotte. They were all alerts from JOYFULL.

IT'S BEEN 15 DAYS SINCE YOUR LAST CHECK-IN.

HOW HAPPY ARE YOU?

1 2 3 4 5 6 7 8 9 10

I hadn't talked to anyone at the third-most-popular internet company since we left for our babymoon. Someone, probably Jamie, had been in touch with them; I could remember an enormous bouquet of flowers hovering somewhere near my hospital bed.

But the third-most-popular internet company didn't matter. All that mattered was my hand in the space capsule, her hand clutching onto mine. Between visits, I would lie in the darkened bedroom, under a downy white comforter that seemed too clean and light for the way I felt. I slept hard and deep. I should not be sleeping this well, I thought, but Jamie said it was good, Kumiko said it was good.

My father didn't appear to sleep at all. He was always cooking, things I didn't know he knew how to cook, mild, soothing dishes that he would convince me to eat even though I wanted to eat nothing: miso soup with strings of seaweed; sushi rice, barely seasoned with sugar and rice vinegar, sprinkled with sesame seeds; agedashi tofu, drizzled with soy and dotted with slivered green onions.

Jamie had told me that my father had been a huge help; he had talked to the doctors, to the insurance people, to the doctors, to the insurance people. He drove us to and from the hospital, sometimes coming in with us and sometimes remaining in the waiting room, intently reading whatever magazines were sitting there, fanned out on the small side tables. He had kept the kitchen stocked, kept everyone fed. I had thought it was Kumiko, but no, Jamie said, it was my father.

"I made this for your mother," my father said to me, standing in the kitchen one night over a pot of rice. "Towards the end, she couldn't eat much."

I waited for him to tell me that he really loved her, that sometimes he worried I didn't know that, that I was a lot like her, that she would have been proud of me, that she would have loved to meet her grandchild, that everything was going to be okay. But he didn't say any of those things.

"Eat," he said, pushing the bowl of rice into my hands. "Eat."

⁂

At night, I pressed my face into Jamie's back, nestling it between his shoulder blades.

"Are you asleep?" he whispered, after we had lain like that for several minutes.

"No," I said, my lips moving against his skin.

"Me neither," he said. "I keep thinking, if she's at the hospital, then why are we here?"

Neither of us said anything for a few moments.

"It's my fault," I said, my mouth still pressed against his back. "It's my fault, it has to be."

Jamie didn't say anything. I was afraid to raise my face and say it again, like the more I said it, the more it might be true, but it was something I needed to say, needed Jamie to hear. I pulled my face away from his body.

"It's my fault," I said again, this time clearly and loud.

Jamie rolled around to look at me. In the darkness, the edges of his face were slightly blurred. He looked tired, and worn.

"I should have known that something was wrong," I said. "I should have felt it."

"There was nothing for you to feel, Ev," he said. "There was no way to predict it."

I closed my eyes. I imagined what it would feel like to hold her, not through a space capsule, but against my body. To feel her heartbeat next to mine. I started to cry, a cry with no noise, only pure physicality, the grief rolling through my body, my shoulders, my ribs, my pelvis, pulsing along the scar that ran across my stomach.

"Hey," Jamie said, reaching his arm out and pulling me to his chest. "We don't know what's going to happen yet. And no matter what happens, it's not your fault. No one thinks that it's your fault." He held me to him and said more comforting things, things based in logic and reason, and I let him hold me to him and say these comforting, logical things. But I knew he was wrong. It had been my job—my one job—to keep her safe, and I had failed.

Outside, it was still raining. It had not stopped since I left the hospital.

I fell asleep without realizing that I was falling asleep, but I must have been asleep because then I was dreaming that I was caught in a river, the current pulling me downstream, its flow fast and unceasing. I was not supposed to be in this river. The river was not supposed to be like this. I felt my mouth fill with water, I felt its icy touch on my skin. I was struggling, hard, grabbing at anything I could—low-hanging branches that cracked off in my hands, rocks too slippery to grip. I was fighting the pull of the water, trying to get to shore, but the current was too strong. Before me, I could see the river widening out into a great expanse of water, broken only by the line of the horizon. The ocean. It would wash me away, I thought. It would swallow me whole. I was struggling and struggling, but my limbs were tired and heavy. And then, as the river met the sea, my body floating out into the endless blue, I felt a sudden sense of peace. I stopped struggling. I let my body rest.

The next morning, my phone rang.

This time it was the hospital.

She was going to be okay.

TWENTY-EIGHT

After we brought Lotte home from the hospital, I hardly left her side. I don't know what I thought would happen to her if I stepped away. That she would disappear? The doctor said she was ready to leave the hospital but she wasn't ready to travel, so we went on living in the condo, me spending what felt like my every waking moment trying to get her to latch onto my breasts. When she wasn't sleeping or getting her diaper changed, I was holding her body to my bare chest, establishing skin-to-skin contact, dribbling milk into her mouth, doing everything the lactation consultant had suggested. And yet still, Lotte refused.

"She's just used to the bottle," Jamie said. "There's no harm in it, is there?" I knew he was right—it was the same milk—and yet something desperate inside me needed her to latch.

On the advice of the lactation consultant, we tried nipple shields, a clear plastic pacifier-like object—basically the top of the bottle—that I placed over my actual nipple. I supposed the idea was to fool Lotte into thinking I was a plastic bottle, not her human mother. It didn't work.

"It can take months," the lactation consultant said when we went back to the hospital. "The important thing is to stay relaxed and positive."

I was not feeling very relaxed, or very positive.

In the bathroom, I took off my clothes, piece by piece, the soft, stretchy material I had been swaddled in for the past several days. I stood in the shower and let the water pour over the crown of my head, my shoulders, the small of my back. The water stung when it hit my nipples. I toyed with a loose piece of skin on one of them, winced as it came off in my fingers, a tiny fish scale.

I looked down at my stomach. I had spent a lot of time looking at my stomach over the past months, watching it as it grew. My stomach still looked like it was pregnant. Not as hugely pregnant, but still distinctly pregnant, protruding and swollen. No one had told me my stomach would still look like this. I knew what people said, that your body was never the same after giving birth. I knew this was now a part of my body that I should be ashamed of, that I was supposed to conceal with flowing clothing, or tone back into submission through long series of repetitive exercises to make it look like a body that had never carried another being inside of it, that had never been stretched and pressured and pushed to the extremes of what a body was capable of.

Was I supposed to hate my body now?

The place on my stomach where they had cut me open for the C-section was already beginning to heal. I touched the beginnings of the scar, ever so lightly. The skin felt different there, glossy and slick, knotting itself back together so that it looked like a tiny strand of glistening white rope.

I wondered when my body would begin to feel like my body again.

I wondered if my body would ever again feel like my body.

❄

A few days after bringing Lotte home, I heard my phone ping. I had been ignoring it—not hearing it at all, really. But this time I picked it up.

I was so unused to looking at my phone that at first, the screen looked almost foreign to me. Pressing the buttons felt unfamiliar and strange. The words on the screen swam before me and then settled into place:

ARE YOU HAPPY NOW?

○ YES

○ NO

○ NOT SURE

I knew that I should click YES, that I was supposed to click YES. But what did HAPPY mean? I did not think JOYFULL meant the kind of happiness that I meant, the happiness that we could each define for ourselves.

I still had not posted Lotte's photo on the social media website where everyone I knew posted photos of their babies. Did that make her less real?

I hovered my finger over YES. If I could bring myself to click YES, then I could go back to my high-earning life at the third-most-popular internet company, to the self-affirming ease it offered.

I could not do it. I pressed NOT SURE.

The wheel on the screen turned and turned. I watched it turn and turn.

The words loaded slowly and then all at once:

WHAT WILL IT TAKE FOR YOU TO BE HAPPY?

❋

Dr. Luce picked up her office phone after only the second ring. She said hello, sounding breathless. I wondered if she had been on the treadmill. She asked about the baby, about my health, said how glad she was to hear from me, how worried everyone had been.

I was surprised by how nice it was to hear someone else's voice, someone who was not related to me or paid to be attentive to me. People had been worried about me.

"I'm sure it's been difficult," she said. "Did you get the flowers we sent?"

I could feel my eyes welling up with tears. I willed myself not to cry—why was I crying now, of all times?—but the tears started to fall, at first silently and then not silently. This was not why I had called her.

"Take as much time as you need," she said. Her voice was so soothing.

I would have six months of maternity leave, she said. But if I needed more, I should tell her. We could work something out. I was valuable to the company.

"I'm not coming back," I said. I had stopped crying, but my voice was still a little wobbly.

"You're not coming back?" Dr. Luce said. Her voice had become mildly less soothing. Now she mostly sounded perplexed.

"I'm not coming back," I repeated, my voice more steady now.

"I see," she said. I thought I could hear her press a button, the slow *whish* of the treadmill coming to a stop, though I might have been imagining it. "Would it change anything if we made your position permanent?"

There it was, the permanent position I had been trying for all year.

"Thank you," I said. "But it wouldn't change anything."

"What will you do?" she asked.

"I'll finish my dissertation," I said. I had spent so many years working up an argument that the mind was all that mattered. But I had been wrong about that, too. The body was undeniable. I was surprised to find that the idea of going back to the unfinished document on my computer made me excited. I was ready to return to a world that didn't believe life could be so easily overwritten, so easily codified.

I thought of all the programs that had told me their predictions over the past year; the programs that had scanned me—the virtual me, and the physical one—and told me what I wanted to buy, what I wanted to see, who I was. I thought about the scans and the tests and the measurements, the constant check-ins to assure me that I was safe, that my baby was safe. But we had not been safe. The whole time, danger had been lurking just out of sight. Danger, I thought, would always be there. There was no way to excise it. You could not predict it away.

"I see," she said again. "Sounds like you've decided."

"I have," I said.

"I shouldn't say this," she said, after a pause. "But you should take the leave. Wait until the end of the leave to give your notice." I started to say something, but she cut me off. "The company can afford it," she said.

I said okay. I thanked her. Then we were both silent for a moment.

"You said you believed that our work would help people," I said, breaking the silence. "Do you still believe that?"

The line went quiet again.

"I do," she said, finally. Her voice sounded just as certain as before, just as determined. "It will."

✳

Several days passed. We were still waiting for the go-ahead from the hospital to take Lotte back to California. We settled into a routine: my father and Kumiko heading out in the morning to do the day's shopping; Jamie going out for a run on the beach midday. I went nowhere. I sat with Lotte and tried to nurse her. I sat next to Lotte and pumped. I pretended to read, my eyes glossing over the words on the page. We watched daytime television, which had improved a great deal, I thought, since the last time I had turned on the TV midday. Now, instead of shows that featured divorces and affairs and people slapping each other and having to be restrained by bulky security guards, there were many television shows hosted by women, in which panels of women talked about politics and culture and, also, sometimes, shopping.

It had only been a few days, but this routine felt ingrained, immutable. I liked the routine, the safety of it. So when Kumiko and my father suggested we all go for a drive early one afternoon, I was hesitant.

"I'm not sure if Lotte can do it," I said, but what I really meant was that I wasn't sure I could do it.

Everyone assured me that Lotte would be fine. That it would be good for both of us to get out. I looked at Jamie—wasn't he supposed to be on my side in this?—but he was oblivious. He was excited, I realized, about the prospect of a drive.

I changed from my sweatpants into a floral dress that Kumiko had bought for me on one of her many trips to the nearby big box store. It seemed a little odd to me that she had bought me a dress—it wasn't something I would normally choose for myself—but it fit fine. When I emerged from the bathroom, everyone was waiting for me; Kumiko was wearing an off-white linen dress, and my father was wearing khakis and a polo shirt, tucked in. Both of their outfits looked freshly pressed. I thought this, too, was a little odd, but I didn't have time to dwell on it. We clipped Lotte into the car seat my father had bought at the super store and installed in the back seat of the gold convertible, and then the rest of us piled in, my father and Kumiko in front, Jamie, Lotte, and me in the back. We kept the top up, and inside, it felt snug and secure. I hadn't wanted to leave the comfort of the couch, of the condo, but here we were, and it was fine. Actually, it was beautiful. The rain had ended, and the island seemed to shimmer with the influx of all that life-sustaining water, the plants breathing their verdancy back out into the air, which felt crisp and clean.

We drove for a few minutes through the streets in town before merging onto a two-lane highway that followed the coast. I had not seen the ocean since the day at the former leper colony. There it still was, sparkling out to the horizon.

"That's the ocean," Jamie whispered to the top of Lotte's head. She looked to me like she was fast asleep. She made a small snuffling sound.

We drove for several minutes in silence before exiting the highway onto a road that grew narrower and narrower as it wound up the mountains. My father seemed to be driving with a destination—or at least a route—in mind, but he shared no information about where we might be headed. I leaned back into the leather seat. On the side of the road, people had set up small stands where they sold breadfruit tacos, banana bread, avocados. The foliage became thicker, the road carving into a dense wall of plants, the light increasingly dim. And then, after a few more minutes, we emerged into daylight once again, a vast green field ahead of us, punctuated by a small speck of white in the distance. As we grew closer, I could see that the speck of white was a church.

"Well," my father said, slowing down the car. "What's this?"

"What a beautiful church!" Kumiko said, turning around and looking at us. "Isn't it a beautiful church?"

"It's a beautiful church," Jamie said, nodding.

I waited for my father to start driving again, but instead, he put the car in park.

"Let's go take a closer look," he said, practically springing out of his seat.

Kumiko hung back, making sure we got out of the car okay. Jamie had already begun the process of unclipping Lotte, wrapping her up in a complicated piece of fabric that I had not yet mastered and attaching her to his chest.

"I'm going to stay here," I said. "You all go ahead." If I stayed in the car, I could have a few moments to myself. I hadn't had a moment to myself in weeks, possibly.

Kumiko looked oddly stricken.

"No, no," she said, her voice insistent. "You must come." She held the car door open, waiting. I looked at Jamie. He was standing a few feet from the car, Lotte clutched to his body like a limpet. He was ready to help me, ready to do anything for either of us, things that he would always be there to do. Was it possible he had planned this whole thing? No, I thought, he would never. Still, I couldn't help but look at him. I could tell that he knew immediately what I was asking. He shook his head vehemently.

"I have no idea why we're here," he said. He looked at Kumiko. "Well, I guess I have an idea, but it has nothing to do with the two of us."

I was still in the car. If it had nothing to do with the two of us, then that meant it had something to do with the two of them, my father and Kumiko. Could I just stay in the car forever? I got out. I looked at Lotte, affixed to Jamie's chest. It was hard to believe that I had ever been this small, hard to believe that now I was the one responsible for someone so small.

My father was waiting at the door to the church, an immense grin on his face.

"Ready?" he asked us, but he seemed to mostly be speaking to Kumiko. She nodded. He pushed open the door and took her hand; Jamie, Lotte, and I followed behind. Inside, the church was plain but welcoming; its pews were made of a warm wood with an orange cast, oak or fir. There was little decoration, only a few large vases of flowers on the altar. Narrow windows ran along the sides, letting light stream in.

A middle-aged Asian man entered, younger than my father but older than me. He was dressed in what I would call "Hawaiian business casual": nicely pressed khakis, a short-sleeve button-down tucked in, and a pair of brown loafers.

"Pastor," my father said, walking over to greet him. They clasped hands, and my father led him back to where the three of us were standing, made introductions. My father and the pastor stepped to the side, busying themselves looking over a sheet of paper in the pastor's hands.

"We found this church when we were out for a drive one day, after you'd brought Lotte home," Kumiko said. "We thought it was the right place, the right time. All of us together. I hope you don't mind?"

"Of course we don't," Jamie said. I was relieved he had answered for both of us. He reached over and gave Kumiko a squeeze on the shoulder. He was always good at things like that.

Jamie and I sat in the front pew, Lotte still wrapped to his chest, sleeping. Kumiko and my father stood at the front.

It was a short ceremony. The pastor said a few words about marriage, about new beginnings, about the beauty of finding a partner at any stage of life. Jamie reached over and took my hand. Lotte continued to sleep. As they exchanged their vows, I saw my father's face quiver. I wondered what his life had been like, all these years without my mother. All this time, I had tried not to think about how he spent his time outside our once-a-month visits. What were his days like, his nights? I knew that he had been lonely, all these years. That now he would not be lonely anymore.

Outside the church, the day had become even more radiant. It seemed strange to get in the car right away, and so we stood in a small cluster on the expansive green meadow and made small talk. Jamie, Kumiko, and the pastor did most of the talking, mostly about Lotte.

At some point, my father wandered off to a different corner of the field. I followed a few steps behind. I was wearing sandals and I could feel the grass brushing against the sides of my feet, velvety and soft.

"Dad," I said. He turned, and we embraced awkwardly. His body felt smaller and bonier than I remembered. "I'm happy for you," I said.

And I was. It was a complex kind of happiness, with sadness and longing and mourning all mixed in, but it was happiness none-theless.

TWENTY-NINE

The day before we left Hawaii, I was finishing up my packing when Lotte began to cry. Only seconds passed before I heard Jamie comforting her and the crying stopped. When Jamie picked her up, she quieted almost immediately. She did not have the same reaction to me. I knew I should feel lucky that she responded so well to one of us, at least, but instead I usually felt jealous, and slightly resentful, and then hated myself a little for feeling jealous and resentful when I knew I should feel grateful that we had Lotte with us at all. But there was no one way to feel. No one way to be.

After carrying Lotte's body for months, after being the only one who really knew her, I didn't like feeling superfluous, unnecessary, even for a minute. But of course I was necessary. And they were necessary to me. Jamie and Lotte, my father; possibly even Kumiko.

I emerged from the bedroom to a beatific scene. Jamie sat on the sectional with Lotte pressed to his chest, swaddled in a blanket and deeply asleep. The bit of her face I could see looked pink and raw, this little animal who had so recently been inside my own body. My father and Kumiko sat on the sectional across from the two of them, holding hands and—it seemed to me—doing nothing but staring at the sleeping baby.

I sat down next to Jamie. He smelled the way he always smelled, earthy and sweet, like mushrooms and fresh dirt. I was still learning Lotte's smell, like cottage cheese and pancakes. I knew all about the new baby smell, how our primal bond meant I should be able to pick her out of a baby lineup based on smell alone. There were so many things that mothers were supposed to be able to do instinctively, easily. I doubted I was capable of recognizing Lotte's scent, but who knew? I had made it from the leper colony to the hospital, blood pouring out of me, and both of us had survived. When I thought back to that day, I felt not horror, but rather pride and wonder. My body was capable of things I could not even imagine.

Lotte burbled as Jamie shifted her on his chest, but she did not wake.

"I was thinking," Jamie whispered to me. "You haven't had any time to yourself since the hospital. Why don't you go for a walk?"

I hesitated. My father and Kumiko smiled at me encouragingly, in a way that made me think the three of them had probably discussed that it would be good for me to get out of the condo. I did not want to leave. What if something happened while I was gone?

"Nothing will happen," Jamie said. "Everything's under control here."

I put my phone in my pocket, the ringer turned all the way up, ready for emergencies. I walked a few blocks toward the ocean. A man rode by on a bicycle, one hand on the handlebars, the other arm holding his surfboard. A teenage girl clattered by on a skateboard. Out on the beach, people were playing Frisbee, volleyball, paddleball; they were tossing a small foam football; they were eating picnics out of plastic coolers, Tupperwares of poke, slices of pineapple and mango, bags of rippled potato chips, two-liter bottles of soda; they were running into the water and jumping into the waves; they were screaming with delight; they were running back up the sand, flopping their bodies down onto their beach towels, the fabric comforting and warm from lying in the sun. I took my shoes off, felt my feet in the hot sand. I went down to the waterline, where the sand was cooler and firm. I walked for several minutes, the scene around me changing as I walked but only minutely: a red cooler instead of a blue one, a football being thrown instead of a Frisbee. All around me, people had put up structures to shield their bodies from the sun, umbrellas and tents and canopies in bright primary colors. This was the scene here every day, I thought; this was what it was like on the day I went to the hospital, on the days Lotte struggled for life, on the days we stood beside her spaceship in the NICU and squeezed her tiny hands.

In the far distance, I saw what looked like a large gathering of people. I wondered, briefly, if I should go back to the condo. What if something had happened to Lotte? What if something had happened and there had not been time to call me, and when I returned it would be to an empty house, an empty crib? I pulled my phone out of my pocket and checked it. No missed calls. It felt strange, to be so unencumbered out in the world. I was no longer an unencumbered person. I had a baby. Soon, I would have a husband.

I walked through a tangle of seaweed, the strands rough from the sun. I stood at the water's edge, hesitating, then I stepped in, but only up to my shins, the water soft and undulating. I stood in the water and surveyed the ocean. Directly ahead of me, a family was playing in the waves. When a big wave came in, the father would direct the children to wait—wait for it, wait for it, he said—and then, all together, they would dive under and come out the other side. Every time, the children had a look of shock and joy on their faces, the surprise of emerging unscathed.

I stepped out of the water and continued to walk along the packed sand at the water's edge. Up ahead, the gathering was getting closer, and I could see what looked like a piece of machinery, a small crane, sticking out over the crowd. A few minutes later, I made it to the knot of people, but I still couldn't see what it was that everyone was looking at. Bodies were crowded in, shoulder to shoulder, but for such a large crowd, it was strangely quiet. Several people had their phones out, recording video, but I could not see what they were recording.

I asked the woman standing next to me what was happening.

"Humpback whale," the woman said. "Beached itself this morning. A female." She explained that the Coast Guard was trying to dig enough space out from under the whale so they could attach a special harness to her body to lift it with the crane. You couldn't drag the whale or push it, she said, that was a common misconception. She told me this in a way that implied that she was some kind of amateur whale expert. I knew she was not a professional whale expert, because if she were a professional whale expert, she would not have been standing on the outskirts of the crowd with me.

We stood in silence for several minutes. Through the crush of bodies ahead of me, I caught a glimpse of glossy black. The whale's body.

"It's terribly sad," the woman said, as though our conversation had not paused. "But really they should euthanize her. Beaching causes massive damage to the body—instead of being suspended in the water, the whale's entire weight is pressing down on her internal organs, slowly crushing them. And even if they are still intact, she's probably been separated from her pod. They could be days ahead of her on their migration. She might never find them."

I nodded and tried to edge away from this whale doomsayer. She stayed back on the periphery as I maneuvered through the crowd, trying to find a gap. I was focusing on not putting my own body in anyone else's way, but when I stopped and looked up, suddenly there wasn't anyone left in front of me. I could the see the whale in its entirety, or rather, I could see as much of her as the human eye could see, from that close up. She was probably thirty feet long, if not more. I was positioned somewhere around her vast middle, near the fin, so when I turned my head to the left I could see her head, and when I turned my head to the right I could see her tail, but I could not see all of her at once.

Now that I was closer, I could see people in uniform shoveling away the sand around the whale, carefully but quickly. Several other people who looked like civilians were shuttling back and forth to the ocean, carrying buckets of water that they would toss over her to keep her cool and hydrated. Her eyes were closed, as if she were asleep, and her great wrinkled mouth seemed to be melting into the sand. Hundreds of barnacles studded her skin, artifacts of a life spent under the water.

There was no way to know what the whale was thinking, how she was feeling, but I imagined she must be scared. Tired and scared. How could she not be? This ordeal had been going on for hours upon hours. Her body had found itself in a place where it should not be, and there had been no escape.

All around me, people were holding up their phones, taking photos and recording video, posting them to this or that site, messaging them to this or that friend or family member. I wondered if I should take a photo and send it to Jamie, but when I raised my phone and looked at the whale through the camera, she looked so different from what I actually saw before me that I couldn't bring myself to take the picture. It wasn't right, I thought. The photo didn't look like the way it felt to be standing there, at that moment, wondering if the whale would live or die. I put my phone away.

An hour had passed since I left the condo. The men in uniform continued to shovel and the people not in uniform continued to run back and forth with their buckets of water. I felt a buzz from my phone.

Where are you? Jamie had texted. *Are you okay?*

I started typing, started telling him about the whale, but nothing I wrote seemed adequate.

I'm okay, I texted back.

I reconsidered. This was probably not actually enough information.

I'll be there soon, I wrote.

I knew I should go back. I had been gone too long. Soon, I knew, my breasts would begin to ache. But still, I stayed on the beach.

The men began to thread the harness under the whale's body, moving carefully to avoid any sudden movements of her tail. If she tried to move, she could crush one of them in a moment. But she lay perfectly still, as though willing herself to endure. Her eye was at least the size of my hand, fingers outstretched, but she kept it closed, a thin black slit almost indiscernible from the rest of her body. Her mouth had opened a crack, and I could see the rows of baleen, thousands of bristles ready to take on the pressure of the ocean. Now that I was closer up, I could see all the things her body had withstood. There were deep gouges along her flippers that had healed into white scars; places her flesh had met rock, had met coral, had met the unyielding teeth of another animal, one that she had evaded or defeated in battle.

By the time they hoisted her up with the crane, the sun's angle had changed, and the crowd had begun to dissipate. I stood among the small group of onlookers who had stuck it out. The wind was picking up. They had warned us to stay back; men in neon orange vests stood in a loose perimeter around the crane, around the body of the whale, which looked far too large for the straps they had secured around her, laced around her middle. I watched as they hoisted the whale higher and then, slowly, began to drive the crane down to the water. The whale dangled before it, majestic and helpless. Up there, she looked almost weightless, like she could float or fly.

I knew that so many things could go wrong. The whale was tired and weak from hours on land. Something had caused her to beach herself in the first place, something that might be fine, or might prove fatal. She might be battered by the currents, she might be attacked by orcas or by sharks, she might be caught in the cast-off nets of commercial fishermen, trawling the waters and leaving behind their deadly debris. She might not be able to swim; she might never find her pod. She might wander the ocean alone, calling out for them in whale song, receiving no answer.

After the crane had driven as far into the water as it could go, they began to lower the whale. When her body hit the water, her tail instantly began to thrash, moving side to side like the awesome beast she was. She lifted her left flipper and then her right, twisting her body this way and that, reawakening it. She was no longer docile and passive, her body flattened and immobile on the sand, but unpredictable and alive.

They released the harness so that she floated free. For a moment, she remained suspended in place. A wave came in, pushing her back toward the beach. But she recovered quickly, and when the wave went back out, she carried herself out with it, her body skimming along the water's surface with unimaginable grace, then dropping below. I watched her for as long as I could, marking her progress by the trail of white froth she left behind. I caught glimpses of her hump, her tail, but they became harder and harder to make out as she moved away from shore and toward the darkening horizon.

Even after she had disappeared from view, I remained on the beach, watching.

I imagined the whale swimming, her great body cutting through the water at speed, unavoidable, unstoppable.

I imagined her making it out to sea.

ACKNOWLEDGMENTS

Thank you to Jacqueline Ko for seeing this book so clearly and truly, and to Lindsey Schwoeri for editing with such thoughtfulness and care. Thank you to Kristi Murray, Allie Merola, Ivy McFadden, Lynn Buckley, Lucia Bernard, Megan Gerrity, Sara Leonard, and to everyone at the Wylie Agency and Viking who helped put this book out into the world.

I found inspiration in many sources, and I am especially indebted to the "High Voltage (Emotions Part Two)" episode of the podcast *Invisibilia*, for introducing me to the idea of *liget,* and the "Animal Misfits" episode of the PBS show *Nature*, for teaching me about the minute leaf chameleon, the big-headed mole rat, the kakapo, and many other "nonconformist" animals.

I am grateful to all my teachers, and especially to Fred D'Aguiar, whose guidance changed the way I saw my writing, and who helped me stay true to my work. Thank you to Julie Schumacher and Charles Baxter, for your foundational insights and tireless generosity. Thank you, also, to the UCLA Department of English, the University of Minnesota MFA Program, the Kimmel Harding Nelson Center for the Arts, the Brush Creek Foundation for the Arts, and the Loft Literary Center.

Thank you to Liana Liu, my first reader, for always understanding. Thank you to Sara Culver for your incisive reads and for giving me space for a mini writing retreat.

Thank you to my fabulous and loving aunties, for taking such good care of me while I've been living in LA.

Thank you to Peter Sowinski, who has been by my side this whole time, and who helps me see the beauty and the joy every day.

And to my parents, Don Stanford and Michi Kawachi, for immersing me in art and literature from the very start, and for your unending support, belief, and love.